Andrew Christie lives in Sydney
where he writes a blog about eating.

This is his first novel.

LEFT LUGGAGE

Andrew Christie

PAINTING THE BRIDGE BOOKS

A Painting the Bridge Book
paintingthebridge.com

This edition published 2016

ISBN 9780992574703

For Strop
who always has the best lines

Paris, August 1975

Rashid jammed the battered blue Deux Chevaux into gear and sent the car lurching out into the traffic on Avenue de Flandre. The Portuguese had rung him that morning, whining like a little dog about his woman, *la pute Australienne*.

"You have to take the suitcase away. I can't have it here anymore," he said.

So now Rashid had to find somewhere new to keep the guns and the money until the Germans were ready. All Jorge had to do was look after the suitcase for a couple of weeks, till Gunther's team could move. It was nothing difficult, nothing dangerous, just hold the suitcase. But Jorge had shown he was just another bourgeois coward, more worried about keeping his woman happy than doing anything useful. All these intellectuals were the same. They made lots of noise, talking about standing up against imperialism, but none of them were doing anything. Apparently looking after a suitcase for two weeks was too much trouble.

A taxi stopped suddenly in front of him to avoid a dog that had run into the road. Rashid braked hard, making the old 2CV wallow on its soft suspension. "*Merde. Qu'est-ce que tu fous?*" he muttered as he swung out into the next lane, working the gear stick and the accelerator to get the underpowered car back up to speed again. It was a hot day and Rashid was sweating underneath the black leather coat he wore to cover his shoulder holster. He wished he had taken the time to roll back the cloth roof of the car before he had left– the little fold-up windows didn't let enough air in to cool the car.

None of it would have been a problem if the Germans had known what they were doing. Rashid had expected that they would be serious operators, professionals. After all, the Syrian himself had chosen them. "They have an important job for us, give them what they want," he had said when Rashid had last been in Marseilles. It turned out that what they wanted was money and automatic weapons.

Well, these Germans might know how to shoot, but they didn't know how to plan. Rashid had done his part, bringing the guns and the money to Paris, only to find they weren't ready.

"What are you waiting for?" Rashid said. "I thought it is a big urgency, that the timing was critical."

"It's Lutz," the leader, Gunther, had said. "He is gone for his holiday, to Bordeaux. We only now found out that he goes every year to Bassin d'Arcachon. He won't return to Paris until two weeks. We must wait, there is no point if he is not there."

"What am I supposed to do with the guns till then?"

"It is just two weeks. When Lutz is back we will go to work. It is a better time anyway, after the holidays. People will take more notice."

If you kill the ambassador, Rashid had thought, *people are going to notice.*

So the raid was delayed, and Rashid had asked Jorge to hold the suitcase for him. But now he had changed his mind, and Rashid had to find somewhere else to store it until Lutz returned, and the Germans gave the go ahead.

The Île de la Cité was packed with tourists and the little Citroën got stuck behind a sightseeing bus that seemed to be intent on travelling as slowly as possible. A *moto* came past on the left, weaving through the traffic. The girl on the back was blonde; long hair and sunglasses with blue circular lenses. She took a long look down at Rashid, a big smile showing her perfect teeth when he turned and looked back at her. He saw her fingers tap lightly on the shoulders of the man in front of her before they accelerated away, disappearing up the side of the bus.

On Rue Saint-Jacques there were still plenty of tourists on the pavements, but the traffic began to move a bit more freely. Behind him a blue van turned off into a laneway, revealing the taxi he had swerved around before, two cars back. Rashid checked the other cars. There were none that he recognised, none that looked suspicious. He checked his mirror again. Two men were in the taxi, the passenger sitting in the front beside the driver. He made a right onto Rue du Sommerard, driving a slow loop around the Jardin Médiéval. When he came back out onto Rue Saint-Jacques there was no sign of the taxi.

He was glad of the weight of the Makarov beneath his arm. The taxi was probably nothing, but you could never be sure. He had vowed at the start that he would not let himself be captured. Not like Baader and Meins. If it came to it, he would take as many of the pigs as he could, then use the gun on himself. Rashid had no fear of death.

He turned on the radio, listening and singing along when his favourite song came on, a French version of Del Shannon's "Runaway", while his eyes flicked back and forth from the road in front to the mirrors. Still nothing.

At L'institut Océanographique he turned left onto Rue Gay-Lussac and found a parking place opposite Jorge's apartment building. It was one of a row of seven-storey buildings that opened directly onto the street. Rashid sat in the car for a couple of minutes, watching. The street was quiet. There was nothing that looked out of place.

The Portuguese must have been watching the street too, because he opened the door before Rashid had a chance to press the buzzer. Jorge was a tall man but soft. Today he looked unhappy.

"I'm sorry, Rashid."

"*Fermés la gueule*. I thought you were a friend. I thought I could rely on you."

"I am a friend. You know that. But you didn't tell me it was guns."

"You opened the suitcase?"

"Yes, but ... What the hell are you doing with guns?"

"What do people usually do with guns? Do you think we are playing games?"

"No, of course ..."

"Where is it?"

"Upstairs." Jorge held the door open.

Rashid turned to check the street again before he went inside. The taxi was there, double parked. The driver and the passenger were getting out, looking at across at Rashid and Jorge. "*Traître*," Rashid said under his breath, his hand sliding beneath his coat. He turned and shot Jorge in the face.

There was a shout from across the street. The men were running now, drawing weapons. Rashid stood his ground and fired. The first man went down, hit in the chest. The second man took cover behind a blue Renault as Rashid's shots shattered its windows. A large black sedan skidded to a stop in the middle of the street. The back doors flew open and two men came out holding automatic weapons. Rashid fired at them, then made a dash towards the taxi. The man behind the Renault stood and fired but missed. Rashid shot back as he ran. He missed too, but he kept going, kept running. He had his hand on the door of the taxi when the GIGN anti-terrorist team from the second car opened up with their MP5s. Two bursts of automatic fire slammed into Rashid's chest. The Makarov dropped from his hand as he fell against the taxi and slumped face down on the pavement.

ONE

Photojournalist of the Year

John Lawrence closed the sliding door and adjusted the vertical blinds, narrowing the slices of late-afternoon sun that cut across the pale carpet, reducing the light in the room to a soft glow. He had spent all day moving the furniture in, arranging and then rearranging it, getting ready for his mother's arrival in the morning. Looking around the small sitting room now though, the pieces of furniture he had chosen sat awkwardly with each other, like strangers in a doctor's waiting room. Well, it was too late to change; his mother was certain to have her own ideas anyway, and he could move things around however she liked. They could even swap the furniture for some of the other stuff in storage – there was more than enough there. Hell, they could buy all new furniture if she wanted. It was up to her.

The apartment was on the ground floor, a 'courtyard apartment', in the Forest Court Retirement Community. He had chosen the retirement village in Glebe so his mother would be close to him: it was two kilometres from his house, a distance that he thought should provide enough separation, allowing them to have their own lives, but close enough that they would still be in easy contact with each other when they wanted. There were other, newer, retirement villages with bigger apartments and better facilities, but they were all much further away, out in the suburbs. He knew his mother would want to be in the city, close to things.

The furniture was what he thought were his mother's favourite things. The two old armchairs that had been in the living room of her apartment in Montparnasse he had eventually put against the end wall. An oak dresser, the old kitchen table and a couple of bookcases didn't leave room for any other furniture. The long wall opposite the window was now covered with framed photographs. To one end were a group of awards. *Betty Lawrence - Photojournalist of the Year, 1972*. A couple of *Time* magazine covers too, Vietnam and Lebanon. His mother in her heyday, when it wasn't really a war until Betty Lawrence photographed it. Who had said that? One of her journalist mates, he thought. The photographs and awards had been on her walls in Paris. They were the first things he unpacked in her new apartment.

The photos of his mother showed her as a small woman with intense pale eyes, blonde in the older photographs. John took after her in his face and especially his eyes, but his size came from his father's side. That was what she always said. John had only seen his father in photos, a big, dark, unknowable man. John's hair was light like his mother's, but more brown, and clipped short. On the side of his neck was an angry red mesh of scar tissue that was all his own. It disappeared beneath the neck of his white T-shirt, reappearing on his right arm, and extending all the way down to his wrist, ending abruptly where his combat glove had protected his hand from the flames in the cab of the Bushmaster.

His mother owned a lot of books. They had filled the

bookshelves lining the hallway of her old apartment. There wasn't room for them all here, so John had made a random selection, just enough to fill the two low bookshelves. Some of the novels he recognised, but most of them he'd never heard of. There were books on fashion and art too, even some on Aboriginal art. The art books were all in French, but some of the novels were in English.

In the kitchen he washed up the mug and plate he had used for lunch, and put a new liner in the bin. He took one last look around the sitting room, trying to see it the way his mother would in the morning. It would have to do, she was going to have to make it her own.

It was a short drive from Glebe to where John lived in Camperdown, in an old mixed industrial and residential area. His house was jammed between a warehouse that had been converted to trendy loft apartments and a row of terrace houses. It was the odd one out, older than its neighbours, and set further back from the street. Despite the shiny new corrugated steel roofing, it looked dark and uncared for. Bigger than the terrace houses, it would have once had land all around it, but now the side yards had gone and the newer buildings were hard up against his walls. Still, he had a big backyard and a rear lane, and one day he'd have a garden too.

When he had bought the house at auction, the word most frequently used by the agent was potential, because it was the only selling point. The house had been neglected for the last thirty years, owned by an old woman who had aged with the house, eventually dying in it; her life shrunken down till she was living in two rooms on the ground floor, leaving the rest of the house to decay around her. It was a fixer-upper's dream, the agent said. Nightmare was more like it, but John did see potential. For him it was the chance to reshape his life, to build something solid. He ignored the smell of damp and the rotten floorboards.

At the auction, the first wave of bidders were the romantics and the wishful thinkers who thought they might pick up a bargain. He waited till the serious bidders began to stir, leaving the optimists shaking their heads and muttering about the price of Sydney real estate. These were the ones with experience, semiprofessional renovators who bought old houses, fixed them up and resold them. They had a keen eye on the costs and on what they could realistically expect to get for the place in a year or two. John came on strong, raising the price by $10 000 with his first bid, then sat back and harassed them, raising every bid by $1000. Calm, tenacious, letting them know he wasn't going away, he wasn't worried about a bottom line. He needed somewhere to live, something to do. He was buying a life. One by one, they dropped out until John became the owner. That was when the real work started.

John parked his battered Hilux ute in the street, emptied the letterbox and let himself inside. A bare bulb lit the dirty walls and worn floorboards of the hall with hard white light. The second thing he had done to the house, after putting a new roof on, had been to get an electrician in to completely rewire the house and put in new lights. The rotten insulation and bare wires had been a death trap.

The old roof had let in so much water that the ceilings had collapsed in the upstairs bedrooms and the floors were dangerously rotten with gaping holes in some places. The house still smelled a bit of damp and mould, but it was getting less every day. He had the living room and kitchen in habitable condition, having completely stripped them back,

9

rebuilt the floors and relined the walls. The rooms were bare, but they were dry and mostly clean. The laundry was serving as a temporary bathroom and his bed was in the living room: a mattress on the floor and a sleeping bag; basic but adequate. This was the base he would use to take on the rest of the house, room by room. That was the plan.

John threw the mail onto the table in the kitchen and poured himself a glass of Bowmore. With the whisky warming his throat, he sorted the mail. There were a couple of pieces of junk mail, an electricity bill and a letter from France. It was from the *notaire* in Paris who had arranged Betty's affairs for the move, something about furniture still in storage there. John dropped the letter back on the bench and pulled out his sketch book. He'd worry about Betty's furniture once he had got her settled in. The sketch book was nearly full, the pages covered with neatly drawn plans, different versions of his future home. At the back there were lists of materials and contact numbers for plumbers, electricians and timber merchants. Last night he had been working on an idea to knock out the wall between the living room and the front bedroom, to make it all one big space, and bring a bit more light through into the middle of the house. The trouble was that the wall was load bearing. When he'd finished the whisky, the only conclusion he'd come to was that he needed to talk to an engineer.

Large Phil Waters ordered a bourbon and Coke, and turned to take stock of the bar. He had a good view of the room and both doors from where he was, so he eased his buttocks onto a stool and took a sip of his drink. Whoever gave Large his nickname believed in stating the obvious. He was a big man, tall and wide, with sandy hair and a wide red face. It didn't seem to matter what he wore, it was always a tight fit.

It was a mid-town pub, on a busy corner between a burger joint and a city church; the sort of place where no one looks out of place. Unfashionable, but convenient for an after-work beer, no matter what time of day it was. Further north the pubs were full of suits, and women looking for suits. Here there was a mix of workers who hadn't figured out how to go home yet, some in hi-vis, some in polyester, and even a few in lightweight charcoal wool mix. And backpackers at a corner table, laughing and showing off lots of sunburnt flesh, straight from a day at Bondi, learning to surf, but not learning to spot a rip. In the other corner, looking like out-of-work waiters, a table of men in cheap tuxedos, most with their clip-on bow ties in their pockets and their shirts unbuttoned. Probably kicking on after some cocktail hour function

"I'll find you," was what the guy had said. Large couldn't see anyone who looked particularly interested in him so he waited. Give it half an hour. He kept one eye on the room while he watched a twenty20 cricket match on one of the many screens fixed high on the walls. The game was all colour and movement, no subtlety. After it had become obvious that this form of the game wasn't going to die a natural death, Large had found that he could bear to watch it as long as he thought of it as a completely different game from the test cricket he had grown up with. It was a pretty easy delusion to maintain. He finished his drink and ordered another.

"Phil Waters?"

One of the off-duty waiters had detached himself from his table and was standing next to Large at the bar. Not looking at him, watching the barman instead. Cautious. Large didn't turn his head either. "You Dennis?"

"Yeah. I won't be long, the others will go after this round. They always do. We can talk then." He turned to Large. "That okay?"

Large gave him a toothy smile. "It's okay. As long as what you're offering is worth the wait?"

"Yeah," Dennis said, "it is." He picked up a tray full of beers and made his way back to the table.

Large went back to watching the cricket.

Twenty minutes later the men at the table started to leave. Dennis began to go with them, but turned back, heading for the toilets. When he came out, he went straight up to Large and stuck out his hand.

"Hope you washed that," Large said, watching the man's eyes as he took his hand and shook it.

"Of course ..."

"So who are your mates?"

"Choir. We had a gig at the Town Hall tonight."

A choir. "No shit. What do you sing?"

"Schubert, tonight."

"Schubert?" No shit.

"Yeah. Do you want another drink?" Dennis asked.

"Nah. Let's go get something to eat, I'm starving."

They went to a Chinese restaurant in Sussex Street. A big place with white linen table cloths and plenty of waiters, all dressed up like Dennis's choir mates.

Large watched Dennis settle himself in his chair and pick up the vinyl-clad menu, then he stood up. "Something we need to do first. Come with me." He led Dennis back across the dining room and downstairs to the toilets.

"I just went, in the pub ..." said Dennis.

"I'm going to need to know that you aren't wired up."

"Oh."

Large took a yellow "Toilet Closed for Cleaning" sign

12

from behind the door and put it out in the corridor. He shut the door and leaned back against it. "Strip," he said holding out his hand and snapping his fingers.

"Strip?"

"Everything. All off. Otherwise how do I know I can trust you?"

"But ..." Dennis looked at Large for a moment, then began to take his clothes off, passing them to Large to hold.

"You understand I have to be careful," Large said after he'd made the man spread his buttocks and lift up his scrotum.

Dennis didn't meet his eyes as Large passed his wallet and jacket back to him, just muttered, "Sure. Careful."

Back at the table, Large ordered steamed dumplings, roast duck and a bottle of chardonnay. "Don't worry, it's on me," he said. "Expenses. Anyway, now I know a bit about you, Dennis. And if I may say, you're in pretty good shape for a man your age. Could lose a little bit of weight, but then I'm in no position to comment on other people's weight issues." He tried a grin but Dennis didn't respond. "Anyway, the important thing is that I trust you. Which I do. For now. So what can I tell you about me?"

Dennis looked up from studying his hands. Eventually he said, "What do you want to bring through?"

Large let the grin fade from his face. "Guns."

Dennis's eyes widened.

"You look surprised," Large said. "What were you expecting?"

"I don't know. Drugs, I suppose, some kind of drugs."

TWO

Welcome Home

It was getting light when John woke. Nearly five thirty. He watched the minute hand of his watch creep towards the six, when the alarm in his phone would go off. He lay on the single mattress looking up at the new unpainted ceiling for a moment, as grey morning light filled the room, listening to the currawongs calling to each other, warbling away from the fig trees in the park at the end of the street. His mother's flight didn't get in until nine forty.

He dressed in shorts and a T-shirt, and pulled on his running shoes. In the park he did a few quick stretches before setting off at an easy pace, across Parramatta Road and down towards Rozelle Bay. The water was silver, shifting softly against the sea walls and the boat wharf. Even though it was early, the parks and ovals were starting to fill with runners and dog walkers. John enjoyed the companionable silence, everyone out early before the heat made it unpleasant, just getting on with their routines, minding their own business. He followed the shore around the bay then headed up through Lilyfield, over the ridge and down through the grounds of the old mental hospital at Callan Park to Iron Cove. The long kikuyu grass was wet with dew and soaked through his shoes so he was glad to reach the broad and well-made path that ran along the shoreline of the cove. This path was always popular and it was starting to get crowded now, with more runners and dog walkers beginning their day. John picked up his pace, overtaking people on the path, keeping an eye out for cyclists and unpredictable dogs. He came back across the Iron Cove Bridge and headed for home along Victoria Road, ignoring the noise and smell of the traffic.

It was beginning to get warm when John got back to the house, walking now but covered in sweat. He was armed with bread and the newspaper from the corner shop in Australia Street. The kid, Billy, was waiting on the veranda, sitting on a paint-spattered plastic chair.

"Morning," said John, holding out the folded copy of the *Telegraph*.

"Morning," said Billy, taking the paper and following John into the house. He perched himself on a stool and opened the paper while John went out the back door to the laundry, pulling off his sweaty T-shirt as he went. Shower first, then breakfast, that was the deal. If Billy went to school like he was supposed to, John let him help with the renovations on Saturdays. Breakfast and thirty dollars was the going rate.

The shower felt great, hard and hot. Plenty of pressure – no water-saving devices here. John pulled on his last clean T-shirt and yesterday's jeans. Tomorrow he'd have to do some washing.

Back in the kitchen, Billy had made tea and poured it into two mugs. Now he was bent over the newspaper sipping his tea and reading something about a celebrity John had never heard of, who had disgraced herself somehow.

"I have to go and pick up my mother this morning,"

John said.

Billy nodded but didn't look up. "Yeah, you said last week." One thing about the kid, he listened, even if it was hard to tell sometimes.

"I'll probably be with her all day. You be alright on your own here? Keep working on stripping back those window frames?"

Billy looked up. "Sure," he said. "Did you buy more sandpaper?"

"Yeah, it's in a white bag, beside the tool box."

"Okay. What's she like, your mum?"

"I don't know. She's just my mum." John shrugged. "I suppose she's a bit unusual. Mostly French nowadays, but still Australian. Come over tomorrow if you want, I'll introduce you."

"Maybe," Billy grunted.

John squatted down in front of the old bar fridge and pulled out eggs and a white paper package of bacon. "The usual?" Billy nodded and turned back to the paper.

John put a couple of thick slices of sourdough bread in the toaster, then set about frying the bacon and the eggs. He assembled the bacon and egg sandwiches on a couple of mismatched plates, adding barbecue sauce to both, but tabasco only to his.

"Here," he said, sliding Billy's plate across and pulling up a stool in front of his own.

Billy handed over the paper and turned his attention to the food. They didn't talk much; Billy was intent on his food, John reading the paper while he ate.

He had first met Billy outside the house, just after he had moved in. He was getting started with the renovations, stripping out the water-affected rooms, filling a skip with barrow loads of damp plaster. Billy was outside on the

16

footpath each time he came out. The boy was skinny and dirty. Just watching John, not saying anything. After five barrow loads, John spoke to him.

"Did you want something mate?"

"No," the boy said, looking away but not moving.

"Just watching are you?"

The boy nodded.

"You live around here?"

"Not really."

John pulled off his gloves and scratched at his scarred arm. Sweat made it itch like a bastard.

"Annandale," the boy added.

So, not a neighbour. Annandale was fifteen minutes' walk away.

"Do you do this often – just watch houses, people working?"

The boy didn't say anything.

"'Cause I reckon it could get a bit annoying," said John, "me working up a sweat, you just watching. Know what I mean?"

The boy lowered his eyes, shuffled a bit, but stood his ground. "Used to be my gran's house," he said. "Mum says we should have got the house. By rights."

Christ, thought John, this was just what he needed. He turned and looked up at the house. "The old woman, Mrs Sheehan? She was your grandmother?"

"Yeah," said the boy. "My dad's mum."

"How come the hospital had it then? I bought it from them."

"Granny left it to them, when she died. 'Cause Dad had cancer," Billy said.

"So she didn't leave it to the family," said John.

"Dad died a long time ago." Billy scratched his face.

17

"Granny and Ma didn't get on. Hated each other."

"What about you?"

"I used to come here. When I was little," Billy said. "Before Dad died. Ma wouldn't let Granny see me and Tom after that. Guess that's why she didn't leave it to us."

"So why're you hanging around?" said John.

"Dunno. Heard they sold it. Thought I'd come see."

"It's pretty run down," said John.

"Ma says it's fucked," said Billy. "Water damage."

"Yeah, well, she's not entirely wrong. Structure's still good though. Good bones," John said, pulling his gloves back on.

The boy looked dubious.

John wheeled the barrow back into the house. The boy was gone when he came out again with the next load.

But he was back the next day, late in the afternoon. This time with a black eye and a cut on his cheek.

"Been fighting?" John asked.

"No."

"Who hit you then?"

"No one."

"If you say so."

"It's alright. It's been worse."

"Come inside. I'll put something on that cut. It looks a bit nasty."

"'S'alright."

"Nah. It's not alright. What's your name anyway? I'm John, John Lawrence."

"Billy."

"Okay, Billy, come on. I've got a first aid kit inside."

The cut was long and jagged. John cleaned it and the rest of the boy's face, but he wasn't sure where to stop. The boy was filthy. "You stink," he said. The boy glared at him. "No, really. You do. When'd you last have a shower?" The boy

18

didn't say anything but made to move for the door. "Alright, just the cut then," John said. He put some iodine on it and a couple of butterfly strips. "Try and keep it clean for a couple of days." He closed the first aid kit and put it back on top of the fridge. "Want something to eat?"

"No. I'm alright." But he changed his mind when John pulled a container of leftover pasta out of the fridge and began heating it in a frypan. He looked uncomfortable in John's company but he was clearly interested in what John was doing to the inside of the house.

"Gran had a big clock over there," he said, nodding towards a corner of what would have been the dining room. "Grandfather clock, she called it."

"Yeah? Did she have nice stuff, your grandmother?"

"Some. Old stuff anyway. Lots of little china things. Like little statues. The hospital sold all that too."

"That's a pity. Does this happen often?" John asked, putting a bowl of pasta in front of the boy.

There was no reply – the boy was too busy filling his mouth with food.

"Because you should tell someone. The cops or someone."

"No," said Billy.

"Why not?"

"They'll stick me in a group home."

He was probably right, thought John. If they took him away from his family, at his age, he wasn't going to end up in some neat suburban foster home. And he wasn't a big kid, he'd struggle in a group home.

"Okay, tell me then. Who hit you?"

No reply, nothing, just more pasta going in.

"You can't let them get away with it."

The boy ignored him.

"You've got to do something about it."

Billy looked up at John, his loaded fork quivering in midair. "Yeah, what? Can't do nothing. Just makes it worse."

"Cops'll do something."

"No, they won't." It was the voice of experience.

Maybe not but they'll get you off my hands. "I'm taking you home or to the cops when you've finished eating. Doesn't matter which to me, so you better choose," he said.

Billy looked at John. "Home," was all he said.

Billy tried to run as soon as he was out the door, but John grabbed him by the collar. "Nice try. Now behave and get in the ute. We're going to have a quiet word with your mother."

"You'll be lucky."

"What do you mean?"

"Mum doesn't do quiet," said Billy. He was right about that.

Miller Street was wide and lined with huge fig trees that cast deep shadows. The roots of the trees were busy tearing up the footpath. Fruit bats screeched and chittered above them and John hoped he didn't get shat on as he picked his way carefully along the heaving footpath. Billy's house was a single-storey terrace set back from the street. The small front yard had no plants in it, but broken and dismantled bikes and scooters seemed to be sprouting among the deep mulch of leaves that covered the ground. John pressed the doorbell.

"Doesn't work, you've gotta knock." Billy said, stepping past John and pounding on the door with the bottom of his fist. "Still be lucky if they notice."

There was no response from the house, so John knocked again, using the flat of his hand on the peeling wooden door.

There was a brief sound of movement from the house, then it went quiet again. John waited a moment, then knocked again, louder.

He heard the sound of a voice this time, coming from the back of the house.

"Fuck off. I said I'm going didn't I ... well I am."

John looked at Billy.

He shrugged. "Mum."

John nodded.

A light went on in the hall, then the door was thrown open.

"What?" The woman was shrunken and skinny with mad red-grey hair. She wore a short blue robe loosely tied at the waist. Thin white legs connected the robe to the ground. Her red-rimmed eyes looked at John for a second then flicked to the boy standing behind him. She lunged past John, grabbed the boy by the arm and pulled him inside. "Get the fuck inside, Billy." The boy stumbled down the hallway. The woman's attention was back on John now. She looked him up and down. "You a cop?"

"No, I—"

"Fuck off then." She stepped back and started to shut the door. "Fucking do-gooder."

John stopped the door with his hand. "Listen—"

"Get your hand off my door."

"Not till you talk to me about the boy."

"Billy's none of your fucking business, you nosy prick. Now piss off." She tried to swing the door shut again but John didn't move his hand. "Let go the fucking door," the woman shouted.

Then a man's voice called from the back of the house: "Will you shut that fucking door?" Deep bass. "I'm trying to watch the telly here."

21

"Jason, help me. This cunt won't let me shut the door."

"What cunt?"

"This cunt, fucking do-gooder. Acting like he thinks he's a bloody copper. Now he won't go. Won't let me shut the fucking door."

A figure appeared at the end of the hall, silhouetted against the light in the room behind. A big man to match the voice. Billy ducked into one of the doorways, letting the man go past.

"Who the fuck're you?" Jason said, picking up an aluminium baseball bat that had been leaning against the door jamb.

"Fucking interfering do-gooder," said the woman. "Won't piss off."

John didn't like the way this was developing. "Someone's been hitting the boy," he said.

Jason wasn't listening. He smelled of beer and marijuana. "No one wants you here, cunt," he said, raising the bat to his shoulder.

John stepped back. "Take it easy, Jason. I don't want a fight. You'll kill me if you hit me with that thing. I just want to talk about the boy. About Billy."

Jason kept coming "He's none of your business, so you better just fuck off."

"Listen, I don't want a fight," John repeated. "I just want to talk."

"I just want you gone," Jason said, stepping forwards and swinging the bat at John's head.

But nowhere near fast enough. John stepped inside the arc of the bat, trapping it and Jason's wrists beneath his left arm. His right hand came up fast, an open-palm strike. Jason's head snapped back and he went down hard in a flurry of fig leaves. John stepped back with the bat cocked at his shoulder, ready to swing it. But the big man wasn't moving.

"Jason," the woman screamed. "What have you done to him, you bastard? Jason? Jason." She turned and launched herself at John. He caught her and twisted her to the ground.

"Don't think I won't hit you too," he said quietly into her ear. She started to shout again so he hit her. An open handed slap to the ear. She kept shouting. "Shh ... be quiet now. Jason'll be alright. Shouldn't be anything broken."

The woman quietened down a bit. John let her get up. "Alright?"

"Piss off." She rubbed her ear and face.

"Glad to. One thing, though, if I hear about any harm coming to Billy, from you or Jason or anyone else in this happy family, I will be back and I will be breaking things." He went to the door and leaned inside. "Billy? You alright?"

The boy's head appeared from one of the doorways lining the hall. "What?"

"Are you okay? Do you want to come with me?"

"You better go," he said and disappeared again.

John pointed the bat at the woman, who was kneeling over Jason now. "Either of you touch him and I'm coming back. I'll put you both in hospital if I have to."

John threw the bat in the back of the ute and drove off, wondering what the fuck he had got himself into.

The next time Billy showed up at Camperdown he had no new injuries.

"They leaving you alone?"

"Jason left. Mum won't talk to me."

John looked at him. "That's a good thing, right?"

Billy tried not to smile.

"So, if you're going to hang around here do you want to help me? Instead of just watching." The boy looked

23

uncomfortable. "I'll pay you," said John.

That got his attention. "How much?"

"Dunno." John scratched his neck. "Say ten dollars an hour, see how long you last."

Billy nodded his agreement and John found a spare set of gloves for him. They looked huge on the boy, like his skinny arms were sticking out of baseball mitts, but he worked hard, filling and emptying the wheelbarrow. Once they had settled into a rhythm of work they didn't talk much, just got on with it. Occasionally John had noticed Billy looking at his scars, but the boy never said anything.

The Cathay Pacific A330's attitude changed slightly as it began its long descent. Betty Lawrence opened her eyes, leaned forwards and slid the plastic window blind up, letting the pale dawn light slip into the cabin. A bank of cloud lining the eastern horizon was outlined in gold and pink, but the ground beneath her was still dark, just a grey presence waiting for the new day. Waiting for Betty. It was an empty land, its people clinging to the edges in the east and south. That was where she was going, to the far side of the continent, back to Sydney.

She had to come back because she had fallen down. Just a few steps, just enough to change her life. She had told Madame Chaput about those worn steps. More than once, but nothing was done. The maddening thing was that she knew she was going to fall. As soon as she put weight on the foot she could feel it. But there was nothing she could do about it. Nothing. She tried – she grabbed at the balustrade, but that sudden movement just unbalanced her more. Her foot slipped. Her arms flailed for balance, for a hand hold that wasn't there. Madame Chaput was standing at the bottom of the stairs, their eyes met for a single moment before Betty landed hard on her hip, and slid down. Each jarring step a new slice of pain through her shattered femur.

She was in hospital for two months. Her leg was full of plates and screws now, she had to tell them about it every time she went through the security check at the airports.

So here she was on her way back to Sydney. After forty years away. A lifetime.

John had insisted. "You can't stay here, Mum, you've got a broken leg. What are you going to do? Your apartment is on the fourth floor. There's no lift. There is no one left here to look after you. Your old mates, they've all gone away. *Temps de partir*. It's time, Mum."

But Paris was her home. Since 1966, since she was twenty-five and in love. "It's your home too," she said to John, "you were born here."

"I know, Mum, but I live in Sydney now. I'm more Australian than French, I always have been. If you wanted me to be French, why did you send me to school in Australia? You made that choice for me."

He had said the same thing many, many times over the years, reminding her of her shortcomings as a mother. Betty didn't need reminding, by him or anyone else; she was well aware of them.

"Sydney is my home now, Mum. It's where I live, and I'm the only one left to look after you."

Yes, yes. He was right. He had an annoying habit of making perfect sense. Always had, even as a little boy. Betty knew she wouldn't be able to get up the stairs or walk to the little market near the Métro to get her vegetables and meat. John, always very rational, very sensible. Well, fuck rational. She had every right to be angry. At the world, at John, at Madame Chaput and her stupid stairs, but mostly at herself for being so careless. For becoming so dependent.

While she was in an awful rehabilitation hospital near the Gare Montparnasse, waiting for her old bones to mend, John had packed up her things and let her apartment go. Shipped everything back to Australia. Now it was all waiting for her there, he said. John being practical, efficient. She presumed he had got that from the army. Certainly not from his father, the romantic. Betty supposed she had been a romantic too. Once upon a time. That was how she found herself in Paris in the first place, following her heart. Following the bastard Michel. Following his soft, dark eyes, and that sexy voice. He was like something out of the movies. Totally different from the men she had grown up around in Sydney, and the men she had met in America. How could she not fall in love with him? She had watched him working in Alabama, the Civil Rights marches and Bloody Sunday. Betty the awkward amateur, feeling her way on her first paid assignment, Michel the slick European professional, at ease in any situation. He always seemed to know what was going to happen before it did, was always able to put himself in the best position to get the best shot. He always looked cool, laughing and joking with the rest of the press corps. Noticing her, smiling at her.

After the march on Montgomery, she followed him to Paris. She was in love. For a few months she lived in a dream, in love with being in love, in love with being in Paris. The city overwhelmed her, the light and the smells and the tastes. Her senses were alive for the first time, it seemed. She was so young. Just a baby.

When they weren't in bed she went exploring, wandering the streets, soaking in the romance of the city. At first she looked at Paris with her photographer's eyes, a collection of wonderful images. Later she learned to go for walks without her camera, content to just be part of the scene. It was her first time in Europe and she was entranced by the textures of the city. So different from Sydney, where you could still see the first scars of history being laid down, the native landscape being hacked back for new suburbs. But Paris was layered with stories, reflected in the buildings and the streets. And the food. In Paris she discovered real food: patisserie. In Sydney, her culinary highlight had been vanilla ice cream with hot butterscotch sauce at Cahill's. She was amazed and delighted by the importance that was placed on the preparation and consumption of food in Paris. Michel enjoyed cooking, enjoyed cooking for her. He was very proud of his skill in the kitchen, nearly as proud as he was of his skill in the bedroom. On weekends they went out, shopping at the little markets or walking hand in hand along the Seine. In the evenings they went to jazz clubs. Michel took her to see Miles Davis at Salle Pleyel. She fell for the music, and the man. The king of cool. That was when she started to buy jazz records.

Betty became a *flâneuse*. When Michel was working, and when the weather allowed it, she would be out, strolling about Paris on her own. In a daze, her eyes and ears wide open, telling Michel each evening what she had seen during the day. He laughed at her. "But of course. It is Paris – what did you expect?" She didn't know what she had expected, but it hadn't been the beauty, or the light. Nor had it been the people. At first they intimidated her with their assurance and their indifference, but she found they could be won over. This tiny blonde Australian was so obviously in love with their city, so keen to speak to them in their language, and so willing to try anything, that they embraced her. With her schoolgirl French she struggled to make herself understood, but she persevered and found she learned quickly the more she threw herself into life in Paris.

But the dream of Paris did not last. After three months,

Michel told her she had to leave because his wife was coming back.

Wife? The bastard.

She cried, she shouted. She hit him, threw things at him. Then she packed her bag and walked away. But where could she go? She spent an afternoon crying at a café on the Boulevard Saint-Michel, her bag tucked under the table and a café crème going cold on top of it. She couldn't stop crying. The bastard. She loved him, she had loved him. Had he loved her? Hadn't he? Was she just ... What had she been? A convenience? Until his wife came back? Was this how people lived in Paris? She drank the cold coffee and ordered a glass of wine, making it last, not knowing what she was going to do next, where she could go.

Eventually the exasperated waiter spoke to her. "Mademoiselle, you must stop crying, you are upsetting the other customers."

Betty looked around, catching a number of patrons suddenly returning their gaze to their own business. Betty sniffed and blinked dumbly up at the waiter.

"No man is worth this many tears," he said.

This set Betty off again, appalled that her miserable plight was so obvious, that she had fallen for the oldest, most clichéd betrayal of all. Such a fool.

She left the café and wandered aimlessly, immersed in self-pity. Swinging like a pendulum between grief and anger. She caught sight of her reflection in a jewellery shop window, a small pathetic figure. With her suitcase in her hand, she looked like a refugee, like an image from the World War Two newsreels she had grown up with. It shocked her: this was not who she was, not how she had grown up thinking of herself. The world had not ended, she had just fallen in love with a shit. She was not the first to have made a fool of herself for a man. She didn't expect she would be the last either.

That night she found a hotel and sat up, deciding what to do. She didn't want to leave Paris. She didn't want to go back to Sydney, to her father, having to tell a tale of betrayal and failure to everyone who knew her.

In the morning she looked up the telephone number for Hubert Foss. She had met Hubert at a party, one of many she went to with Michel that spring. Between glasses of wine, he had talked about starting a new photographic agency. He wanted to develop the work of new young photographers. She had told him about her work photographing the Civil Rights movement in Mississippi and Alabama. At the time she thought that maybe she could get some work through the new Agence Foss but hadn't done anything about it.

Hubert was surprised to hear from her. "Betty? Oh *oui*, Michel's little friend. *L'australienne*." Yes, Agence Foss was still looking for new photographers. Betty got the impression that it was struggling to get established. Hubert liked her work. "You have an eye for the heart of a scene, for the emotional detail," he said after he had finished flipping through her portfolio. So she went to work for Agence Foss.

The plane was much lower now. Khaki paddocks with scattered gum trees had given way to farmland, a patchwork of browns and dull greens. The rivers and creeks had water in them, and the roads were more frequent. Some of them were even sealed. Civilisation. They must be close to the coast now.

The assignments took Betty all over Paris. To places she would not have seen otherwise, to crime scenes, factories and political rallies. She was an outsider, but she gave Hubert something that his local photographers did not. Details and juxtapositions they did not notice. Fresh eyes, he called her.

It was only three months after she started working for

Hubert that he sent her to the war in Vietnam. In Saigon, her senses were assaulted by the glare and the smells, but she fell in love again. It was her first time in Asia and her first experience in a war zone. She found that she got on well with the soldiers. Being a woman helped of course, an outspoken Australian, her blonde hair shining against her oversized jungle greens. The local Vietnamese ARVN and the Americans looked after her and in return she tried to portray the war, particularly their experience of it, with honesty and compassion. That first trip was only for two weeks, but it changed her. It was horrific, but also exhilarating. Addictive.

When she got back she decided that if Paris was going to be her home she would embrace it. No more sweaty, borrowed jungle greens, no more living out of a suitcase. Now that she had a bit of money, she was going to enjoy herself, enjoy Paris on her own terms. She found an apartment in the 14th arrondissement near Montparnasse, bought herself some beautiful clothes, made new friends. Took new lovers. She immersed herself in indulgence and beauty, slipping easily into the new social milieu that Hubert introduced her to. His friends were more interesting and more fun than Michel's stuck-up crowd. They were journalists, photographers, models and designers. Of course, Hubert fell in love with her. Betty let him down as gently as she could. Pressing her fingers to his lips to stop him talking. "Hubert, no. I'm sorry, no. You are like my brother." Hubert took the rejection with good grace, as if it was just something that had to be settled. He became her friend and mentor. Paris became her home.

Betty felt the plane bank and looked out the window again. Bushland slid past below her, then yellow sandstone cliffs glowing in the morning sunlight, and the sea. Beyond the fringe of white foam at the foot of the cliffs, the ocean was flat and calm. A fishing boat on its way down the coast was cutting a brilliant white vee across the deep blue surface.

"*C'est votre première fois en Australie?*" The businessman in the seat next to her was leaning over to see out the window.

"*Non, je suis de retour,*" said Betty. "This is where I came from."

When she had eventually given in and agreed to be shipped to Sydney, she thought she was going to be living with John.

"No, Mum," John had said on the phone, "my place is no good. I'm renovating, I've only got floorboards in one of the bedrooms, I told you that. Don't worry, you'll like Forest Court. It's in Glebe, close to everything, not far from me."

An old people's home. Independent living, they called it in the brochure John had sent, but it was just an old people's home. What else do you call a place full of old people?

Glebe. She couldn't remember what Glebe was like. Near the city she thought.

The plane levelled out of its long turn and they floated over Cronulla Beach and Kurnell. To the west Betty could see the edge of Botany Bay. Ramsgate and Brighton-le-Sands, her old haunts, flat, built on ancient sand.

Then they dropped onto Sydney, shiny and bright in the morning sun.

Welcome home, thought Betty.

The flight was twenty minutes late. John stood with his back to the wall and sipped suspiciously at a cup of coffee while his eyes scanned the arrival hall. He still didn't like crowded places. There were too many people, too many possibilities – and too few of him. He knew it didn't make sense, it was just training, conditioning. The plastic brain, rewiring itself. Always on the lookout for threats. He knew he had to let all that go, but he didn't know how. They didn't tell you how to unwire your brain. How to forget. He finished the coffee and binned the paper cup. It had been better than he expected airport coffee to be.

John was tall enough to see over the crowd to the two exit ramps his mother could appear on. He scratched idly at the twisted flesh above his elbow while, behind black wraparound sunglasses, his eyes scanned the crowd, sorting out the family relationships and then reassessing them when new arrivals turned up. Looking for the anomaly, the one that didn't fit – vaguely amused by the thought that this was probably him. Lots of Asian and Middle Eastern families here today. A few groups of Islanders too. The people coming down the arrival ramps from the customs hall split about fifty-fifty, he guessed, between those being greeted by family groups and those just trying to find a quick path through the crowd to get a taxi or to change some money. Backpackers, young surf dudes with curly blond hair and unwieldy surfboards. A couple of old surf dudes too, fit and very tanned. Young women in sarongs, some in ugg boots and track suits. Business men in blazers over polo shirts, minimal luggage, travelling light, in a hurry.

Then his mother was coming down the left-hand ramp. She looked tiny and frail in the wheelchair. A big Indian-looking man steering her down the ramp, leaning over and saying something to her. His mother nodded and looked up for the first time, peering out across the crowded arrivals hall. If it had been anyone but Betty, John would have thought she looked scared. He started to move through the crowd, navigating a route to arrive at the bottom of the ramp at the same time they did. She's changed, he thought. It was only three weeks since he had seen her at the rehab hospital but she seemed different now, smaller somehow. Maybe it

32

was just the wheelchair. He squeezed past a large group of Chinese tourists, sidestepped an errant luggage trolley and stopped in front of his mother.

"Hello, Mum. Welcome home," he said, smiling and bending down to kiss her on both cheeks. Then he straightened up and smiled at the wheelchair pusher. Not sure of the niceties, he stuck out his hand, "Hello, I'm John. Betty's my mother."

The man smiled, lots of white teeth in a brown face, and shook his hand briefly. "Here she is then, all safe and sound, and here is her luggage," he said pointing to a luggage trolley another man had pushed up beside them.

Betty was looking up at them, eyes flicking from one to the other. The man who had been pushing Betty bent down over her. "Goodbye, Mrs Lawrence, I hope everything works out at your new home."

"*Merci*, Sajit. You have been very kind to me, but I can walk from here."

"Are you sure?"

"Yes, of course."

John held Betty's walking stick while Sajit put the brakes on, folded up the foot plates and helped Betty to stand. She wobbled a bit then took the stick from John. "Which way?" she said.

Sajit nodded to John then the two men disappeared into the crowd, making their way towards the staff security door.

"*Et le pourboire?*" said Betty.

"*Non, je ne le pense pas.*" John looked at her then back at the men moving quickly through the crowd, "Not in Australia. We don't tip, not in airports."

"It is too late now anyway," she said. "We better go, we're blocking the way here."

She was right, the ramps were becoming crowded as

people tried to make their way through the crush at the bottom. "Yes, okay," he said, stepping behind the luggage trolley. "Straight ahead, through those doors. I'll follow you."

Betty set off at a slow hobble, past a a small woman in a sari guarding a trolley carrying an unstable-looking mountain of suitcases. John was glad they didn't have to go far.

Forest Court Retirement Village was in a wide, tree-lined street within strolling distance of Glebe Point Road. It was a genteel place, made up of two-storey apartment buildings, tastefully arranged around shady courtyards, hidden from the street behind a high brick wall.

John unlocked the gate and held it open for his mother. Inside the gate were tidy gardens and little lawns cut by pathways. They moved slowly, Betty hobbling along with her stick, John following with her bags, pointing out the sights. The administration building, where the manager's office and the mailboxes were, the common room and laundry over on the right. They passed a pair of old women chatting in a courtyard. One of them was leaning on a four-wheeled pusher, the other was sitting on a bench with a newspaper folded in her lap. John smiled and nodded to them. They smiled and nodded in return, conversation suspended, their eyes following Betty, who hadn't stopped, hadn't smiled.

Betty's new home was apartment number 12, on the ground floor of a block towards the rear of the village. John opened the door and stood back to let Betty in. When she didn't make a move to enter, he slipped past her and carried the bags through into the sitting room.

"*Tu es très occupé*," said his mother following him inside.

John looked around at his mother's old furniture in this new room, at her photographs on the wall. "Just trying to

34

make it look a bit like home."

"It has not worked. *Ce n'est pas du tout comme chez moi.*" She crossed the room to her lumpy old armchair, leaning her stick against the over-stuffed arm and easing herself down. "*Vas-tu m'offrir une tasse de thé?*"

"Of course. I'll put the kettle on."

When John came back with a tea pot and two cups, his mother was staring at the dresser, at the *objets* he had arranged there, souvenirs she had brought back to Paris from the various battlefields and hell holes she had worked in: a little ceramic tea pot from Vietnam, a carved cedar tree from Lebanon, and a beaded elephant from somewhere in Africa.

She is never going to forgive me for bringing her here, he realised, as he passed her the tea.

Later, after they had shared an early lunch, Betty put herself to bed and slept for most of the afternoon. John stood in the doorway watching his mother sleep. She had always been a bundle of energy, but now she was old. Her skin was thin and almost translucent, wisps of grey hair curling across her cheek. There were photographs of her from Vietnam, all blonde hair and cheeky grin, usually surrounded by soldiers. She had been beautiful then, but now she looked frailer than he'd ever seen her.

John wasn't sure what to do now. He couldn't go home and leave her alone. Not yet, not on her first day. He turned on the television with the sound down low and watched a show about antique fairs. The point seemed to be for people to buy things and try to resell them for a profit. Mostly they didn't. The host was a bizarrely dressed Englishman with a bow tie and bulging eyes. John turned the television off again.

In the kitchen he took the chicken he had bought the

35

day before out of the fridge and looked at it. He had meant to roast it: a welcome home dinner, roast chicken with all the trimmings. But now he thought chicken soup might be a better bet.

Betty never cooked much when he was a kid. When he was home from school they would always go out to eat, sometimes at friends' houses, but mostly cafés and restaurants. She knew all the people who ran the local cafés, greeting them by their first names, asking about their families, gossiping about the other regulars. She would miss all that here.

It was after five when Betty woke up. Making her way to the living room via the bathroom, she sat herself back down in the lumpy armchair.

"How are you feeling?" John asked.

"*Je me sens mieux maintenant.* Better for being in my own bed, even if it is in a strange room. What is that smell? Have you been cooking?"

"Chicken soup. Thought we'd have some for dinner."

"You're making soup?"

"Yes."

"I thought you lived out of cans."

"Yeah, well, I still love canned tomato soup, but I can cook a bit. Have done for years. I was going to do you a roast chicken but thought soup would be better."

"Do I seem sick?"

John shrugged. "Out of sorts, jet lag. It's only natural."

John finally left when Betty was asleep for the night, snoring softly in her own bed. He had done the washing up and put the leftovers in the fridge while he waited for her to relax enough to go to sleep. As he locked her in, he thought, *This is do-able, she'll settle in. It might take time but she will get used to things.*

THREE

Rules

Betty woke early to the sound of once familiar birdsong, sounds half-remembered from her childhood. Her new bedroom was strange, all her old things, but in a new place. It was disorienting, familiar and alien at the same time, like being in a dream. She remembered similar feelings of disorientation when travelling in new countries, especially in supermarkets, the spaces and colours familiar, even the brand names, but when you looked closely, things were different, unintelligible.

The new apartment was small. Just a single bedroom, a sitting room and a tiny galley kitchen, making her feel big, like Alice after she had eaten the cake. The sitting room opened onto a little terrace that in turn opened onto other courtyards. The architecture was old-fashioned, minimalist, all pale bricks and dark timber – from the sixties, she guessed. It added to her feeling of disorientation. She was like an exile, but in a country that she had left a long time ago, when Kennedy was the president in the United States, young and good looking, and still alive.

Paris had been her home all her adult life. It was her

heart, it was in her. John didn't understand that. She had nothing in Sydney anymore except old memories. There was John of course, but all her family were long gone. Her father Jack, and Emily, her stepmother, had died in 1998, three months apart. Her own mother had run off when Betty was five; just after the war, leaving Betty and her father behind in Kogarah. No, she had been away too long. Sydney would never be home again.

She had left in 1962 to look for her mother, meaning to come home again, hoping to bring her mother back with her. But she didn't find her mother, and once she got out, it was such a long way to come back. Well, it was then, in the sixties. And there was so much happening out in the world.

It was not long after the Cuba crisis, Kennedy and Kruschev standing toe to toe. She read the reports and listened to the broadcasts, hoping one of them would blink before they managed to destroy the world. Betty was working in the classified advertising section of the *Sydney Morning Herald* then, having to listen to that fool Frank Thompson saying neither of them had the guts to do it. Talking as if he wanted them to launch the missiles, press the button, or whatever they did. Start a new war. The man was an idiot, swanning around the office like he owned the place. Supposed to be an account manager, but he still had pimples. Frank Thompson said even if they did do it, we'd be alright. Australia was too far away, the other side of the world. But Frank was talking out of his arse as usual. He didn't know, no one did – that was the point.

Hiroshima and Nagasaki were fresh memories then. Her father had been to Hiroshima, had worked in the occupation force after the war. He said you wouldn't believe anything could do that. A single bomb. There was nothing left of the place.

When the Russians turned back their ship, it seemed that the whole city began breathing again. But then everyone just got on with things, as though nothing had happened, everything back to normal. But for Betty the world had changed: after Cuba, they were always going to be on the brink of disaster. It was too easy. Too easy for one side to misjudge the other, misread the signals, let things get to a point where there was nothing left to do but launch the missiles and hope that someone would survive.

After Cuba, time was no longer limitless. Betty had things she wanted to see, things she wanted to do before it was too late. She wanted to speak to her mother again for one thing. To find out why she had left Betty behind, why she hadn't come back, hadn't sent for her like she'd said she would.

Mary Lawrence had followed an American sailor to San Francisco, leaving Betty behind with her grandparents in the weatherboard house in Kogarah. She had some memories of her mother in the last years of the war, beautiful and young, sometimes sad, sometimes full of life and laughter. There were hot days in the backyard, her mother happy, smiling, bending over Betty, blonde hair falling around her face, glowing in the sunlight like a halo. Blue eyes, white teeth, red lips. Smelling of soap. There were memories of a dark, powerful man too, who was so big he seemed to block out the sun. He might have been Mary's sailor, Pete Connors, but Betty didn't know for sure; she could be remembering a different American. She didn't imagine her mother had gone out with just the one.

Betty had no memory of the day Mary left. She just wasn't there anymore, replaced by a man who turned out to be Betty's father. Jack Lawrence was a quiet, thin man. He must have been an angry man too, coming back from Japan to find his wife gone. But he kept all that inside himself, never talked about Mary, just got on with things. Went back to work at the Bank of New South Wales.

There had been three letters from Mary in America. The first letter was long and rambling, full of excitement and descriptions of the new country she found herself in. Looking forward to settling down somewhere with Pete. Missing Betty. When Pete got a job they would send for her, and what a life they would have together in America. The other two letters weren't so excited. They were sent from different places. Pete and Mary were moving around looking for work. The last was from Texas: Pete was trying to get work in the oil fields. Mary said she missed Betty. That letter was the last any of them heard from her.

After Cuba, Betty went to America to find her mother. Or at least to find out what had happened to her. She was young then, she didn't believe that people could just disappear. But they could – Mary Lawrence and Pete Connors had. After Texas there was no record of them anywhere that Betty could find. She had no money to hire an investigator, so she did what she could herself, talking to the Navy, following their trail to Texas, talking to the police. She put ads in newspapers and kept looking until what money she had ran out. Then she hitchhiked to the east coast and picked up some waitressing work. In New York she met some students who were starting a newspaper. When she said she had worked for a paper in Sydney, they didn't ask what she had done there, just lent her a camera, said take some photos of a picket line for us. So she did. Turned out she was good at it.

Betty had only been back to Sydney a few times. The last two trips had both been in 1998, for her father's funeral in May and then Emily's in August. So close together.

In the tiny kitchen. Betty searched through the cupboards and drawers till she found her crockery and cutlery. There was food too, milk in a plastic bottle, Greek yoghurt, butter. No bread though. She found a brand new electric kettle on the bench and her old tea pot that John had left on the draining board. She made herself a cup of tea, and went into the sitting room, carrying the cup in her left hand and wielding her stick with the right. Just outside the living room window there was a little terrace and beyond it she could see gardens and lawns. There didn't seem to be anybody else about yet.

The door slid open easily and Betty hobbled outside, settling herself on one of the two new-looking chairs arranged either side of a small round table. It was a warm outside, a dry heat that prickled at her skin. It was going to be hot later. She remembered Sydney in February, hot days punctuated by dramatic storms. Southerly busters, Emily had called them. Dark clouds rolling up the coast, bringing relief at the end of long, stinking-hot days. She remembered standing out in the back garden under a sudden downpour, squealing with delight while her father yelled at her from the shelter of the veranda to get the hell inside.

A tabby cat joined her on the terrace, yowling a greeting and rubbing against her ankles. Betty bent down and rubbed its ears, "*Bonjour*, kitty. *Comment tu t'appelles?*" The cat didn't tell her its name, but it did purr and lean into her hand.

The edge of the terrace was lined with pot plants that were old and struggling to compete with the flourishing weeds. They must have belonged to the previous occupant of the apartment. Who would that have been, she wondered, another old woman? Dead now, no doubt.

Betty dragged the chair over to the nearest pots and began pulling out weeds, pausing every now and again to sip her tea and rub the cat's head. Before long she had a little pile of weeds beside her chair.

"Young Terry's going to be annoyed with you."

A man was standing on the edge of the courtyard watching her.

"I'm sorry?"

"The gardener, Terry. Calls himself a gardener anyway," the man said, giving Betty a grin. "Wouldn't know a rose bush from a coconut tree if you ask me, but he's supposed to do all the gardening round here." He stuck out a large-knuckled hand. It was a working man's hand, strong fingers, the back covered in thick white hair and liver spots. "Ken," he said, "Ken Mallard. You must be the new girl."

Betty looked at the hand for a moment then offered her own but quickly withdrew it when she saw the dirt caked on her fingers. "Sorry. I will have to get some gloves." She looked up at the man. He was wearing a cloth cap, slacks and a light jacket. Very neat. Betty was wearing her old red dressing gown. "I am Betty Lawrence," she said.

"Betty," he said, trying the name out. "It's good to meet you. We need a bit of new blood around here, new faces." He looked around at the gardens. "Like I said, theoretically you're doing young Terry out of a job,"

"Theoretically?"

"I don't think Terry really believes in work."

"I can tell," said Betty looking at the pile of weeds she had produced.

The cat picked itself up off the bit of low wall it had been sleeping on and yowled lazily at them. "You're blocking its sun," said Betty.

"Sorry, Tiger," said Ken Mallard, stepping sideways to move his shadow away from the cat.

"Who does it belong to?" Betty asked.

"Oh, it's just the village cat, doesn't really belong to anyone. Just appeared one day, a skinny, beaten-up tabby, looking very sad and sorry for itself." He gave the cat a rub behind the ears. "Weren't you, mate? Can't remember who came up with the name, but it stuck."

Betty thought it was an unlikely name. The cat may have been lean and hungry when it arrived, but now it was fat and happy.

"Tiger's daily routine involves dragging himself from one patch of sunshine to the next and visiting one old lady after another. He's the luckiest cat in Sydney – a village full of cat ladies all to himself."

"There are worse fates for a stray cat."

"Sure. They all love him. And they all feed him, which is why he is so fat. But none of them will own up to it because we're not allowed to have pets. Against the rules."

"Oh," said Betty. "Rules."

"Oh yes," said Ken. "There are rules."

Billy was leaning against the bonnet of the ute when John emerged from the house on Sunday morning. "I want to meet your French mum," he said. "See what she's like."

On the way to Forest Court they stopped in Glebe Point Road to buy some croissants for Betty. The smell in the little Vietnamese-run bakery was fantastic. John bought three *pains au chocolat* as well as the croissants.

Betty was sitting with her cameras on the table in front of her, cleaning them with a soft cloth.

"Morning, Mum." John bent down and kissed her. "This is a friend of mine, Billy Sheehan. He's been helping me, working on the house."

"*Bonjour*, Billy," Betty said, looking at the boy then back at John, before she went back to polishing the Leica.

"Um, hello, Mrs Lawrence," said Billy.

"You found the cameras then?" said John.

"Obviously," said Betty. "Here they are."

John had told Billy about his mother, the broken leg, bringing her back to Sydney to live. Billy had helped John move Betty's things into the apartment and had been fascinated by the cameras when they had unpacked them.

"You were a photographer?" said Billy.

"Photo-journalist," said Betty.

"What did you photograph?"

"Wars mostly," said John, looking at his mother.

"I photographed all sorts of things," Betty said to Billy.

"But mostly wars. Vietnam, Lebanon, Rwanda," said John, slipping into a familiar routine but unable to stop himself.

"There were a lot of wars to cover," said Betty.

"Still are."

"You should know, you are the soldier." She turned to Billy and smiled. "It was a long time ago. I'm retired now, but I like to keep my cameras in good condition. It is just a habit."

"Mum was famous for a while," said John. He was aware of Billy watching them, mother and son, performing.

"I should show you my portfolio some time, Billy. My photographs."

"Yeah. That'd be good," said Billy

The cameras didn't need polishing. John had checked them before they were packed away. Not that she used them now she was retired anyway. "What would be the point?" she had said once when he asked her why she didn't take photos any more. "It was never a hobby, always a job."

She had only kept two cameras when she retired, the Leica and her first Nikon. The favourites. They'd had a rough life but still shone through all the scratches and dents. John didn't think she would ever own a digital camera. He assumed

44

that she kept cleaning them because she liked the familiar feel. The tools of her trade. He had been the same in the army. The hands remembering what to do, without thinking, the familiar feel of the weapons. Reassuring. Comforting.

Billy hadn't seen a film camera before. Betty showed him how they worked, taking the 50mm lens off the Nikon, showing him the mirror, opening the back to show him where the film went. Then she cocked it and fired the shutter. The old camera still made a crisp click as the mirror flipped up and the shutter opened and closed, all in the blink of an eye.

Billy was amazed at the complex mechanics of it. "Used to take weeks to see the photos in the old days, didn't it?" he said.

"Not necessarily. If you have a darkroom, you can process the film yourself," said Betty.

"Yeah?" Billy sounded sceptical.

Betty twisted the lens back into place and held up the camera "Here, you have a try."

Billy held the camera up to his eye and pressed the shutter release. Nothing happened.

"You have to cock it," said Betty. She showed him how to use the lever that advanced the film and cocked the shutter.

Billy tried again, grinning when the camera clicked. "Can I take it outside?"

John nodded. "Yeah, but don't drop it. And don't go taking photos of old people getting dressed."

John sat down next to Betty while Billy wandered around the courtyard with the Nikon pretending to take photographs of flowers, birds and an old tabby cat. "I got a letter yesterday from Jacques Poirier about some more furniture in Paris," he said.

"The lawyer?"

"Yeah. Do you know about that? More furniture in storage there?"

"My furniture? It's here, isn't it?"

"Yes, your furniture is here. All that was at Rue de Gergovie – that was all I knew about. It sounds like he's talking about some other stuff that's still in Paris, in storage."

"I have more furniture than is here. In this apartment. Is the rest still in Paris?"

"No. All your stuff is here, in Sydney. There was too much for the new apartment so I put it in a lock-up. A storage unit. I'll take you and show you sometime. I think the lawyer is talking about some other furniture that wasn't at Rue de Gergovie. Furniture in storage in Paris. Do you remember what it might be?"

Betty looked at him then turned to watch Billy squatting in front of the cat, talking to it as if it was a fashion model, while he clicked away with the empty camera. "Jorge's things," she said quietly.

John watched his mother. She didn't look up at him.

"Dad's things?"

Betty nodded, watching Billy.

John's father had died before he was born. All John had ever had of his father's belongings were some books and photographs. "You've had Dad's things in storage all this time? Why didn't you tell me?" He stood up and walked away from her, then turned back and stood over her. "It's been forty years, Mum."

"Don't shout."

John sat down again. "For fuck's sake," he said quietly. "Why didn't you tell me?"

"When he died, it was very sudden. It was too much, too much to deal with. And later … it just seemed simpler. To forget."

46

"Simpler to forget? He was my father."

"He was my love."

John couldn't believe that she had never told him that there were things of his father's in storage. All that time. "I don't understand you. Didn't you think I'd want to know? That I had a right to know? *Il était mon père pour l'amour de Dieu.*"

"You weren't born yet. You didn't know him."

"No, I didn't, did I? That's the problem, I didn't have the chance."

"Please don't shout at me."

They glared at each other.

He hadn't been bloody shouting. John tried to put his anger aside. "What is there? What furniture did he have? Why did you keep it? Why not sell it, why leave it in storage?"

"I don't know why. It was too painful. You were on the way. I was alone. It was just too much."

"So what was there? Didn't you pack it up?"

"No. After he died, I let the removalists pack it up. There will be his furniture," said Betty. "I don't know what else. He had some nice furniture. Books, of course, lots of books."

John turned and looked out the window. Billy had stopped photographing the cat. He was talking to a white-haired man who was carrying plastic shopping bags. The cat had changed allegiances and was busy rubbing itself around the old man's ankles. Billy was looking embarrassed, not sure what to do with his hands or with the camera hanging around his neck. The man said something and Billy pointed to John and Betty.

"Who's that talking to Billy?" John asked.

"Oh, I met him this morning. Ken, that's his name." Betty went to the window and waved him over. "He's pleasant enough."

Ken came over and smiled at Betty. "Is this your family?"

"No," said Betty. "Well, yes, my son is, John, but this young man is his friend Billy. I've just been showing him my cameras."

Ken shook hands with John. "Good to meet you. Young Billy here seems to be trying to turn Tiger into a star."

"The cat," Betty explained. Tiger was sitting in the middle of the lawn watching them.

"He's wondering why he isn't the centre of attention anymore," Ken said. "Anyway, I better get my ice cream in the fridge before it melts. Nice to meet you."

"We better get going too," said John.

John didn't say much as he and Billy drove back to Camperdown. On the way they picked up some lunch in Stanmore. Hamburgers, fries and Cokes, which they ate sitting in the shade on John's back veranda, looking out on the overgrown kikuyu grass. John ate silently, methodically, but apparently Billy wanted to talk.

He sucked on his Coke till the straw was just pulling air, watching John chew his fries. "How come you aren't French?" he asked.

John looked at him. "I am. Technically."

"What does that mean?"

"I was born there, and I've got French and Australian passports."

"Can you have two passports? From two countries?"

"Yeah. I was born in Paris, but Mum sent me to boarding school here, in Sydney, when I was six. She wanted me to be Australian even though she never wanted anything much to do with Australia herself."

48

"Why not?"

"Dunno. I used to stay with my grandparents down at Kogarah in the holidays. I only went home to Paris at Christmas."

"What was it like in Paris?" Billy asked.

"Cold mostly. So cold after Sydney, and dark. Short days," said John. "Food was good though, particularly after boarding school food. I used to miss the beach and my friends. I never had a proper summer for a long time." He remembered days stuck in the apartment, and following his mother through the cold streets to parties and restaurants. Playing with kids he only saw once a year. "I think I would have been better off going to school in Paris. I would have had more friends, but Mum was always travelling overseas for work."

"Taking photos?" Billy said. "Sounds like a sweet job."

"Dangerous, if you're taking photos of wars." John scrunched up the wrapping from his hamburger and shoved it into his empty drink container.

"I suppose so. Do you speak French?"

"*Oui*," said John, "It's English I have trouble with."

"I wouldn't mind boarding school," Billy said. "Not have to go home every day. Never have to see Tom."

Tom was Billy's older brother. "I thought he wasn't at home much anymore."

"Yeah, he spends a lot of time with his girlfriend. Unless she kicks him out. Then he comes crawling home. Trying to bludge off Ma and telling me what to do all the time." Billy peeled the plastic lid off his drink container and peered inside at the ice filling the bottom now that he had sucked out all the cola.

"How old is he?"

"Seventeen," said Billy. "He's got a new girlfriend now. Called Jenny. Dark hair, big mouth. Big tits. Ma hates her.

49

Reckons she's a bloody prossie. 'What's he bloody hanging around with her for?' she says. I reckon the big tits might have something to do with it." Billy snorted. "She's nice though, to me. Smiles, that's more than bloody Tom does. He couldn't give a rat's. She's got a tat of a red rose winding up her arm."

Billy didn't think Jenny was a prostitute. John thought Billy had a big crush on the girl.

"Not that I'm gonna ask her," Billy said. "Tom would kill me. Seriously. Kill me dead. Even Ma wouldn't ask, and she'll ask anyone anything. She once asked Uncle Teddy if he was a poof. Just like that, to his face. We were sitting around watching telly. *Big Brother* or some shit. They were just about to kick someone off, when Ma pipes up and says, 'So Teddy, you a poof or what?'"

"Who's Teddy?" asked John. He was having trouble keeping up with Billy's family.

"Uncle Teddy. He's not really an uncle, just a friend of Ma's brother, Peter. The one who got killed in Vietnam, not the other one, Kevin. He's up in Western Australia somewhere, working in the mines. Don't think I've ever met him. If I have, I can't remember. Peter and Teddy were in the army together, in Vietnam. Anyway we were all sitting around when Ma asks Teddy if he's a poof. Tom was home then – this was a couple of years ago – Tom gave a huge snort of surprise halfway through having a pull on his VB. Beer came spurting out his nose, made a mess on the rug. Mum jumped up shouting at him to get out, saying he was too young to be drinking anyway, what the hell's he think he's doing? Tom's got beer and snot all over him, yelling at Ma to shut the fuck up and go get a towel. I was nearly wetting myself, but trying not to let Tom see. In all the shouting and carrying on, Uncle Teddy left. Just snuck out the front door.

"Course, Teddy is a poof, gay, whatever. Everyone knew it, but Teddy didn't know everyone knew. He thought it was a secret still. I don't care if he is, though. I like Teddy, he's about the only person I know who's never hit me." He looked at John. "Apart from you."

"Give me time," said John, "you haven't known me that long."

"None of us cared really. It's just who Uncle Teddy is. They make jokes about him, when he's not around. Well, mostly when he's not around. He just pretends not to hear if he is around."

"So Teddy's a friend of this dead uncle, Peter?" John said. "Was he gay too?"

"Don't know. No one jokes about whether Peter was a poof. He's a dead hero. I don't think Teddy would be so quiet if they did."

FOUR

No One Gets Out Alive

Betty hated the new apartment. It was too small and it was too different. It wasn't her home. She was trapped there unless John came and picked her up in his little truck. Compared to her home in Montparnasse, it was pokey and characterless, all modern and bland. It felt temporary.

Betty couldn't get used to it, couldn't settle into a routine. She had trouble remembering where things were. Even though the kitchen was tiny, she still could never find anything, opening, then banging closed, every one of the cupboard doors before she found what she was looking for – sometimes forgetting what it was she wanted in the first place. John said that he could take the doors off the cupboards if she would prefer that, but it would look terrible. It was designed to have doors. Why they couldn't just put in nice simple shelves, she didn't know. She didn't need much in the kitchen, just two of everything, It wasn't as if she was going throw a party. No one visited her but John.

The food was all different too. When John took her shopping, she could only rely on guesswork in the huge supermarket. There were no brands she was familiar with, so there was no way to know which ones she would like. The supermarket vegetables were all big and shiny and flavourless. Even the meat was all wrapped in plastic. John tried to help but it soon became apparent that their tastes did not overlap. Sometimes she chose the cheapest, sometimes the most expensive, but it didn't seem to make any difference. It was like learning how to live again. Which crackers, which tuna, which soap? And there was only her to feed so if she bought the wrong thing it took a long time to use it all up. John said she should just throw it out if she didn't like it, but she wasn't going to waste things she had paid good money for. She should be glad to live somewhere where there was choice, but that was no use when all the choices on offer were wrong. In Paris, Betty had done her shopping at the little street market, just down on the corner. It was only open on Wednesday and Sunday but it had everything she needed, and they all knew her and they knew what she liked. Chèvre from the Loire and those little pork *saucisse*, her favourite weekend breakfast. She missed gossiping with her neighbours while they shopped, and buying fresh flowers for the apartment each week. She missed it all, she missed her life.

Now she spent most of her time reading, and looking out the window. There was an enormous new television in the sitting room but it never seemed to work properly for her. It was fine when John was around, he could always get it to work straight away, making her look like a bloody fool. But when he wasn't there it refused to do what she wanted. Not that there was anything on television that she was remotely interested in. It was all American and English shows, except for SBS. France hardly got a mention. The radio was worse. She had no idea what the talk shows were always so indignant about. She wanted a little bit of jazz to listen to but apparently that was too much to ask for in Sydney. She did have her CDs at least. And her own old CD player. She knew how to make that work. In the afternoons Mingus, Coltrane and Davis slid around the apartment, weaving spells, while she read. She was gradually rediscovering her old books, exploring the bookcases that John had filled at random from different parts of her collection. She found once familiar titles in strange new associations, many she hadn't looked at for years. They took on a new light, covers she remembered well, but the details long forgotten. She spent hours sitting in her old chair, listening to her old music, reading her old books while outside the sun glared hot and white. Through her windows she could see the other residents walking or hobbling through the courtyard.

John had arranged for a physiotherapist to come twice a week to oversee her rehabilitation. Stephan – "with an A" – was a horribly cheerful young man, and far too familiar. "Have you been doing your exercises, Betty?" *No I have not, it hurts too much. And it's Madame Lawrence to you*, she thought, trying to swing her leg out against the pull of a big rubber band that was tied to the leg of the bed. Despite her grumbling at the exercises, Stephan's relentlessly cheerful encouragement did produce results. Betty found that her leg got stronger and hurt less each week. By her second month at Forest Court she was moving around the village with the aid of her stick. Not that there was anything to see, but she did go to the letter boxes each day, to collect what was mostly junk mail, and she started going to the communal laundry to do her washing.

Moving around the village put her in contact with more of her neighbours. Most were completely boring. She should have expected that in an old people's home, but she hadn't expected them all to be so poorly dressed. There was an awful lot of knitted polyester, mostly shapeless, mostly beige. Some of them even got about outside in slippers.

They were Christians generally, which was understandable, seeing that Forest Court was a church-run place. To her atheistic eyes, however, it made them even more alien and incomprehensible. They talked about things she had no knowledge of, and less care for. At first they seemed interested in her, asking questions about where she came from, what she had done. When she tried to tell them all about Paris, about her work, their clouded eyes would glaze over and they would nod then take the first chance to shuffle away. They had nothing in common with Betty, nothing to share.

Nearly everything about Sydney and the village annoyed her. "My God, the heat, how do you stand it? And the noise? Those damned cicadas, I can't hear myself think." Betty knew that she was always complaining about Sydney but she didn't know how to stop.

There were a couple of inmates whose company she enjoyed. Ken Mallard was one. Betty got in the habit of sitting outside on her terrace with a cup of tea each morning, about the time Ken came back from his daily constitutional, as he insisted on calling his morning walk. Ken reminded her of men from her parents' generation, hardworking and with a dry-as-dust sense of humour. The two of them shared a wry view of where life had led them. Ken had worked on the railways, a fitter and turner in the workshops at Redfern. "A good union man I was, until it turned out most of the bastards were corrupt all along. More fool me. It was all comrade this and comrade that, meanwhile they were lining their pockets. I was sick of the whole thing by the time I retired." His wife, Louise, had died in 2001: "Bowel cancer. A stroke finished the old girl off."

"I'm sorry," said Betty.

"Well, no one gets out alive, do they?"

"No. That is true."

"What about you, Betty? Were you ever married?"

"No. Not married. Jorge, John's father, he died before John was born. 1975, a long time ago."

"Long time to be alone."

"Yes."

There had been men of course, affairs but no relationships. She had never wanted a replacement for poor darling Jorge.

Helen Hayes was another one that Betty liked. She had worked in the government, "Before I became old, before I became an aged-care consumer." Helen was a striking woman, tall, and always dressed in strong, bright colours, her long grey hair pulled back in a plait that hung down her back. Helen said what she thought, which Betty liked, and was a bit left-wing, which was appealingly unfashionable. *We were all socialists at one time*, thought Betty, but everyone seemed to get more conservative as they got older.

Betty found that despite herself she enjoyed Ken's and Helen's company. They had a bit of spark about them, and were interested in life. The two of them tried to get her involved in the village activities, but Betty resisted.

Rosemary Bennet, on the other hand, was someone she tried to avoid. A recent widow, Rosemary was younger than most of the village residents. She was a busy woman, always doing things for others. "Always sticking her nose into other people's business," Betty complained to Ken and Helen. "Trying to fill her life with other people's problems so she doesn't have to deal with her own." There was no beige knitwear where Rosemary was concerned. She was always neatly turned out. It seemed to Betty that Rosemary had not changed the way she dressed since she was in her twenties, when someone must have told how to dress to make the most of her figure. It was the Rosemary Bennet uniform, a fitted linen jacket over a T-shirt, and linen slacks or skirt. It would be chic if it wasn't always exactly the same.

Rosemary was always on the alert for any unexplained absences. If she hadn't seen someone for a day or two, she would virtually send out a search party. "We have to make sure we're all still ticking over. Can't have anyone left behind," she said. Betty would be very happy if this annoying woman would leave her behind, and she thought a lot of the others would too.

Rosemary was the chief instigator of organised activities. Shopping trips, excursions to the art gallery, *boules* in the courtyard. They called it *boules*, but it wasn't anything that Betty recognised. Just a bunch of old people lobbing steel balls around a tiny lawn. The most entertaining part was watching them bend over, trying to pick the *boule* up after each round.

Card games were another Rosemary special event – she organised them every Wednesday afternoon in the common room. Betty went along just the once. When Rosemary said cards, Betty heard poker, and was looking forward to winning a bit of spending money. But the game turned out to be canasta. No gambling was allowed, apparently. Rules. "Just as well," said John when she told him, "the way you play. You won't make any friends if you take their pensions off them every fortnight."

"That is the trouble with this place. You have to be careful in case you upset anyone. They are all too bloody sensitive," Betty said.

"I haven't noticed it cramping your style. You just go ahead and say whatever is on your mind."

"Yes? What else should I do?"

Despite Betty's efforts to dissuade her, Rosemary took a shine to her. She did some research and was very excited by what she found out. "Oh, you have had such an interesting life, Betty." She had tried to get Betty to give the residents "a slide show and a little talk, show us some of your famous pictures". Betty didn't think so, not without a gun to her head.

As much as she tried to avoid Rosemary, it wasn't always possible. That was the problem with sitting out on her little terrace. It was the best place to be at the end of a long hot day, with a nice glass of wine and something to read, but there was no privacy.

"Hello, Betty, what a lovely evening." Rosemary was apparently on her way to the bins, a white plastic garbage bag in her right hand and a stack of newspapers tucked under her left arm. "Did you hear what happened to Sue Hodges?"

Sue lived across the courtyard, a very quiet woman who kept to herself. She had collapsed in the communal laundry the previous morning. Taken a turn, was what Ken said. Bad heart, was the rumour. She had been carted off to hospital in an ambulance.

"Yes," said Betty. "It is bad luck for Sue, missing her washing day, she will have to wait a whole week before she gets another chance at the machines."

Rosemary ignored her. "Poor woman. I wonder how long she will be away for?" They both knew Sue probably wouldn't come back. These events were not uncommon at Forest Court: a natural form of attrition, and a topic of conversation for the next week or so. Ken said that four of the residents had been carted off in the last year. Someone was always having a fall or some other health crisis. Usually they didn't come back, instead they were shipped off to a nursing home, the next stop in their inevitable decline. There were a couple of vacant apartments now. Waiting for fresh meat, Betty supposed. Ken said that they liked to wait till there were two or three vacant so they could get a cheaper price for renovating them.

"I'm afraid poor Sue will miss the party next week," Rosemary said. "Did you see my notice?" Betty had, but hadn't planned on going. "When I say party," Rosemary went on, "it's just a bit of get together, just some tea and cakes. No particular occasion. Do come, it'll be a good chance to get to know some of the others. Ken and Helen are going." Betty probably should go, at least to see if there was anyone there worth talking to. She didn't suppose there would be any dancing – not for her anyway. John offered to get her a little wheeled pusher to lean on, but Betty preferred her stick. She enjoyed the thought that she could poke things – and people – with it if necessary.

She had recently started to explore her new environment, beginning with the local corner shops, gradually extending her range to Glebe Point Road. There were plenty of cafés in Glebe, but Betty found the coffee was too strong, and there was nowhere quiet to drink it. All the cafés were too noisy, full of music or television screens, and young people with computers and mobile phones.

John had given Betty a mobile phone when she started going out on her own. "Look, it's really simple to use, green to call, red to hang up," he said, holding it out to her. It was an ugly black thing with big buttons and big numbers, designed for a half-blind person with clumsy sausage fingers. Anyway what did she want another phone for? She had no one to call except John, and he always called her on the house phone in the sitting room. She didn't want him calling when she was out somewhere.

"It's just in case you get stuck, Mum. Have an accident or

something. So you can call me."

Betty took the damned phone in the end, just to shut him up. She kept it in the top drawer with her lingerie.

Against her better judgement, Betty told Ken and Helen that she would go to Rosemary's party. When she settled down in front of her mirror to do her face she realised how long it had been since she had made herself up properly. Most days she just slapped on a bit of lipstick. For the party, she chose her favourite blue dress, one she used to wear in summer in Paris. It would be fine for an autumn evening in Sydney. She wore a lemon silk scarf with it, and considered leaving her stick behind, but decided that was just a foolish vanity.

A woman that she thought was called Philippa greeted her at the door of the common room with a pot of tea. "Yes, thank you, just a drop of milk," Betty said, peering around her. Rosemary was in the little kitchen rallying her troops, standing over Jennifer Hewitt, watching her cutting the crusts off chicken and mayonnaise sandwiches and trying to squash them onto an already full plate. Rosemary looked as if she was trying hard to stop herself from slapping Jennifer. Instead, she passed across another plate.

"Here, Jenny, some of those sandwiches can go on this one. There's no shortage of plates."

"Oh, I suppose so," said Jennifer, "but it's another plate we'll have to wash up."

"You're standing in front of a dishwasher, you know. Here, let me get these out of the way." Rosemary picked up two full plates and marched out of the kitchen, nearly bumping into Betty, who was juggling her tea cup and her walking stick. "There you are, dear, I'm so glad you came. Would you like a sandwich?"

Betty took one of the sandwiches and made her way through to the main room.

Ken stood up and offered her his chair. "This party is eating into my drinking time," he said, glancing at his watch.

"Oh, sit down and keep us company," said Helen. "The pub will still be there tomorrow."

"Do you have these things often?" Betty asked. She hoped not. It was not really her idea of a party. There was no wine for a start.

"A couple of times a year," said Ken.

"When the mood takes Rosemary," said Helen. "Something to look forward to, she reckons."

"I suppose it is a chance to meet the other inmates," said Betty looking around the room. She didn't think she had ever seen so many cardigans before.

"Inmates?" Helen laughed. "Yes, that's what we are. For the term of our natural lives."

"At Her Majesty Rosemary's pleasure," added Ken, draining his tea cup.

The pub Ken frequented was called the Bulls Roar. It was a small place tucked in with a collection of local shops at Forest Lodge. "It's a nice pub," he told Betty, "quiet, and they've got decent beer."

It was only two blocks from Forest Court. Betty stumped along the narrow footpath, occasionally stopping for a short rest, leaning on her stick in the middle of the footpath, ignoring the other pedestrians, who stepped around her. It was nice to be out on the streets, the area was busy with lots of people going about their business under the bright blue autumn sky. Betty was tired by the time she pushed through the pub's door, leaving the light of the street outside, replacing it with cool gloom and the smell of beer.

The smell took her straight back to her youth, before she left home to try to find her mother; drinks after work with the girls from the typing pool. The smell was still the same but everything else was different. The pubs she remembered had tiles everywhere to make them easy to hose out in the morning. This one had carpet, and there were tables made from barrels, and high stools along the bar. A television screen was located high up in the corner showing a cricket match from somewhere overcast and dull.

Ken was there, sitting at a table at the back. He had a glass of beer, nearly empty, and a newspaper spread out in front of him open at the crossword page. He looked up as Betty came in, and smiled.

"Mind if I disturb you?" she asked.

"Come and help me with this bloody crossword."

"I don't know if I will be much help. These days my French is better than my English," she said. "Can I get you another drink?"

"No, no. You sit down. I'll get this round. You can get the next one." Ken got to his feet and pulled out a chair for her.

Betty was grateful to sit down. She lowered herself into the chair and balanced her walking stick on the arm.

"What would you like?" Ken asked.

"Oh, a glass of wine please, white. Anything white will be fine."

While Ken went to the bar, Betty pulled out the mail she had collected from her letter box. There were two letters, one from Hubert Foss in Paris and one with a government crest from Canberra. She opened Hubert's letter first and quickly scanned it, smiling at the gossip and local news. When Ken came back with the drinks she put it away to read properly later.

Ken put a glass of white wine in front of her. Beads of condensation were forming on the outside of it. "Pinot grigio, is that alright?"

"Wonderful. *Merci.*" She took a sip. It was cold, dry and very welcome. The letter from Canberra was from the National Gallery of Australia, from a photographic curator.

Ken sat down with his beer. "What's that you've got there?"

"It's from the National Gallery, in Canberra. They want to talk to me about my work, about my photographs."

"Really? That's great. Are they going to buy them?"

Betty laughed. "I hope so, but it doesn't say, it just says that they want to talk to me." She put the letter away in her handbag. "How is the puzzle?" she said, nodding towards the crossword in the paper.

"Not very good. I'm trying to do the cryptic one."

"Cryptic?"

"It means the clues are written by a smartarse. They're puzzles. Like this one, eleven down, 'Strong enough or not to break.' Six letters."

Betty looked at him blankly. "What does it mean?"

"Exactly. What does it mean? 'Strong enough or not to break.'"

"Strong enough for what?"

"Last letter might be a T." Ken tapped his pen on his teeth. "If eighteen across is really opportunity."

Betty smiled. "Sorry, I have no ideas."

"Me neither. Let's have a go at the quickie."

"Pardon?"

"Quickie – crosswords for dummies."

"Ah, like us." Betty sipped at her wine.

Ken shifted the paper and read out: "One across: 'Region of contact between nerve cells', seven letters?" He looked at Betty, drumming the pen against the side of his jaw.

"Could it be synapse?" said Betty.

"Dunno. What's a synapse?"

"It is something to do with nerves. And brain cells."

"Never heard of it."

"You probably kill them if you drink too much beer."

"Mine are probably all gone then, why I've never heard of the buggers. How do you spell it?"

Betty spelled out the word while Ken filled in the white squares. The barmaid came past collecting empty glasses. When she walked back to the bar, Ken's eyes followed her. "Very nice," he said, mostly to himself, before taking another drink from his beer.

"Ha. You are too old, Ken. You could be her grandfather."

He grinned. "Sure, but seeing a pretty girl gives me a reason to go on living."

By five o'clock they had worked their way through half of the crossword. "That's me done," said Ken, downing the last of his beer. "If I have any more I'll be up all night going to the loo."

"Thank you for the wine," said Betty. "I think I will walk back with you. It's been good to be out of the apartment for a while."

"Yeah, you've got to get out and about. Some of the old dears in the village just sit around moping. Rotting away."

As they made their way slowly back along Norfolk Street, Ken paused, and said, "Robust."

"Pardon?"

"'Strong enough or not to break': robust. It fits."

"If you say so," Betty said.

Billy Sheehan was waiting outside the gates when they got back to Forest Court. "Hello, Billy," Betty said. "Did you want something?"

"I just wanted to show you this." Billy held up a camera that was hanging on a cord around his neck.

"You have a camera?" said Betty. "Why don't you come in and show it to me. I'm a bit tired, I need to have a sit down."

The camera was small and digital, the plastic case worn and scratched. Betty opened the lens cover and the little camera hummed as the lens extended and the viewing screen lit up. "I'm afraid I don't know much about digital cameras, Billy." She lifted the camera up and took a photo of Billy, the flash startling them both. Betty looked at the image on the screen then showed it to Billy. "We're going to have to learn how to use your new camera. Where did you get it from?"

"It's my brother Tom's. He never uses it. I'm just borrowing it."

"My first camera was my father's Box Brownie." Betty wondered what had ever happened to it. Disappeared, like so much else, into the void of the past. She held Billy's camera up to the light and read from lens bezel. "Canon, 6.0-22.5 – I wonder what that is equivalent to in 35mm? It's reasonably fast for a zoom lens, f2.0."

"Fast? What's that mean?"

"Means how big a hole the lens can make to let light in. Big hole, lots of light in a small time, fast shutter speed. Small hole, you need to keep the shutter open longer to get the same amount of light."

Billy was looking confused.

"It's not complicated really, but it's good to know these things if you want to take photographs. If you want to get the most out of your camera. I could teach you."

Billy's face lit up.

"But not this afternoon," Betty said. "I need to have a rest."

Billy stood up. "Yeah, sure. Thanks, Mrs Lawrence."

"Betty, call me Betty. Mrs Lawrence is some old woman. Not at all young and sprightly like me."

Billy grinned at her.

"Can you come and see me after school tomorrow?"

Billy nodded. "Sure."

"And see if you can find the manual for that camera. So we can learn how to work it."

FIVE

Prepaid Only

"Hello?" John called from the door. His hands were full with plastic shopping bags from the supermarket.

"We are in here," Betty replied.

John managed to open the screen door without having to put the bags down, and went through into the kitchen. He had run out of food at home and had decided to shop for both of them while he was at it. He left the groceries on the bench and found Betty and a young woman in the sitting room. There were empty tea cups on the table, and a couple of Betty's portfolios.

"This is Annette," said Betty. "She's from Canberra."

John took the offered hand. It was small and plump like the rest of its owner. The handshake was brief and firm but accompanied by a smile that started at her mouth and lingered in her eyes.

"John," he said. "I'm Betty's son."

"I know, Betty's been telling me all about you."

"Oh. Has she?" John looked down at his mother.

"Don't worry, nothing too dreadful," the young woman said, still smiling. "So far."

John guessed she was in her mid-thirties. Dark hair, nice eyes. Nice smile.

"Annette works for the National Gallery, in Canberra," Betty said. "They want to do an exhibition of my work."

The young woman retrieved a business card from the large black handbag at her side and passed it to John. Beneath a commonwealth crest in black, the white card said *Annette Morgan, Photography Curator, National Gallery of Australia.*

"National Gallery. That's the big time, Mum," he said, putting the card in his pocket.

Betty beamed. "I know."

"How come? Why now?" he asked Annette.

"We have a program. Each year we try to do a major retrospective of a single Australian photographer. We don't have the funds to do more than one a year. I was trying to get in contact with Betty in Paris. I didn't know she was back in Sydney until I spoke to her agency. I'm so glad she is, it will make life much easier. For me, I mean; I've got two kids. I'd love to go to Paris, but I wouldn't be able to leave them for that long."

"Oh, you'd love Paris," said Betty. "I miss it very much."

"I'm sure you do," said Annette. "But it's lovely here, isn't it?" She looked around her. "And you've got that fabulous courtyard. So close to everything too, Glebe shops just up the road, all those cafés." She smiled at John. He was glad that she was talking-up Glebe.

"Annette needs to go through all my portfolios," said Betty. "So we can choose which ones to have printed up. Where have you put them?"

"They're in storage. I can get them out." He turned to Annette. "Do you need all of them?"

"Preferably."

"There are a lot. Do you want to take them back to

Canberra? Have you got a car?"

"No, I flew up. I wasn't planning on taking them back to Canberra. I can do it here."

"My apartment isn't big enough," said Betty, looking around the crowded room.

"No," said John, "it's not. But my place is. You could use my front room."

"No. Your house is horrible," said Betty. She turned to Annette. "John is renovating his house. *C'est un gâchis.*"

Annette turned to John and raised her eyebrows in a query.

"She says it is a complete mess," he explained. "It isn't. The front room is fine, I can tidy it up."

"Are you sure? It needs to be dust free."

"It will be fine. I'm just using it for storage at the moment. What do you need?"

"Oh, just a table and a chair. And some decent light. Power for my computer."

"The front room's got big windows, and there's a good lamp you could use," he said.

Before Annette left they arranged for her to return the following Friday. John would have all the portfolios at Camperdown and the room ready for her by then.

After she had gone, Betty told John about Billy and his camera.

"He's a strange kid, Billy. Full of surprises. You must have impressed him."

"I think he just liked my cameras. Do you know when his birthday is?"

"His birthday? No idea, why?"

"I would like to buy him a camera. A good one that he can learn with."

"That's a bit extravagant isn't it? You hardly know him."

"But you know him, and you like him, don't you?"

"Yes. Of course."

"Well then, find out when his birthday is."

"How am I going to do that? I take it you want to surprise him."

"Of course. That is the fun of it. Ask his mother."

"No. I don't get on with his mother. I don't think anyone does." John scratched at his neck. "Leave it with me, I'll find out somehow."

The next day John caught up with a couple of blokes from the regiment. He hadn't seen Sam Morris for five years, and it was even longer for Tommy Jackson. They were consultants now, high fliers in corporate security, although John had heard they still had ties to the government and the spooks. Everything was tax deductible for these guys. Sam had rung John out of the blue, invited him to lunch. "Might be able to put a bit of work your way, if you're interested. If not, well, be good just to catch up, sink a few."

They had lunch at an expensive restaurant, all linen tablecloths, discreet staff and expansive views of Circular Quay. The food and the wine were excellent.

Sam and Tommy were based in Brisbane. "We're in town to talk to a new client. Thought we'd look you up. See how life's treating you," Sam said.

"Heard about your adventures at Chahar," said Tommy.

John wasn't really surprised. That kind of fuck-up tended to get talked about.

"Yeah," said Sam. "You get any blowback from that?"

"Not so far. Where'd you hear about it?"

"It's an incestuous business. People like to gossip. Why the hell did you get mixed up with those IRC idiots?"

"Seemed like a good idea at the time," John said. Chahar had been his first and only job for IRC. A new company, good pay – he should have known better. After the regiment, after the IED and the burns unit, John had worked for a few years for private security firms. It was good money and mostly straightforward work, usually keeping some rich prick alive, even if most of them didn't deserve to be. Chahar was the last. Things went wrong and good people got dead along with the bad. He'd been lucky to get out in one piece.

Chahar Qal'eh was a village about forty kilometres outside Kabul, just off the A1 on the Kabul-Behsud highway. Not much of a village, just a collection of low mud compounds strung out along fertile riverside land, and overlooked by steep, dry hills. John had been part of a three-man IRC team. The client had his own bodyguard and drivers. The team leader was a young Pommie guy called Mike, ex-para; chatty, confident. Management material, but he seemed to know his shit. The other guy was a heavy-duty local called Mahmoud. Mahmoud was solid. John had worked with him before, and was glad to find him on this new gig. The guy had started out fighting the Russians when he was just a kid. He'd been fighting ever since. The fact that he was still alive said it all.

The client was young, close to someone in the government, according to Mike. He had business in the village, some land deal. So they had rolled out in the morning. Three soft-body SUVs, client in the middle with Mike and the bodyguard, John up front, looking out for trouble, and Mahmoud bringing up the rear with his M249, ready to discourage anyone following them.

The meeting was in a family compound on the eastern edge of the village. They arrived just before 11am, and Mahmoud and John went in first to check the buildings while the others waited outside with the vehicles. It was dark

71

inside the thick walls. The family watched, their eyes shining in the gloom, as John and Mahmoud moved from room to room. The buildings were clear, just the family. No fighting-age men, no children. No weapons visible, which was the best you could hope for in Afghanistan. Mike and the bodyguard went inside with the client to do the deal, leaving John and Mahmoud outside with the drivers. Mahmoud took a position by the gate, watching the road and their vehicles, John stayed inside the compound, by the door to the main house. It was all fine till the shooting started inside.

Two shots. John called to Mahmoud, then went through the door with his M4 up. First room was empty. Shouting from the next room, sounded like the client. John crossed to the door fast. There were women screaming.

"Don't. Fuck—" That was Mike, his voice cut off by more shooting: two shots followed by a burst from an M4. John went through the door, crouching. Mike was down, the old guy from the family was down too. More women screaming. The bodyguard had a big pistol out, coming round at John. He didn't wait, he put the bodyguard down, a three-shot burst, head and throat. The client shouted something and pulled a pistol.

"Put it down!" John heard himself shout but the gun kept coming and John fired again. Screaming, lots of screaming. The tables with tea and little bowls of almonds and dried mulberries had been up-ended. Four down. The client and the bodyguard dead. The guy from the house and Mike bleeding badly. The women shouting and screaming. Mike screaming. Total fuck-up.

John heard Mahmoud shouting from outside then the heavy rattle of sustained fire from his machine gun. A young man with a weapon appeared at the back of the crowded room. John fired over the heads of the family and the guy disappeared through the door. John grabbed Mike's webbing and started dragging him out of there, keeping his weapon on the people in the room. Mike's blood left a long red streak across the floor.

Mahmoud was crouched by the front door. He pointed to the other side of the courtyard near the corner of the house where there were two bodies on the ground. "There are more."

"There always are," said John.

There was no sign of the drivers so John hoisted Mike onto his shoulder and ran for the closest vehicle. Mahmoud covered the house and the walls while John lifted Mike into the back seat. The Englishman had been hit in the chest and thigh and was white, in shock. Bleeding out. He'd been screaming before but he wasn't making any noise now. Mahmoud jumped in the front seat and got them moving. John stripped off Mike's webbing and went to work trying to stop the bleeding. It was no good – Mike died before they got near the hospital.

John had no intention of waiting around for whatever local justice or family retribution may follow. "I need to get to the airport. What about you?"

"I will go north. To my family."

"Time to go home."

"Certainly."

They left Mike's body at the hospital, and drove north out of Kabul. Mahmoud dropped John at Bagram and kept going. A US Air Force major who owed John a favour got him a no-questions-asked lift on a medevac flight to Ramstein. Two days later he was back in Perth via London. That was the last time he'd worked security.

"Come and work for us," said Sam. "We need trainers. No one will be shooting at you – we leave that shit for the kiddies."

"Who are you training?"

"Anyone with the cash," said Tommy.

"At the moment we're working in Malaysia and New Guinea. They're good people to work with," said Sam.

"Funny bastards," added Tommy, grinning, "good sense of humour, and keen as."

"Thanks for the offer," said John, "but I'm okay for money at the moment, plus I'm in the middle of renovating a house. And my mother is here now. I've got to stick around to keep an eye on her."

"That's okay," said Sam, sliding a business card across the linen table cloth. "If you do decide to get back into it, keep us in mind."

After lunch, John led them around the Quay and into the Rocks. Leaving the George Street tourist strip behind, they walked up between the damp sandstone walls of the Argyle Cut.

"Where the hell are we going?" asked Tommy, concerned that they had walked past a series of perfectly good-looking pubs.

"The Hero of Waterloo," said John. "It's worth the walk."

The Hero was a small pub, quiet at this time of day. The walls were lined with raw convict-hewn sandstone blocks, and there were no video screens. John got the first round in and carried them to a table near a big old fireplace.

"Nice joint," said Sam taking his beer. "Definitely worth the walk."

"It'll get noisy later on but it's a great place for a quiet drink in the afternoon."

"Do you hear from Smokey at all?" said Tommy. "He was from Sydney, wasn't he?"

"No. Not for years. Yeah, I think he grew up in Hornsby. Somewhere up that way."

"Bastard seems to have gone completely off the radar."

"I thought you two were pretty tight," said Sam. "Thought he might have kept in contact, after you saved his arse in Uruzgan."

"Didn't save his legs," John said. "We were in different hospitals. I visited him a couple of times ..." He shrugged. "I guess we each had our own problems. Smokey was different too."

"Yeah. Ending up in a wheelchair is bound to change things," said Tommy, finishing his beer. "My round, I think." He stood up, pushing his chair back noisily.

John drained his glass and held it out to Tommy. He wasn't sure why Sam and Tommy were interested in Smokey, they had never been that close in the regiment, but if Smokey wanted to stay dark that was his business.

They called it a day soon after five. The pub was getting noisy, starting to fill with after-work drinkers. Sam and Tommy caught a taxi to their hotel, John decided to take a bus from Circular Quay. John couldn't remember the last time he'd caught a bus.

The Quay was full of office workers waiting for a bus to take them home, and tourists making their way back to their hotels.

"Prepaid only, mate," the driver of the 438 said when John offered him a five-dollar note. "Read the sign."

"What?"

"Prepaid tickets only."

John had no idea what the bus driver was talking about.

"You need to buy your tickets first, we don't sell 'em on the bus. You can get them over there at the information booth." He pointed back over John's shoulder.

John shook his head and got off the bus again squeezing past a big woman with a shopping bag and a young man talking loudly on a mobile phone.

He bought a ten ride ticket at the information booth and joined the crowd waiting for the next bus. When it came, John took an aisle seat next to a small Asian woman. The space between the seats wasn't long enough for his thighs so he had to sit with his legs splayed. His left knee and shoulder were sticking out into the aisle and he was conscious that he was taking up more than his share of the bench seat. The young woman didn't seem to mind though, she was totally engrossed in her phone, sending and reading text messages in rapid succession.

The bus was completely full by the time it reached Town Hall. John's knee and shoulder were getting bumped every time someone moved past in the aisle. A young man dressed in black with big white headphones on his head turned to let someone out and whacked John across the ear with his backpack. John gave the guy an elbow in the thigh and a muttered, "Watch it, mate." The young man turned and glared at John, hitting the woman standing behind him with the backpack this time. John glared back and the boy looked away, the tinny beat of music leaking from his headphones. At Broadway, John decided he'd had enough. He got off so he could pick up some shopping and visit his mother on the way home. Glebe Point Road was crowded, mostly people on their way home. Ken Mallard was ahead of John, walking up the hill with a plastic shopping bag in each hand. John picked up his pace to catch up; he wanted to ask Ken how Betty was getting on in the village. A teenage boy on a BMX-bike darted across the road at the top of the hill and started coming down the footpath towards them. The boy was moving fast, swerving in and out, playing chicken with the pedestrians. Lining them up, veering away at the last minute, laughing, leaving a trail of angry stares and shouted abuse behind him. The people who saw him coming moved quickly out of his way. One man reading a notice in a real estate agent's window didn't, and got knocked face first into the glass.

An old woman with a shopping trolley was ahead of Ken. She moved to get out of the way of the approaching bike but it followed her. She moved the other way and so did the bike, only straightening at the last moment, the teenager grinning as he raced past the terrified woman. Ken was next but he refused to play the game. He just kept walking. When the boy shifted his weight to swerve past him, Ken swung one of the white plastic shopping bags in front of the boy's grinning face. The boy swerved, lost control of the bike and hit the footpath hard, landing on his shoulder then somersaulting onto his back. The bike clattered down the footpath on its side. Ken kept walking.

John watched the boy get slowly to his feet. He looked at his bike then he turned and looked for Ken. When he started to move after him John put a hand on his shoulder.

"Don't."

"Fuck off," the boy spat, knocking John's hand away. He looked back at Ken, then at John, before he went after his bike.

John caught up with Ken near the top of the hill. "Bit of an overreaction back there?"

Ken turned, smiling when he recognised John. "Maybe. He had it coming though. I don't like smartarses."

"No," John said. "You made that pretty clear. I think he got the message. Do you know him?"

"No, just his type. They need a firm hand." Ken kept punching the button at the pedestrian crossing while they waited for the traffic lights to change. "Probably got no dad."

John hadn't had a father, either. "No excuse," he said.

SIX

Large

Large carried his bourbon and Coke and his *Telegraph* through the cool gloom to a table at the back of the bar. He took out his reading glasses and unfolded the paper. "State of Confusion", the headline bellowed. "I'll say," Large muttered, flipping the paper over to the sport section to read about the latest fast bowler to bugger his back. He'd had a difficult day, and it wasn't over yet. There'd been an unusual number of dickheads to deal with, and he was looking forward to a couple of quiet drinks and something to eat before he had to deal with another one.

Jimmy arrived at the pub at 8pm, by which time Large had wrapped himself around a pepper steak, chips and two more bourbons. The skinny young man was dressed to impress: black jeans and black T-shirt, covered by an almost floor-length black overcoat. He even had a black beanie holding his blond hair under more control than it was used to.

"Very fucking *Matrix*, that outfit," said Large. "I didn't see where it said fancy dress on the invitation."

Jimmy looked at his reflection in the glass doors. "The coat? It hides the baseball bat. I cut a hole in the pocket, so I can hold the bat inside the coat beside my leg. No one's the wiser."

"Is that a baseball bat in your pocket or are you just glad to see me?" said Large.

"What?" Jimmy held up both his hands and waved them in front of Large. "No bat. I left it in the van. Didn't think it would be cool in the pub."

Christ, thought Large, *why do I always get the geniuses.* "Did it cross your mind at all that we might not want to draw attention to ourselves by dressing like we're going to a fucking Halloween party?"

Jimmy looked down at himself then looked at the other people in the bar. None were looking at him. "Sorry. Thought it would scare the prick."

"It fucking scares me," said Large. "Get us another bourbon while I take a leak. We've got an hour to kill yet."

By nine thirty they were in Pyrmont, Jimmy driving the white Hyundai van, Large in the passenger seat with a street directory open in his lap. His reading glasses were balanced on the end of his nose. Jimmy had offered the use of his smart phone. "It's got maps," he'd said, "tell you where to go."

Large knew where to fucking go; he didn't need some electronic Simple Simon telling him. "This is it on the left," he said, "Bowman."

Jimmy braked and indicated left.

"Yeah, that's it. Pull in here," said Large. The apartment they were after was on the ninth floor of a sixteen-storey tower.

Large waited in the Hyundai while Jimmy checked the car park. He was back in two minutes, leaning in the window. "It's got those see-through mesh shutters. No blue M3." He looked up and down the street again. "What do you want to do?"

"We wait. He'll be here." It was a beautiful night, the clear sky grading from the glow of city lights into dark blue overhead. There were even a few stars visible. Every now and then fruit bats crossed the sky.

It was ten twenty before the midnight-blue BMW M3 crawled up the narrow street and turned down the ramp into the car park. They had a glimpse of a dark-complexioned young man driving the car that had been stolen and resprayed specifically for him. The one he had neglected to pay for.

"Showtime," said Jimmy, reaching for his bat.

"No rush," Large said. "Let him get comfortable, have a piss, settle down with a drink, put the telly on. We're in no hurry."

Ten minutes later, a pizza delivery scooter pulled up in front of the apartments. "I think that's my cue," said Jimmy.

"Yeah, get going," Large said.

Large watched Jimmy catch the door after the pizza kid had been buzzed in. He locked the van and strolled across to join him.

As they were going up in the lift, he said, "You know the drill?"

"Sure. Course. I don't say anything or do anything unless you tell me."

The lift arrived and they stepped out into a lobby with corridors leading in both directions. "We want to send a message with this guy," said Large. "'Don't fuck with me.' We want to scare the living shit out of the cunt and anyone else thinking about not paying up."

Jimmy nodded and led the way along the corridor. He'd heard this speech before.

"Nine-oh-eight?" said Jimmy, stopping in front of the

door.

"Yeah." Large knocked. Jimmy stood to the side, out of sight of the peephole.

Large produced an envelope from his pocket and when he saw movement behind the peephole he smiled and held it up beside his face until he heard the locks working. The man who opened the door might've been twenty-five. He was wearing gold chains and a white towelling bathrobe. It didn't look like he had anything on underneath it.

"Yes? What is it?"

Large stepped forwards, shouldering the door open and pushing the man back as he moved quickly into the apartment.

"Hey. What the fuck?" the man said.

Jimmy followed them in, peeling off to check the bedrooms and bathroom.

"Who the fuck do you think you are?" the man shouted.

Large put a finger to his lips "Shh."

Jimmy came out of the last bedroom shaking his head, confirming there was no one else in the apartment.

"Get the fuck out of my house or—"

"Or what?" said Jimmy, standing beside the man with his baseball bat out, slapping it rhythmically into the palm of his left hand. The guy pulled his robe closer around himself.

It was a nice apartment. Floor-to-ceiling windows looking north and east over the harbour and to the city lights, great view of the bridge. Large wouldn't mind living somewhere like this, a bit closer to the city. He'd miss the trees though, the birds in his garden. He was checking the framed photographs in the shelved room divider that separated the dining room from the living room. Family photos, a lot of them featuring a pretty girl.

Large turned to the man. "My friends don't like people taking the piss," he said.

"Look, I've got no idea what this is about but ... Do you know who I am?"

"It's Ricky, isn't it? Do you know who I am, Ricky?"

"No, but—"

"Have you got twenty grand, Ricky?"

The man paled visibly. "No—"

Large nodded and Jimmy stepped forwards, swinging the bat hard into the calf of the man's right leg. The pain made Ricky cry out and lift up his leg. Jimmy hit the other leg and Ricky fell howling to the floor. He tried to push himself up again, but Jimmy hit him hard on the upper arm.

"That was by way of introduction," said Large. "A bit of a stinger, to get your attention. You will note that my colleague is starting with the nice, well-padded muscly parts. Next he'll move on to your bony knobbly bits: knees, elbows, shoulders, that kind of thing. After that it'll be your soft, sensitive parts."

As Jimmy stalked around the man on the floor with the bat cocked on his shoulder, Large picked up the remote control and turned on the television. It was a big flat-screen with a surround-sound system, tall banks of speakers arranged either side of it. Large flipped through the channels until he found a rock music channel. *Metallica, very appropriate*, he thought, turning the volume up.

SEVEN

An Extraordinary Australian

"What time is your flight?" John said. "I can give you a lift to the airport."

Annette Morgan had arrived on Friday morning, just after ten o'clock, and had been working through his mother's portfolios ever since. Now it was late afternoon and John had just knocked off for the day. He was contemplating a beer.

"Oh, I'm staying in town for the weekend," she said. "The kids are with their father, so I'm going to catch up with some old friends. And do a bit of shopping. A girls' weekend."

They had arranged that she would come every second Friday to work on the portfolio. It coincided with the weekends her kids were with their father and meant that she could stay in Sydney if she wanted to. John had cleaned up the front room as he had promised. It looked alright too, rough but clean. There were no skirting boards or architraves yet, and the un-sanded floorboards were spattered with plaster and paint, but there was no dust. He had moved out his tools and ladders and replaced them with a stack of boxes that contained all Betty's portfolios and a trestle table set up beneath the tall front window for Annette to work at. He hadn't had a decent chair so he'd bought one from a furniture shop in Alexandria, one with wheels and that went up and down, so Annette could adjust the height to suit herself. He'd even remembered a power board for her computer.

"This will do fine," said Annette when he showed her the front room. "Plenty of light, as you said, and not messy at all." She gave him a smile.

John had showed her around the rest of the house too – at least, all the rooms that had floorboards.

"It's a big place isn't it? Bigger than it looks from the street." She was right, there were four bedrooms upstairs and plenty of room downstairs. A lot of floorboards to be replaced, a lot of walls to reline, and skirting boards to install. "It will be great when it's finished, won't it?"

John was just starting to realise how long it would take to finish.

Annette set herself up at the table with a laptop and the portfolios. John left her to it and went back to pulling up the old floorboards in the back bedroom. He was throwing them off the veranda into the rear yard for the moment. Later he would stack them and cut them up for firewood.

At lunchtime they walked down to the café near the park and bought sandwiches and coffees. Annette paid. "It's my shout." When John protested, she held up her hand. "No, I insist. I can claim it on expenses anyway."

They sat outside on the street overlooking the park. There were a lot of people having their lunch, workers from the university and the hospital mostly, sitting alone or in small groups on the bright green grass.

"Your mother has an amazing body of work," said Annette. "I knew a lot of her famous images, the prize winners, the covers, but there is so much more in her portfolio. She was a wonderful photographer. An exceptional eye."

John didn't know how to react to this kind of praise for his mother. He was proud of her of course, and he enjoyed her photographs as much as anyone, but it seemed that he had been listening to people talking about how wonderful she was all his life. "So you think it will make a good exhibition?" he asked.

"Oh yes. People will love it. They will know some of the images already, the famous ones, but there is so much more, and they probably don't know she is Australian. There is a wonderful story to tell there."

John chewed on his sandwich, wondering if the boy who got sent back to Sydney for school each January would rate a mention. Or Jorge.

On the way back, she stopped on the street, opposite his house. "I love this place. With the park and the café. There's nothing like this in the suburbs in Canberra."

"I bet you don't have trouble finding a parking spot in Canberra though."

She laughed. "Nobody parks on the street in Canberra anyway. They park all over the verges instead, kill the grass."

By four thirty, John had finished stripping out the back bedroom. When he stuck his head into the front room, Annette was sitting at the table with photographs spread around her, typing away at her computer. She had white earphones in her ears and didn't notice him, intent on her work and whatever she was listening to. John watched her for a while, till he realised how creepy that would seem to anyone watching him. He knocked on the door and went over to the table as she turned and smiled. He liked her smile. "I'm knocking off now," he said. "Beer o'clock. Can I get you a drink or something?"

"I'm nearly finished, and yes, a beer would be lovely. Just let me finish with this image."

The photo was one that John didn't remember, which surprised him – he thought he knew most of Betty's work over the years pretty well. It was of an American soldier, Vietnam, judging by the helmet and the M16 lying across his thighs. The soldier was sitting on the front fender of a Jeep, facing the camera, looking directly at it. In the background, slightly out of focus, other soldiers were herding Vietnamese peasants down a road through a village. The soldier's look was a challenge. It was a morally ambiguous image.

It unsettled John, reminded him of too many villages in his own wars, too many judgement calls. Deciding if the guy on the other ridge with a rifle is a threat, up there where every second bastard carries an AK. What are you going to do if he comes this way? How close do you let him get to your OP? At what point do you decide that his life is worth less than the risk to your mission? End his life for tending his goats too close to you?

They sat out on the front veranda drinking their beers and watching people going past on the street. Mostly people on their way to the park, with and without dogs.

"What will you do with the house when you finish it?" Annette asked.

"Live here."

"I thought you might be planning to sell it. Then do another one. Some people I know do that, constant renovation, house after house, year after year."

"No, I couldn't live like that. This one will do me," he said.

"It's a big house for one person."

"Yeah." He shrugged. "I might take in lodgers. It's a good spot, close to the uni and the hospital. Not sure I want to, though. I think I'll enjoy the space."

"You don't have a family of your own?"

"No. I never got around to it, never made the time. Too busy with work." That was what he always said but the truth was he hadn't ever been able to hold on to a woman long enough to form a proper relationship, let alone have kids.

"Work?"

"Army. A while ago now. Bit of private work since. Not anymore though." He watched her looking at the scars on his arm, her eyes following the twisted flesh up to his neck, meeting his eyes. "IED," he said.

She looked blank.

"Bomb. Afghanistan."

"Oh. I'm sorry."

He didn't know what she had to be sorry for.

Annette said, "You and your mother both ended up in up in war zones."

John nodded. "Mum used to say there is always another war somewhere. In the regiment, our greatest worry was that someone would hold a war and not invite us." He took a sip of his beer. "We trained so hard, it was more dangerous than the missions. You go through all that ... You don't want to miss the opportunity to put it into practice."

"To test yourself?"

"Kind of, but it's working together too. The team thing. You're supposed to be the best at what you do, but at some point you need to prove it."

"Not like photography. That's an individual thing, I imagine, and a bit competitive. Trying to get the best image, to get it published first."

"Mum always said it was about telling the story, getting it to a wide audience. The wider, the better." He laughed. "Our lot don't want the story told. Not unless we're telling it."

"What did they call it in Iraq? Embedding? That seems like bullshit."

He smiled at her. "Yeah, bullshit. We'd rather the media stayed home and we emailed them happy snaps." John decided to change the subject. "How about you? You've got kids? How many?"

She smiled. "Two, Chris and Julie, ten and twelve now. They're good kids. Mostly. I'm dreading sharing my house with two teenagers though."

"Husband?"

"Divorced. Five years. Steve's remarried, but the kids see a lot of him, which is good."

John finished his beer. "Another one?"

Annette looked at her watch. "Oh, why not? Then I'll call a taxi. I'm meeting an old friend for dinner at the Opera Bar, but I don't have to be there till seven."

The second time Annette came to work on his mother's portfolio, John asked her to stay the night.

She declined. Politely, but definitely. They were both embarrassed.

"Sorry," said John. "I didn't mean ..." But he had. He didn't know why he had put the thought into words. He just enjoyed her company, liked her smile and her laugh. They got on.

The two of them had been sitting out on the veranda again, at the end of another warm autumn day. John had ordered pizzas, which they ate while they watched the day fade. Just chatting.

Annette had spent the morning in Glebe with Betty. "Talking through her career, getting the timeline right," she said. "I hadn't realised how many wars she had covered."

"Yeah. She was busy. Lots of wars over her lifetime."

"She went to Vietnam seven times."

"That was where she started, where she got hooked. On the drama, the adrenalin."

"She's an extraordinary woman. An extraordinary Australian."

"My extraordinary mum." John raised his beer bottle and took a swig. He had picked up Annette from Glebe at midday and brought her back to Camperdown to work on the portfolio. They had lunch at the café near the park again before getting back to work. This time, John paid. He insisted, she demurred. Afterwards they went back to the house. She went to the front room, he went upstairs to continue working on the bedrooms.

"That is really good pizza, but I don't think I can eat any more," said Annette.

John smiled and looked across at her. She was sitting in a cheap plastic chair with her feet up on an old milk crate. Her smart but sensible white shoes rocked back and forth on the edge of the paint-stained crate. She was wearing a dress today, blue, with a belt and white buttons down the front. She looked far too crisp and clean for his half-renovated house.

John was sitting on the cracked pavement with his back to one of the timber posts that supported the upstairs veranda. He was wearing building clothes: stained shorts, a faded and holey Mambo T-shirt of indeterminate colour, and thick purple socks. He had left the boots in the laundry when he had stopped work.

"That's okay, I'll have the rest for lunch tomorrow. We never had pizza at Mum's place when I was a kid. She hates it."

"How can anyone hate pizza? It's our national dish, isn't it?"

"It should be," said John.

Annette stood up and picked up their empty plates, started walking towards the door. She paused beside him and looked down. "Another beer?"

He nodded, and before she could move away he put his hand on her bare ankle, and asked her to stay the night.

She paused. "No, John. I don't think so."

He removed his hand and Annette disappeared into the house with the dirty plates. John could still feel the warmth of her ankle on his palm and his fingers.

Annette came back a minute later with an open bottle of beer for John. "It's getting late. I should get going."

"Of course." John called her a cab. They sat in awkward silence while they waited. Mosquitos were starting to buzz around them as it got dark, but neither of them wanted to go inside. Eventually the cab arrived, cruising slowly down the street, checking the house numbers. John waved to the driver and the cab swung across the road, did a cumbersome three-point turn and pulled up in front of the house. Annette shouldered her bag, she looked up at John. "Thanks. For the pizza, and lunch too."

"Pleasure. Good to see you again." He offered her his hand, but she looked at it then leaned forwards and kissed him on the cheek.

"Bye," she said.

John watched the taxi drive away then went inside. Tomorrow was Saturday. Billy would be over bright and early. John still hadn't asked about his birthday.

Billy was waiting on the veranda at seven thirty when John got back from his run. After breakfast they started on the new floorboards for the upstairs bedrooms. The hardest part was getting the boards up to the top floor. Instead of bringing them up the stairs they had lifted them up onto the back veranda, Billy down below leaning them up against the house, and John up top, bending over the balustrade, lifting and sliding the four-metre boards across the railing, then carrying them through to the front rooms. It took most of the morning just to get the timber up. After an early lunch they had started fixing them, cutting, clamping and nailing. It had been a good day's work, all the timber for the front two rooms was upstairs, and John could finish the floors during the week. Then they'd be ready for sanding.

By the time they put the tools away for the day, John's skin was stiff with dried sweat and he was itching from the sawdust that had got down his shirt. Billy had sawdust all through his hair. John poured a Coke for Billy and a beer for himself and settled down on the lounge.

"How old are you Billy?"

Billy gave him a curious look. "Twelve. Why?"

"Just wondering. You work pretty hard, you know, for a skinny little kid."

Billy didn't respond and John realised that he had embarrassed him. He was a good kid and John enjoyed working with him but he was looking forward to the boy finishing his drink and heading home. A shower was in order, then a quiet night eating leftovers and watching crap on television. Tomorrow he would have to visit his mother. "When's your birthday?" he tried to make it sound natural. Billy didn't get a chance to answer. He was still looking suspiciously at John when there was a knock at the front door.

The young man on the doorstep was tall, broad shouldered, with something familiar in the eyes and mouth. A young woman was waiting on the footpath. Heavy eye make-up, tight T-shirt.

"I'm Tom," the young man said. "Billy's my brother."

John heard Billy swearing behind him.

"I'm John Lawrence."

Tom looked at John's outstretched hand for a moment then took it briefly.

"What can I do for you, Tom?" John said.

"You fixing the old place up?"

"Yeah. Billy's helping me. He's a good worker, your brother."

"You paying him?"

John glanced at Billy before replying. "Yeah, I'm paying him."

"How much?"

"I don't think that's any of your business, Tom. Billy'll tell you if he wants you to know."

"He reckons you're exploiting him. Child labour. It's illegal."

From behind, Billy said, "I never—"

"What are you, the union?" John said. Smiling.

"This place should have been ours, you know. Ma's anyway, then ours."

"That's not what your grandmother thought, apparently." John stepped forwards, still smiling, but forcing Tom to step back.

"What'd you pay, hey?" he said. "A million? More? That should be ours."

"Time you left, mate," John said, still smiling, though it was becoming more of an effort. "There's nothing here that belongs to you."

Tom tried to meet his eyes, stand his ground. He shifted his weight slightly to his left foot, then he thought better of it. He leaned to the side, trying to peer past John. "Billy, let's go. You're not staying here with this prick. He's probably a

93

paedo. Come on."

Billy didn't move.

"Come on."

"He's not," said Billy. "And I'm not going. Not with you."

Tom looked at John. "This is our place. Always has been." Then he turned and left, storming past the girl, who rolled her eyes and followed him.

John turned back towards Billy. "Your family continues to impress. How'd you turn out not to be a dickhead?"

"Sorry," said Billy.

"Not your fault, mate. We can't help our families." John thought Billy must have inherited the whole Sheehan clan's quota of intelligence and charm. "You going to be alright going home? You can stay here if you want."

"No. It'll be alright. Tom won't go home. They're heading for Jenny's place." Billy grabbed his sweatshirt and made for the door, pausing just before he pulled it shut. "Next month. My birthday is next month."

On Sunday John took Vietnamese take away over to Forest Court. It was a new Sunday night ritual that he and Betty were both a bit surprised to find they enjoyed. Now that his mother had settled in, John was trying to cut down on the time he spent with her, to give her some space, to let her get on with her own life. And him with his. He figured twice a week would be okay. She could call him if she needed anything during the week. Not that she needed much, and the doctors said she was doing pretty well, worryingly healthy now that her leg had healed.

After dinner, John asked Betty about Ken. "You get on alright with him don't you? He seems like a nice bloke."

94

"Yes, he is. He has a good sense of humour. Did you remember to find out about Billy's birthday?"

"Yes. It's next month."

"Good. I'll get you to take me to a camera store." Betty paused and looked out the window. "Will you look at that old fool." She got up from the table and started tapping on the window. "Gino, stop it. Leave the flowers alone. I will prune them when I'm good and ready." The old man stopped picking dead hydrangea flowers, startled by the noise, looking around for the source of the insistent tapping. When he spotted Betty's angry little figure at the window, making shooing motions at him, he gave an apologetic shrug, turned and shuffled off across the courtyard, leaving the dead flower heads on the ground.

"Bloody Italians. They always think they know everything about gardening. If he wants to be a gardener he should get his own plants."

"That's a bit harsh, isn't it?" said John.

"The old fool is demented. Every time he goes past, he cannot resist picking off the dead flowers. Of course everyone is on his side, afraid of a few dead flowers. Probably reminds them what's waiting for them. For us all." She sat down again, but was still fuming. "Everything neat and tidy, that's what they want."

John had just been thinking how good it was that Betty was getting to know the other residents, making some friends. He stood up. "I better get going. Do you want me to put the rest of this wine in the fridge?"

"No, leave it. I'll finish it before I go to bed."

EIGHT

Mileage

Large was in his study with a cup of coffee, reading the newspaper with his feet up on the desk. The study was just a fourth bedroom with a desk, a leather lounge and a television set. No computers, no landlines or faxes. He didn't trust them.

He had a nice house, and a good life, living with Darlene, a tall blonde, and Sharon, a miniature dachshund. He had been with Darlene for ten years but the dog was a relative newcomer, a gift for Darlene for her fortieth. That was two years ago. The gift had generated some memorable thank-you sex, but cute as Sharon was, the little dog had turned out to be a serious yapper, and Darlene an over-indulgent dog owner. On the other hand, Sharon was probably a better intruder alarm than all the electronic systems he'd installed.

Everything considered though, he had a pretty good life. The house was in Caringbah, in a quiet street, surrounded by a leafy garden that gave it lots of privacy, something Large valued in his line of work. Good neighbours too, predictable. Mrs Christopoulos on one side and the Davidsons on the other, Jeff and Lucy. Nice bloke, Jeff; an accountant. He spent a lot of time in his garden, and it showed. The place was immaculate, always looked fantastic, not a leaf out of place. Generous too, always offering to lend Large his weed-eater or hedge shears. Large had never taken up the offer though, he liked his garden the way it was: overgrown, and well screened from the street.

Mrs C was a good gardener too. Vegies were her go, no room for flowers. She had the whole backyard under cultivation. Fucking fantastic tomatoes every year. Never failed to bring over a basket for Large and Darlene. She lived alone, no sign of Mr C, not since Large and Darlene had moved in nine years ago. Large had offered a helping hand if she ever needed anything done around the place, but she said, "I got a big family, Phillip, two sons and two daughters. They look after their mum. But thank you. You are a good neighbour." She was right, he was a good neighbour. Mrs C's kids all had families of their own. Lots of grandchildren, some of them were teenagers now, so she had lots of hands to help out around the house. Good cook too, Mrs C. Darlene was no slouch in the kitchen but Mrs C could do a roast chicken that just about brought tears to your eyes. She did it some special Greek way, with garlic, lemon and olives. Often Mrs C had arrived at the front door on a Sunday evening, after her family had left: "Phillip, here is some chicken. I make too much, the children don't want it. Please, take it for you and Darlene."

"Happy to, Mrs C. That last lot was the best chicken I have ever eaten. I am not joking. It was fantastic. You're gonna have to teach Darlene how to do that."

"Oh, is just roast chicken," she said, but smiling. She loved it when Large flattered her. Lovely woman.

Darlene liked to cook too. Asian mostly. Thai and Vietnamese were her specialities. Some Indian too, not so much Chinese. She was a good cook but sometimes Large hankered for a bit of a roast. Still, count your blessings; the food was good and Darlene was bloody good in bed. Still a looker at forty-two. Blonde. Natural – not a lot of that around these days. Fantastic tits and a nice arse. With Mrs C coming across with the occasional roast chicken, Large didn't have very much to complain about at all.

He was just thinking that maybe he needed a couple of biscuits to go with the coffee when his phone began vibrating and playing the *Ride of the Valkyries*. He grunted, and jammed a pudgy finger and thumb into his hip pocket to prise out his tiny battered flip phone. "Yeah?"

"Phil?"

"Yeah, who's this?"

"Dennis."

What the fuck did he want? "G'day, Dennis, How are ya?"

"Good. Listen—"

"Hang on a sec, Dennis. Is this line cool?"

"Yeah it's … remote. Like you said."

"Good, okay, but let's keep it brief, Dennis. Best to be safe, hey?"

"Yeah, sure. Just wanted to say that it came through this morning. I wasn't expecting it just yet but, you know. But, well, just lucky it was my shift."

"What did?"

"The shipment."

"What shipment?"

"You know. The shipment."

"Dennis, I got no fucking idea what you're talking about."

"Um, fuck. Okay …" There was a pause then, "But listen, Phil, I'm pretty sure this line's okay. And I wasn't followed or anything."

"Listen, mate, if they were onto you, you wouldn't fucking know if they were up your arse or not." Large ran his thick fingers through his hair. "Where are you?"

"Sackville."

"Sackville? Jesus, mate."

"You said call from somewhere remote."

"Yeah, I did, but remote, not foreign." Large sipped at his coffee while he thought. "Dennis, I've got no idea what fucking shipment you're talking about. Our shipment isn't coming for three weeks."

"Three weeks. Yeah, well that's what I thought, what I was expecting. And you were gonna let me know the box number before."

"Yeah, that's the plan."

"Well, that's not what happened."

"Just fucking tell me what did happen."

"Okay, sure. A container came through this morning with a suitcase in it, like you said. Loaded – guns and money."

"Shit."

"Yeah. I wasn't expecting it. Just lucky I was on the scanner. Nearly shat myself when I saw the guns. But no one else was paying attention so I just cleared the screen and let it through."

"Fuck." Large swallowed the rest of the coffee, burning his mouth. "Okay, okay. Listen, Dennis, I need to make a call, find out what the fuck's going on. Call me back in two hours."

"Okay."

"And use a different location, don't hang around in fucking Sackville, you'll stick out like dog's balls."

Large snapped the phone shut and put it on the desk. Outside he could see Darlene putting out the washing. There was some high cloud about but it was still warm, with a breeze tickling at the gum trees next door. Good drying weather. He gave the phone a flick with his finger and watched it spin round and around. When it stopped spinning he picked it up and flipped it open again. His big thumb moved quickly over the tiny keypad, entering the number.

The phone rang twice then it was answered. "Large, what's up?"

"Jimmy. I need you, we might have a problem."

"What?"

"Get over to my place, I'll tell you when you get here." Large pulled the phone away from his ear and squinted at the little clock at the top of the screen. "Say half an hour. Be here before ten."

"Okay, but—"

Large snapped the phone shut then slid the cover off the back. He dropped the battery out onto the desk and pulled the SIM card out, replacing it with another from his wallet. Then he tapped in a text message to a number in Germany. Two minutes later the reply came through.

~all on schedule no changes problem?

Large thought before replying.

all good just checking

He hoped he was right. Large had spent a lot of time putting everything in place on this new scheme. Lots of money, and lots of hand holding. But Dennis was the key. Large was all set to bring in a case of Glocks every two months. Now this. Nothing was ever simple.

It was right on ten when Sharon started yapping and scrabbling at the front door. Large was on his way to let

Jimmy in, but Darlene beat him to it, scooping the dog up before she opened the door.

"Hey, Darlene," Jimmy said, coming in and nodding to Large.

"Hey, Jimmy. How are you?" Darlene said. She closed the door and put Sharon down. The little dog immediately jumped up on Jimmy's legs, licking at his fingers. He squatted down and it rolled over, presenting its long stomach to be rubbed.

The fearsome attack dog, thought Large.

"I'm just about to make a cuppa," Darlene said. "Do you two want some?"

"Yeah, thanks," Large said, already on his way back to the study.

"Thanks, Darlene, white with two," said Jimmy, giving Sharon a last pat before following Large.

Large could hear his phone ringing and vibrating on the desk as he walked up the hall to the study.

He picked it up and said, "Hello."

"Phil?"

"Where are you?"

"Bundeena."

"Jesus, Dennis, I hope you're not gonna claim mileage," Large said, sitting down behind the desk. Jimmy pulled a car magazine off the shelf and sat down on the lounge.

"No. Of course not—"

"It's not ours."

"What?"

"The shipment, it's not ours."

"How—"

"You let through somebody else's suitcase full of guns and money."

"Fuck."

"Fuck, yeah. Some other prick is using our operation to bring in their own hardware."

"Who—"

"Dunno. Any number of cunts probably, but we're gonna find out. Tell me about the guns."

"Um, they were machine guns."

"Jesus. What sort?"

"I don't know. They were smallish, you know like the movies. Like the ones gangsters use."

"Assault rifles? Sub-machine guns? Machine pistols?"

"I don't know. They were small, maybe you'd call them machine pistols."

"How many?"

"Not sure exactly. I cleared the screen as soon as I realised what they were. More than three, maybe four or five."

"Okay, not a big shipment then."

"What's big?"

"Twenty. What about the money?"

"Looked like a lot. Big bundles of notes. And coins, two bags of coins."

"Coins?"

"Yeah. I thought that was a bit weird, but it's probably gold. You get that sometimes."

"Okay. Gold." Large glanced at Jimmy, who was lying on the lounge listening to Large's side of the conversation. "We need to find out where the suitcase went. Did you get a delivery address?"

"Yeah," said Dennis. "Storage units in Stanmore."

"Okay, thanks, mate. Just sit tight. Our job is still on – I'll call you the week after next." Large shut his phone and put it back in his pocket.

"So?" asked Jimmy.

"Storage unit in Stanmore. We better get over there and check it out."

"What about this one?" Betty said, opening the door of one of the fridges lined up on the showroom floor, and letting out a smell of stale vinyl and plastic.

"No, I want to get one with an ice maker. Like this one." He opened the door of a fridge that was taller than him and twice as wide as most of the other fridges on display. He had always wanted a fridge with an ice maker, ever since he was a kid, when he had seen them on American television shows.

They were at a discount appliance store in Alexandria. John had decided that it was time he had a decent fridge to replace the second-hand bar fridge he'd been living out of. He was surprised when his mother had asked if she could come with him. "I'm just looking at fridges, Mum. Nothing exciting."

"Better than looking at these walls. I want to get out and about."

"Alright, we can get some lunch while we're at it." He didn't regret the time that he spent with his mother, but he didn't want to get distracted from the work on the house. Not that he had any hard and fast deadline to meet, but he had a program for the work, target dates, to put some limits on the project. He didn't want it to just drift along. That had been part of the problem after he left the army. No structure. After he got over the burns, he just drifted for a while, convinced himself that he wanted the freedom of being his own boss. But he got bored, got desperate, then got back into it. Private security, but it hadn't been the same.

"What next?" said Betty after John had handed over his credit card and given the salesman the delivery address.

"Lunch? What do you fancy?"

They ended up at a restaurant on a corner among warehouses in Alexandria, where they sat outside beneath giant fig trees, drinking pinot gris and eating rare steaks. Things could be worse, thought John. "I had a call yesterday. My father's things have arrived. Jorge's things. I'm going to go and have a look at them tomorrow. Do you want to come? We'll have to go through it all eventually to see if any of it is worth keeping, and I'm going to need some furniture for my house."

The storage units were in an old brick warehouse set back from the road with a car park out front. Jimmy eased the van into a slot near the door. The rest of the car park was empty except for an aged and neglected green Corolla. Large climbed out of the van, saying, "You wait here. I'll see what I can find out."

There was no one in the front office so he pressed the doorbell button that was screwed onto the counter. Bells chimed behind the flimsy office partition and a young bloke in a collar and tie, too big for his skinny neck, stuck his head around the corner. "Help you?"

"I certainly hope so, mate. I want to find out about a storage unit. Never had one before, not sure how it all works. How big, how much, all that?"

"Ah, yeah. Sure," the boy said, glancing back behind the partition before coming over to the counter, and leaving behind the girl or the computer game that he had been in the middle of before he was interrupted. Expecting a quiet day, no doubt. The boy's name tag said Bevan. What kind of name was that – sounded like a health food.

"Yes, I don't need it for long, I've got a container of

104

furniture coming over from Europe. Nowhere to put it all till I can finish the renos. The builder is running six weeks late. Reckons it's the weather, but it hasn't rained for weeks. I think it's mostly that he's a fucking idiot. Sorry, language, but I should have known better when his price was so low. So, long story short, I need somewhere to store the new furniture in for a couple of months."

"Sure, okay. Do you know what size the container is?"

"Just a regular-size one, not one of the really big ones."

"Twenty footer?"

"Yeah, sounds about right."

"Okay, you'll need a six-by-three."

"What's that – metres? You sure that'll be big enough?"

"Yeah, it'll be fine, we had a container come in yesterday. Twenty footer, went in a six-by-three no worries."

"Okay, you're the expert. Any chance I can have a look at one of these six-by-threes?"

"Sure. I'll just see what we've got available at the moment." He jiggled the mouse to wake up the computer screen that sat on the counter, then began typing. "Yeah, we've got four— no sorry, three available in that size. Yeah three, the other one went yesterday."

Bevan led Large through a side door into the warehouse. It was divided into low corridors lined with green roller shutters. Each of the doors had a metre-high white unit number painted on it. "All the six-by-threes are down here. We get quite a few builders using them. They like 'em close to the front 'cause they're getting stuff in and out all the time." He pulled out an access card and swiped the reader beside one of the doors, then bent and lifted the door.

"Looks secure and dry. S'pose that's the main thing."

"Certainly. Security is very important. We've got cameras on every corridor, covering every unit."

"That's terrific," said Large.

When they got back to the office, Large took a pamphlet with the prices and contact details, and said he'd call back when he had a date confirmed: "Don't want to start paying for it till I need it."

He stepped outside, waiting in the sunshine until Bevan had disappeared behind the partition, back to his girlfriend or his porn or whatever he'd been up to. After five minutes, Large quietly opened the door and went back inside, using the folded-up pamphlet to stop the door clicking shut. Then he slipped behind the counter and jiggled the mouse, bringing the computer screen to life. It was still on the six-by-three storage units page. The last one let was yesterday, unit number 402. Large wrote down the address on a yellow sticky note, then got out of there.

Returning to the van, he said, "I got the number of the storage unit and an address, but I don't know how much good it's going to do us."

"You reckon they'd leave the guns and money here?"

"I wouldn't," said Large, "but maybe they'd take the risk. It's got a fair bit of security, cameras and shit. Might be safe ... But they'll have to move it at some stage."

"Yeah, but when?" Jimmy said, starting the engine and backing out of the parking space. "And who are they?"

"I got a name, but we should take care of the money and guns first. Get them out of the picture then watch to see who turns up looking for them."

"Okay. How do you want to do it?"

"Dunno."

NINE

402

On Wednesday morning, Betty sat outside Forest Court on the bench by the gates, waiting for John. It was overcast and likely to stay that way according to the morning radio, but it was still warm, still pleasant enough. She was early, but enjoyed watching the morning people going past on the street, office workers in a hurry, plugged into earphones, school children dawdling along, talking to their friends.

Jorge's furniture was in storage somewhere nearby, apparently. John was still bitter about it, that she had kept it but hadn't told him. It wasn't her fault, she had just forgotten about it all. It never occurred to her that John would be interested in them. John and Jorge had been separate parts of her life. There was no overlap for her. Jorge had gone, and later John had been born. She had kept them separate, she had put Jorge away in her memories and got on with having a baby, and continuing to work. Continuing to pay the bills.

John pulled his white ute into the kerb right on time. He didn't say much, just gave her a quick kiss and held the door open for her. He was back in the driver's seat and had the engine running while she was still trying to get the seat belt to click.

"Here, let me," said John, taking the buckle from her hands and slotting it into the end of the belt that poked up between the seats.

"*Merci*," Betty said. She didn't understand why they made seat belts so difficult and fiddly.

It was only a short drive. In five minutes they were bumping up over the kerb, and driving right into an old warehouse that provided storage spaces for the people who had moved into trendy new inner-city apartment buildings, only to find that they didn't have enough room for all their junk. The warehouse was huge and anonymous, full of people's excesses.

John steered the ute between white-painted columns, the tyres squealing and squeaking on the grey concrete floor as he spun the wheel and backed up to a green roller shutter with 402 painted on it.

"What a strange place," said Betty.

"It's just a storage warehouse," said John. "Just somewhere to put the stuff till we decide what to do with it."

John got out and came around to open Betty's door. She clambered out and watched while John held a card to a little plastic box beside the roller door. A light changed from red to green and there was a click. John reached down and lifted it with a loud clatter. The space inside was jammed full of furniture. Betty couldn't tell how far back it went, but it looked like a long way. A fluorescent light in the ceiling flickered into life, brightly lighting the top layer but casting deep shadows further down.

"There's a lot," said John, turning to look at her.

Betty didn't say anything. She stood, resting on her stick, just looking as the jumble of furniture started to resolve itself into once familiar shapes. Shapes remembered from another time, another life. All Jorge's things. She could make out the ugly heavy oak desk she had never liked, and beneath it the curves of a lovely Danish chair he had been so proud of. There were bookcases, a leather upholstered sofa, boxes too, a lot of them, stacked up along one wall. So much. Stuff. Just stuff. All of it Jorge's. Forgotten, like him, put away and left alone, not thought about for years and years. Now, here it all was again. Still the same. Betty moved to the door. She ran her hand along the blue upholstered back of the sofa. It was dusty, gritty feeling.

She had met Jorge in 1968, that mad year when anything seemed possible. When the swell of change and discontent that had been building through France finally broke across their lives, turning Paris into a battlefield, littered with burning cars and drifting clouds of tear gas. She was away when it all started, arriving back from Tan Son Nhut, and the aftermath of Tet, to find Paris full of revolution and madness. She took her cameras and went straight to the occupation site in the Quartier Latin and began working.

It was a nightmare scene, the day fading and the streets lit by the glare of car fires. Nervous young people standing around behind their barricades in groups, talking, some holding hands, some standing on top of the barricades, trying to see what was going on, what the police were doing. Others stood ready beside the mounds of cobblestones, pulled out of the road and piled up to serve as barricades, a ready source of missiles to be thrown at the riot police. Slogans and graffiti had been painted across the walls lining the streets. Most of them were revolutionary slogans, but some of the students apparently couldn't help making jokes. Some were enigmatic: *Sous les pavés, la plage!* Beneath the cobbles, the beach! Which was what it looked like: with the cobblestones removed, large sections of the road had turned to sand.

The CRS police formed up in battle lines opposite the barricades was like a medieval scene with their high domed helmets, circular shields and long batons. The attack was preceded by more tear gas. Betty moved to the side of the street, trying to stay clear of the worst of it. A man with a scarf tied around his face emerged from a drift of gas to throw a cobblestone at the police. Through her viewfinder she watched his body leaping and arching with the effort to send his heavy rock at their lines. She was between the students and the police, who moved forward slowly at first, staying in formation, round shields up and long batons in the air. Betty kept her camera visible and tried to get out of their way. When the police charged, she backed herself against the building, seeking shelter in a doorway, still working her camera, still getting the shots. Then they were on her, police swinging their batons, protesters swinging long timber poles. A cop fell against her, swore and lifted his stick ready to hit her, but she fell back with the door as it opened behind her. A big man pulled her into the hallway and slammed the door shut on the policeman. That was Jorge.

John was dragging some of the furniture aside so he could get at the boxes. He pulled some out and put them down near the tailgate of the ute. He used a large folding knife to prise the wooden top off one of the boxes. Books. Betty ran her hands over them. Jorge had so many books. She pulled one out, half remembering the grey cloth cover. Balzac. The smell, it was his office, lined with bookshelves, the green reading lamp on that awful desk. Jorge looking up, smiling. *Oh Jesus*, she thought. *Dear Jorge*.

They had spent the night in the front room of his apartment overlooking the street, with the sound of shouting and sirens building and fading outside. Drinking tea, talking quietly. At first about the riot, then about themselves. When the riot quietened down they went to bed, made love, slept in each other's arms.

It was a fine Sunday morning when they emerged to find the street littered with burnt-out cars and vans, and the smell of tear gas still in the air. There were other people wandering about too, looking at the damage, as if unable to believe what had happened the previous night. In those few weeks the crescendo of turmoil in the city built and built and then faded away as the street protests gave way to strikes. In the end the revolutionaries lost the political battles but they had changed something in France. It was never the same again. And Betty and Jorge continued their affair. In July they had moved in together. Stayed together until Jorge was killed.

John emerged from the back of the storage unit dragging an expensive-looking suitcase. It was held closed by a wide leather belt looped through the handle. He set it down on the floor in front of Betty.

Oh dear God, not that. Not after so long, it wasn't possible. "No," she said quietly to herself. Surely it had gone. The police had taken it. She was sure it had been gone when she got back, when it was all over. Betty felt cold, her leg was trembling. Her stick clattered to the concrete as her hand lost its grip.

"Mum? Are you okay?" John asked, concern in his face and in his voice. He put his arm around her as her legs gave way.

By the time they got in to see a doctor, Betty was feeling a lot better. She just wanted to go home, but the young female doctor insisted on examining her. John agreed with the doctor of course – "Just in case," he said. The doctor said her blood pressure was a bit low, told her to rest and then sent them on their way. Betty could have figured that out for herself.

John picked up some fresh bread on the way back to Forest Court and made sandwiches for lunch. They ate, sitting together in the old armchairs. John was watching a news channel on the television. Betty was looking at it, but not watching. She was thinking about the suitcase.

It was the same suitcase. Not Jorge's though; it was Rashid's. The last time she had seen it had been in 1975, sitting in the middle of her Persian rug while she and Jorge shouted at each other. Now here it was, back again, in Sydney. Betty had presumed that the police had taken it when they searched the apartment. Thirty-seven years ago. Before John was born.

In the end they did it the old-fashioned way. Jimmy went in just on closing with a balaclava on his head and interrupted Bevan's computer game by sticking a Glock in his face. The kid nearly pissed himself at the sight of a real gun. Jimmy took Bevan's access card and locked him in an empty unit, saying, "Don't make any noise. You really don't want to make me come back here and have to shut you up." Then Jimmy opened up a few random units and made a bit of a mess, took a few bits and pieces. There wasn't that much to take anyway, it was mostly just furniture and weird sporting equipment. When he got to number 402 it was much the same – just older stuff.

"Shit," said Large, driving the van west on Parramatta Road.

"Shit yeah."

"You looked—"

"I looked all through that fucking unit," Jimmy cut in. "No suitcase. Nothing but old, ugly furniture and books. A sofa, a couple of armchairs, desk, couple of wardrobes." Jimmy counted them off on his fingers. "And yes I looked inside the wardrobes. I looked inside every fucking thing, even the boxes. Nothing but bloody books – no fucking suitcase full of guns and money." He had crawled all over that unit, dragging the sofa and armchairs into the corridor so he could open the wardrobes.

"They must've moved it already," said Large.

"Yeah? You reckon?"

Large hit him without taking his eyes off the road, the edge of his left hand slamming into Jimmy's nose. "Don't get fucking lippy with me, you prick."

"For fuck's sake." Jimmy was bending over holding his nose. "It's not my fault," he whined through fingers rapidly filling with blood.

Large just kept driving, concentrating on keeping his speed in check, keeping the van between the lane markings, remembering to stop at red lights. Pushing his rage down.

TEN

Pike

The water in the swimming pool was perfectly aquamarine and clear as crystal. The cloud had cleared away overnight and the mid-morning sun reflected a liquid tracery onto the white rendered walls of the house. A slight breeze, sneaking into the garden between the house and the garage, was the only thing moving the surface of the water. A wattlebird hopped busily around in the big grevillea by the fence. Its detailed investigation of each of the spidery flower spikes was interrupted when Large stepped onto the terrace, naked except for a white towel around his neck, his pale, freckled skin stretched tight over solid muscle and fat. The wattlebird flew up into the Davidsons' lemon-scented gum, as Large dropped his towel on the sunlounge, took three strides across the slate paving, and sprang into the air. He caught his left knee in both hands and planted an enormous bomb on the unsuspecting pool. The delicate play of reflections on the walls smashed apart in a shower of light and water. The plume of white water displaced by Large seemed to hang in the air as if unwilling to share the pool with him, until gravity made the choice for it. Large stayed on the bottom while the surface slapped and slopped at the pool edge trying to regain its equilibrium. His eyes bulged and stared, and a small stream of silver bubbles leaked out of his nose as he fought the urge to breathe. When he couldn't hold on any longer, he pushed off with his legs, shooting out of the water like a missile from a submarine, sucking in a huge gasp of air, and crashing backwards onto the water. He floated on his back with his arms stroking the surface, sucking in air, and watching a plane pushing its way into the clear blue sky over Botany Bay. Large turned over and set out to swim his usual twenty fast laps of the pool. It didn't take long, the pool wasn't that big. When he had finished the laps he pulled himself out of the water and dried his face on the towel, leaving the rest of his body to drip dry as he lay on the banana lounge. Only ten minutes in the sun, then he'd go inside. With his fair skin he was a prime candidate for melanoma, that's what the doctor reckoned.

He hadn't decided what to do yet. His gut said they're onto you, run for it. Those machine guns cannot mean anything good. Maybe they're setting you up, maybe they are just seeing how the system works. Either way, if it was the jacks, he didn't want to be anywhere near the shipment of Glocks. But his head said it was too weird, too untidy a setup. Dennis wasn't supposed to be working that day, he only swapped shifts at the last minute to help a mate out. If he hadn't been there the guns would have been found and all hell would have broken loose. No, it made more sense that someone was trying to piggyback on his setup. But he couldn't get past the coincidence, the fact that Dennis wasn't supposed to be working that shift. It was only an accident that he spotted them. Could Dennis be playing his own game? It was possible, but Large doubted it. There was no way to be sure. He could send Jimmy over, but he needed

Dennis sweet until the Glocks came through. Conspiracy or cock-up? He usually backed cock-up, but in this case he was betting a long stretch. The whole mess was doing his fucking head in. They had to get the guns, that was the key. Get the guns and then deal with the pricks who had brought them in. He was completely dry by the time he pulled himself off the lounge and stalked back across the hot stone paving into the welcoming shade of the house.

Darlene was having breakfast in the kitchen. She had a piece of toast and Vegemite in one hand while she filled the kettle with the other.

"Morning, Darl," Large said, making straight for the fridge.

"Morning." Darlene put the kettle down and turned it on. She finished the piece of toast, looking Large up and down as she licked butter off her fingers. "Are you going to get dressed for breakfast, like a normal person? I don't need to be looking at your thing while I'm eating."

"Yeah, you do. You love it," he said, grinning. She could hardly talk anyway, swanning around the kitchen in a bikini bra and a pair of very skimpy shorts.

"Not for breakfast, I don't. Do you want some tea?"

"Yeah, thanks," Large said, putting the orange juice, milk and Weetbix on the bench, before going into the laundry and pulling a pair of shorts and a T-shirt out of the basket of clean clothes.

"You know I'm going down to Monique and Tina's place on Saturday don't you?" Darlene called from the other room.

"Yeah," he said even though he had forgotten. Monique was Darlene's twin sister. Identical twins. She and Tina ran a little antique business down in Berry. They seemed to do alright at it too. They were dykes of course, not that Large cared, although it did seem to be a waste. Monique was a stunner, just like her sister. Tina was a bit butch for his tastes, but they were a lot of fun. Good senses of humour. Large and Darlene spent Christmas with them in Berry each year and always had a good time. Of course, when Large had found out that his new girlfriend had a lesbian twin sister the obvious thoughts had arisen, but he knew better than to say anything. Not if he wanted to keep his balls. "When are you back?" he said, trailing his hand across her buttocks as he crossed the kitchen.

"Thursday. Don't worry, there's plenty of food in the freezer. Even though you'll just go to the pub every night."

Large shrugged, putting his usual six Weetbix in the bowl and adding milk.

Sharon started yapping and scrabbling at the front door just before the doorbell rang. The video screen next to the intercom showed three men on the veranda. Large didn't recognise any of them, but they didn't look like cops – too many tatts. Not that tatts really meant much these days when every bastard seemed to be inked up from head to toe. He pressed the intercom button. "Yes?"

"Looking for Phil Waters."

"Do I know you?"

"We're friends of Mick Cole."

"Yeah? What can I do for you?"

"Business."

Business? Must be a lot of business, needs three of them. "Okay. Hang on a sec." Mick Cole was a Chief, and one of his biggest customers. He had some kind of ludicrously pretentious official title in the motorcycle gang hierarchy, but basically he was their armourer. He bought guns from Large, but he usually came himself, and alone. Large glanced at Darlene, at all the skin she had on display. "You better stay in here. Till I find out what these jokers are after."

He went through the living room and grabbed his Sig from the drawer in the hall table, breeched a round, checked the safety, and slipped the gun into the waistband of his shorts at the small of his back. He sold Glocks, but for his own personal protection he preferred a Sig Sauer P229, on the basis that if it was good enough for the US Secret Service, it was probably good enough for him. And they were a better-looking gun.

Sharon went straight through the door as soon as Large opened it, sniffing at the men's feet and jumping up against their legs. "Don't worry about her, she's a lover not a biter," Large said, sticking out his hand. "Phil Waters. Everyone calls me Large."

The one at the front was the tallest. Short black hair, wraparound sunglasses. He looked at Large's hand for a moment then took it. "Pike," he said, not bothering to introduce his friends.

Large nodded to them. The two heavy-set men obviously weren't there to do any talking. They weren't quite as big as Pike, but they were big enough. Plenty of muscles on show under their tatts. "Come in," Large said picking up Sharon and tucking the dog under his arm. "How is Mick anyway?"

Pike stopped in the lobby. "He says to say g'day. Bit too busy to drop by himself."

"No worries, come in, have a seat. Can I get you boys something? A cuppa?"

"No, thanks. We won't be staying long."

Large put Sharon in the kitchen and closed the door on it and Darlene while the men seated themselves in the living room. The three men had spread themselves out, Pike in the centre of the big lounge, one of his mates was to the left on a lounge chair and the other to the right in Large's favourite leather recliner. Large pulled over a dining chair. It gave him a slight height advantage but the three of them had spread themselves out so he had to turn his head to keep an eye on them all. "What can I do for you?"

"A friend of mine has been hurt. Someone did him over with a baseball bat."

"Oh yeah? Sorry to hear that. Is he alright?" Large leaned forwards to free up the gun at his back, wondering how fast he could get it out. "When you say friend ..."

"Sister's boyfriend. He's a prick, but he's still shacked up with my little sister."

Large shrugged, as if to say, *Families, what are you going to do?* At least the bloke hadn't been a brother-in-arms, not an actual Chief. That wouldn't have been good. "And what had he done, your friend? I presume he did something, for someone to take to him with a bat."

"That's not the point."

"No?" said Large. "Well, what is the point? Because I'm failing to see the relevance. To me, I mean."

"The point, you fat cunt, is that he is part of my family now, and you beat the shit out of him. My sister is out of her mind because her dickhead boyfriend is in hospital with a lot of broken bones. And she is on the phone to me every five fucking minutes wanting something done. We know the stupid prick owed you money. Me and Joe and Musta here." He turned slightly, indicating his sidekicks.

Large was on his feet with the Sig up in a double-hand grip in the time it took Pike to glance at his friends. The bikie looked surprised to find himself on the wrong end of the gun, not sure whether to get up or stay down.

"You come in my house and start fucking threatening me?" said Large, sounding calmer than he felt. "Who the fuck do you think you are? I ought to put one in your leg just for being a rude bastard." He lowered the gun so it was pointing at Pike's right leg.

The one on the left said, "No, no," and all three of the Chiefs shrunk back into their seats.

"You're a weak cunt, Waters," said Pike, the first to recover his naturally mean composure.

"Oh, I am going to enjoy shooting you," Large said. He moved across the room, keeping the gun on Pike, but narrowing the angle he needed to cover all of them. The Chiefs turned their heads to follow him, but they didn't attempt to move. Large backed up to the front door and opened it. "Okay, on your feet. This audience is at an end. Get the fuck out and don't come back."

They stood slowly and filed out, watching Large all the way. Part of him really wanted them to try something. He would enjoy shooting them, but he knew the momentary satisfaction it would give him wouldn't be worth the shitstorm that would follow. Not to mention explaining it to Mick Cole. Pike was the last out. "This isn't over," was all he said.

"I think you better to talk to Mick, 'cause if I see your face anywhere near me again, you can all kiss those Glocks goodbye. And tell your sister's boyfriend to pay his fucking debts next time. Save us all a lot of grief." He watched them get into a white Land Rover that was sitting in the middle of the driveway. They backed out and drove away, far too slowly for Large's liking.

Back in the kitchen he found Darlene putting the Browning pump-action back in the broom cupboard where it belonged. "What the fuck was that all about?" she said, closing the door.

"One of the arsewipes that owes money turns out to have connections to the Chiefs. Nothing to worry about."

"You sure?"

"Yeah. I'll talk to Mick." Large put the Sig away. He needed a drink.

In the kitchen, his Weetbix had turned into a sodden grey mass. He poured himself a serious rum and knocked it back before he picked up his phone and punched in Mick Cole's number. It rang three times, then Large heard Mick's deep croak.

"Large, how's it hanging, mate?"

"Good, Mick, now that I've had a drink."

"Yeah? You're starting early, what's up?"

Large switched ears and refilled his glass. "I've just had a visit from a friend of yours."

"Yeah? Who?" said Mick.

"Prick called Pike. It wasn't a pleasant experience."

"What d'you mean? What'd he want?"

"You know him? 'Cause he used your name."

"Yeah, I know him. What'd he want?"

"Apparently a bloke I had some professional dealings with is a sort-of relative, his sister's boyfriend," said Large.

"Boyfriend?"

"Yeah. His sister isn't happy, apparently. Pike's, I mean." Large sipped at his rum. "Listen, I don't want to step on Chief territory, you know that. As far as I know this boyfriend has no connections. He owes, and he won't pay, so I do my thing. It's just business. Then this Pike prick shows up. At my house, mind, with a couple of muscled marvels in tow, more tatts than brain cells, and he's demanding that reparations be made."

"What'd you do?"

"I asked him to leave."

"And?"

"They left. I was quite persuasive—"

"Jesus, you didn't—"

"Course not, he said he was a friend of yours. I might have threatened him a bit but no actual harm was done."

"Good."

"Listen, mate, who is this bloke? I mean, I assume he is what he says he is. Otherwise I wouldn't have been so polite."

"Yeah, he's new in town. I don't know him well, but he comes with a rep."

"Yeah?"

"Hard man. From down south, they brought him up to run a few things. Very connected."

"Yeah? He needs to learn some fucking manners."

"I dare say," said Mick

"Can you have a word with him?"

"Yeah, I'll see what I can do. It might need some grease."

"You do surprise me. How much you reckon?"

"No idea. I'll let you know."

"Okay."

"Don't worry, I'll sort something out."

"Thanks, I appreciate it."

"Alright, say g'day to Darlene."

"Sure." Large pressed the red button and dropped the phone on the kitchen bench. "Mick says g'day," he said to Darlene, who was bent over, scraping his Weetbix out of the bowl and into the bin.

She didn't reply.

Large wondered whether to believe Mick. He'd known him a long time, since before the Chiefs, but Large was still an outsider. They could all be fucking with him. There was no way to tell. Could this shit be related to the guns? The only way to find out was to get hold of the fucking guns. He picked up the phone again and called Jimmy.

John was putting floorboards in the back bedroom when he got the call from the storage unit manager asking him to come over.

"Why? What's happened?"

"There has been a break-in. A number of units have been gone through. Yours is one."

"How is that possible? You're supposed to have a manager on site."

"They were armed. The manager's still at the hospital getting checked out."

"Jesus. Yeah, okay, I'll be there in ten minutes."

His father's furniture and books had been pulled out of the lock-up and strewn about on the floor where they were mixed up with the contents of the units on either side, which had been opened as well. Boxes of books had been emptied on the floor, wardrobes opened. The big desk was on its end.

There was a police officer in blue overalls examining the lock of one of the opened units. The manager was talking to a pair of uniformed policewomen. He looked worried. John introduced himself.

"Which is your unit, Mr Lawrence?" asked the older of the policewomen.

He pointed. "Four-oh-two."

"What was in your unit? What were you storing?"

"There, you can see. Furniture and books mostly. My dad's stuff. I hadn't had a chance to go through it yet. Mum hasn't been well."

"We'll need you to tell us if anything is missing, but don't

123

touch anything yet. You'll have to wait until CSOB have finished looking for prints."

The police gave him a card and asked him to come and make a statement after he had checked the unit. John didn't know what was in it so he could hardly say if anything was missing.

When the crime-scene guy had finished, John started packing books back into the boxes. It didn't all fit back in, of course. The manager helped with the furniture and left John with insurance forms to fill out. The desk and the wardrobe were badly scratched and some of the books were torn or had their spines broken. Nothing else seemed too bad. John figured he had got off lightly.

"What do you think they were after?" he asked the manager.

"No idea. They might have just been looking for anything they could find."

John looked dubious.

"Or maybe they thought someone was keeping drugs or money here. Maybe the police will find out."

"Maybe," John said.

The white Commodore braked suddenly to avoid hitting a bicycle weaving across Glebe Point Road. The driver, known to his mates as Brain, was a heavy-set young man with short-cropped dark hair and a droopy left eye, the lasting result of an intensive counselling session administered by the guards in his first stretch at Bathurst. The fingers wrapped around the steering wheel were covered in prison tatts.

"Take it fucking easy," said Large from the back seat.

"This is it, next left," Jimmy said, "Norfolk Street."

"Jesus will you look at all these wankers around here,"

Brain said, braking and indicating left.

"Yeah," said Jimmy, "all think they're so bloody cool. Look at that one with his flat cap and his fucking Ned Kelly beard."

Jimmy and Brain had known each other forever. Grown up together, wagged school together. Mugged people for money to buy grass and speed together. During that time Jimmy had managed not to come to the attention of the law, but Brain hadn't been so lucky. Now they worked for Large together.

"What's with all the fucking Chinese around here?" said Brain.

"They're taking over the bloody country," Jimmy replied. "Buying up the farms. Up north, all those big bloody farms, so they can grow more rice. That must be the place." He pointed at a driveway entry flanked by tall brick walls.

"Yeah, pull in here," said Large. Brain parked opposite the entry driveway. "Yeah, that's it. Go and have a shufty, Jimmy. Brain and I'll wait here."

They watched Jimmy cross the road and disappear through the gates. Brain began drumming his fingers on the steering wheel. Then he turned to Large, "You mind if I turn on the radio?"

"Yes."

Jimmy was back ten minutes later. "It's a bloody old people's home."

"What?"

"It's not flats – it's an old people's home. Look, there's a sign, it says Forest Court Retirement Village."

"Forest Court? You're kidding."

"Yeah. It's not that big, far as I could tell from the outside. It's got a security gate, you've gotta get buzzed in. Inside there are lots of small buildings with gardens and courtyards between. Backs onto a little park on the other side."

"Get in from the park, you reckon? Over the wall?"

"Probably could, the wall's pretty high, but no barb wire or glass. It's not high security or anything. People are coming and going all the time, you'd be better off just following someone in the front gate."

"I don't fucking get it," said Brain. "Little old ladies smuggling machine guns?"

"Gotta be fronting for someone," said Jimmy. "Just using her name and address. Pretty clever."

"Maybe," said Large, staring at the gates.

"Get some old wrinkly to front for the shipment. Wonder if she's in on it or just a stooge."

"Dunno," Large said. "Let's go."

"She'll be some bastard's mum, or maybe auntie. Probably doesn't even know what's going on," said Brain.

"Just drive, will you," said Large.

ELEVEN

A Bit Famous

John slowed as he came over the top of the hill at Glebe Point Road. The footpaths were crowded with commuters and school kids taking part in the morning rush. At the lights he jogged on the spot while a 370 bus lumbered across the intersection, fan belt squealing. He crossed the road, not waiting for the lights to change, and ran up past the church. It was only a short run this morning, a couple of laps of Wentworth Park then back through Glebe and the university. It was a route that would take him past Forest Court but he wouldn't drop in. It was too early. He needed to fill in the insurance forms and go to the police station to give a statement anyway. As far as he could tell, none of his father's things were missing, but he probably should get his mother to look at it, see if she thought anything had been taken. But after the way she had reacted when she had seen the lock-up on Tuesday, he didn't think it was worth the drama.

Away from Glebe Point Road there were fewer people on the footpath. John felt himself relax, stretching out and picking up his pace again. He still felt uncomfortable in crowds. They made him anxious. Too many variables, too little control. It was something he had to work on. One of the many things. Maybe he should have listened to the shrink, settled for a small town. On the coast maybe, instead of trying to take it head on by living in the city, confronting it. But he knew he'd go crazy hiding from his demons in some small town. Not enough stimulation, he'd end up killing himself – or someone else. Anyway, he wanted to be able to look after his mother. He owed her that. And she owed him a few things too.

He wanted to talk to her about his father, but he didn't know how to go about it without her shutting down. And without him losing his temper. He was depressed by how little he knew about his father, and ashamed at how little curiosity he had shown about him when he was growing up. All he really knew about Jorge was that he was an academic of some kind in Paris, and that his family came from Portugal. He had been killed by a terrorist. Some random act of pointless savagery – wrong place, wrong time. If he was truthful with himself, his father's death was one of the reasons he'd wanted to join the regiment. Not that he'd ever admit that to anyone. The man who killed his father was long dead, but John still recognised a deep desire for revenge. If he couldn't kill that man, he could kill others like him. And he had done that.

These were not motives that would be accepted in the regiment and he had duly kept them well buried. But they were there still. He had killed some who may have been terrorists, and some who probably weren't. They would all have thought they were freedom fighters, though. Everyone's cause was legitimate in their own eyes. He recognised that he too had become a man who brings death to other people's doorsteps. In the end it just gets down to sides. Like rugby in the school yard. Whose side was he on now, he wondered.

Friday morning was warm, and the day promised to be another clear, warm day. The weather forecast said it would get to twenty-three in the city. Betty sat outside on the terrace. She was enjoying the autumn weather but she wondered when it would get cold. She had a cup of coffee and a copy of Paris *Vogue*. The magazine had arrived in her letter box the previous week. She presumed that John had organised a subscription, though he hadn't said anything about it. And she hadn't asked. It was kind of him, and this morning she was glad to have the distraction. Anything to keep her mind off Jorge.

She flipped through the thick magazine absentmindedly. There was a time when she would have known most of the photographers and models in it. They were part of her Paris, a relief from her work, a relief from her wars. But now all the faces were unfamiliar, and the names too. Jorge never liked her friends from the fashion world; he thought they were all too frivolous. And he was right, they were. Totally self-absorbed, devoted to fashion, to the image – that was the point. They ignored the ugliness of the world. They made their own world, and their own rules. Jorge, the intellectual, couldn't stand that lack of curiosity, the refusal to engage with the "real" world. For him, the only things that mattered were literature and politics. Everything else was a meaningless waste of time. Except food. He took food very seriously. In their first years together he began teaching Betty how to cook, starting with the basics. His first lesson was how to cook the perfect omelette: "It's like music, first you learn the

rules, then you learn how to break them, how to improvise."
He taught her about love too, on that big old bed in the
front room. Occasionally they would make excursions to buy
food, but in her memory that first summer was washed in
the soft northern light from the two windows. They spent a
lot of time in bed. Touching each other, exploring, fucking;
sometimes gently, carefully, sometimes frantically. As if time
was short.

The breeze was increasing in strength, picking up leaves
and grass clippings, and spinning them in an eddy across
the terrace. Betty picked up her cup and the magazine and
moved back inside.

It took a moment for her eyes to adjust to the gloom, so
she didn't notice the two men until she had closed the sliding
door and pulled the curtains across. When she turned around
they were standing in the middle of the room, grinning at
her. Two young men, one tall and skinny, the other big and
heavy.

It was the heavy one who spoke. "Hello, granny," he
said. There was something wrong with one of his eyes, it was
droopy.

"Who the hell are you?" said Betty.

"Keep your pants on," said the skinny one. "We're just
going to go for a ride, just want a quick chat with you."

"I'm not going anywhere with you two idiots."

"Don't be a smartarse. granny," said the big one, pulling a
big black pistol from behind his back and pointing it at her.
"We're not in the mood today."

As John came over the hill and down towards Forest
Court he could see Ken Mallard talking to a school kid on the
footpath. He was surprised to realise it was Billy. John hadn't

ever seen the boy in his school uniform before. It looked as if he had a camera around his neck. He was a funny kid, strong and independent despite his bully of a brother and his dysfunctional mother. John liked the way he had taken a shine to Betty, and was getting into photography. He had even asked John if he could take some photos of the house. Before and after shots. It was a nice idea. If there were any good pictures, John might get them printed up, hang them on the wall. This is what it used to look like he'd be able to tell visitors. If he ever had any visitors.

John side-stepped some dog shit in the middle of the footpath, and when he looked up again Ken and Billy had been joined by two men coming out of the Forest Court gates. There was someone between them – Betty. A white van pulled into the drive, angling in, forcing Ken and Billy to step back out of the way. John picked up his pace, quickly scanning the rest of the street before focusing back on the scene playing out in front of him. Billy and Ken had stopped talking and had turned to see what was going on. The two men hurried across the footpath, almost lifting a struggling Betty off the ground. Their attention was on the van and they didn't notice John sprinting up the footpath.

"Help me," Betty shouted. "They're—" The closest man put a hand across her mouth.

"Hey, what are you doing?" Ken said, stepping forwards. "Where are you taking her?" The men were both young, one big and dark, the other was skinnier. Blond.

John's feet pounded on the footpath. Forty metres. Too far.

"Betty, are you alright?" Ken said, his voice high-pitched and loud, almost shouting.

The skinny one let go of Betty and opened the side door of the van. Ken reached out and grabbed the arm of the man still holding Betty.

"Hey, I'm talking to you."

Twenty metres. John watched the man pushing Betty roughly through the door of the van, and turning back to Ken, his hand coming up with a pistol.

Ken looked down at the gun then up at the man holding it. He didn't step back.

"Gun!" It was Billy shouting.

John was ten metres from the van when the man fired. One shot. Ken went down. Billy screamed. The skinny blond man shouted something. The shooter turned and saw John now, started to bring the pistol around. But John was too close, coming in low beneath the man's gun arm, launching himself in a diving tackle, driving his shoulder up under the rib cage. The air went out of the man and John felt ribs breaking as he propelled him into the van's door frame. There was shouting from the van and from behind on the footpath. They fell together onto the road, the shooter's head smacking the van's door sill on the way down. John heard the engine roar. He grabbed for the gun with one hand, and held the man's neck with the other. The rear tyres spun and squealed. John felt someone pulling him backwards by the shirt. The tyres found some grip and the van leaped forwards with an awful wet crunch. Tyres screamed. A taxi braked hard, skidding across the road to avoid the van as it bumped over the kerb and back out onto the street.

Billy was still holding onto the back of John's T-shirt, but the boy wasn't looking at him. His eyes were glued to the deformed mess the van's rear wheel had made of the shooter's head.

John tracked the rear of the van with the pistol, but there was no clear target. "Fuck! Fuck!"

Ken was lying in the concrete driveway, a large red stain

blossoming in the middle of his neatly ironed shirt.

The shot had attracted a crowd, people from the street and residents from the village were starting to gather on the footpath.

"Someone call triple 0, now! Ambulance and Police," said John. There was lots of blood. Billy was still staring at the body on the road. John pulled him away, spun him around, got in his face. "Billy. Get over here. I need you." He pulled off his T-shirt and crouched down beside Ken, pressing the wadded-up shirt over the seeping wound. "Here, Billy, hold this. Keep pressure on it. Okay? To stop the bleeding. Listen, okay?"

Billy looked dazed but nodded.

"Keep the pressure on it. Till the ambos get here. Right?" He gave the boy's shoulder a shake. "Right?"

Billy nodded again, looking at Ken then at John. "Yeah. Okay."

Then John was up and gone. The taxi was still in the middle of the road, the driver standing beside the open door talking on a mobile phone. John pulled the driver out of the way, got in and slammed the transmission into drive. They had about a minute start on him. More than enough time to get lost in Glebe or Annandale. Which way would he have gone, Parramatta Road or right on Ross towards the Crescent and Victoria Road? He kept his foot down hard on the accelerator, and the taxi nearly left the ground coming over the hill at Forest Lodge shops, the engine roaring.

He didn't have to decide which way to turn. The van was on the wrong side of the road at Ross Street, wrapped around a light pole. It had tried to turn right against the lights when a 470 bus was coming the other way. The driver of the van and the blond one were out on the road shouting at each other. Both were armed with pistols. The bus driver climbed out of the bus and shouted something at them. The skinny man raised his gun and shot the driver. There was no hesitation.

John braked hard, fighting to keep the taxi under control. The two men turned to the sliding taxi, raising their guns and firing. John threw himself across the seats. The windscreen shattered as the car came to a halt. John crawled over to the passenger side and popped the door, getting out the side of the taxi away from the van. The two men ran behind the bus, across Ross Street and down towards the old creek line. John ignored them, moving around the side of the van with the gun up in two hands. The cabin was empty, the front doors wide open. The side door was mangled where the van had hit the light pole. John went back around the van and popped the rear door, crouching and sweeping the interior with his weapon as the door creaked up.

Betty was on the floor, moaning, blood coming from a cut on her forehead.

"Mum. It's me. Are you alright?"

Her eyes flickered but didn't open. He took her hand and squeezed it, held it.

He could hear sirens now, getting closer. "You're gonna be okay, Mum. The ambulance is on its way." A crowd had gathered on the footpath but they were staying well back, having seen the guns. John left his mother to check the bus driver. He was bleeding from a stomach wound but still breathing. His staring, shocked eyes said how much pain he was in.

Red and blue flashing lights were coming down St Johns Road now. John didn't want to get shot by a twitchy first-responder so he dropped the clip out of the pistol, ejected the breach round and placed them and the gun on the driver's seat.

The first police car pulled up in the middle of the road and two policemen emerged, their weapons out.

John stood still with his hands clearly visible. "The bus driver's been shot. The woman in the van is my mother. She's hurt too, bleeding. Unconscious. Her name is Betty, Betty Lawrence. She's my mother."

"Who're you?"

"I'm John Lawrence. They tried to abduct her."

"He's got a gun too, I saw it," someone in the crowd shouted.

The younger cop put his weapon on John.

"It's on the seat of the van. I took it off one of them."

The older cop, a sergeant, said "Get on the ground. Now."

John knew the drill. He lowered himself onto the road, face on the bitumen, wrists crossed at the base of his back. The young cop cuffed him while the sergeant covered them. Then they recovered the gun and checked on the driver and Betty. An ambulance arrived.

"The men who tried to kidnap my mother are getting away," John said. "They went down the road towards the creek."

The sergeant crouched down beside John's head. "Tell me what happened."

"The two men tried to kidnap my mother— no, there were three of them. A driver and two to grab her."

"Three?"

"One's down. Dead, I think. They shot an old guy, Ken, not sure what his surname is."

"Where?"

"Forest Court, the retirement village. Outside on the street. That's where it started."

"Okay." The cop stood up and started talking into his

radio.

Soon more cops arrived, including a four-wheel drive full of black-clad tactical response police with the full kit: automatic weapons, helmets, vests. They stopped briefly and spoke to the sergeant then drove down the hill the way the two men had gone.

The cops got John up off the road and locked him in the back of one of the vans. "Till we sort out what the fuck's going on," the sergeant said.

"How's my mother?" John asked before he could shut the door.

"The ambos are with her now. She's breathing okay, but still unconscious."

"Where will they take her?"

"Don't know, but I'll try and find out." The cop nodded and closed the door on him.

The back of the van was hot and stank of disinfectant and desperation. John tried to relax, to get comfortable and keep control of his breathing. There was no point getting angry, they were doing their job. He was the only one they had in custody – they weren't going to let him go until they figured out what was going on. Until they were sure they didn't want to charge him with something. Assault, murder, theft of a vehicle, possession of an illegal firearm. They'd have lots of choices if they decided to go after him.

An hour later the door cracked open and the same older cop stuck his head in. "We're taking you to Leichhardt. They want to talk to you back at the station." John squinted in the bright sunshine. Behind the cop he could see more police than before, joined now by the media. Blue and white tape was stretched across the road and uniformed police in fluoro vests were directing traffic and pedestrians around the area. Plain clothes cops were taking details from witnesses including all the bus passengers.

"Your mum's gone to Royal Prince Alfred Hospital."

"Thanks. What about Ken? And the bus driver?"

"Bus driver's gone to RPA too. Dunno about the other bloke," the sergeant said, as he closed the door.

They took John back to the police station, and left him in an interview room.

"You want something to drink?" the sergeant asked on his way out.

"Yeah, water. Please." Politeness counts. "Any chance of a shirt? Getting a bit cold in here now." The room was old, with high ceilings and bare walls. The only furniture was a metal table and four chairs. The cops had probably wound the air-con up to make it colder.

"I'll see what I can do. What happened to yours?"

"Used it as a dressing. On Ken."

The sergeant nodded and left.

The shirt won't happen, thought John. *If I was them I'd let me chill off a bit before starting the questions.* He settled in to wait.

Half an hour later a man in a suit came in with a bottle of water. He was a solid-looking man, not tall but broad, with the heavy shoulders of someone who spends time in the weight room at the gym. He wore a blue-striped shirt under a dark grey suit jacket. No tie. "DS Moreton. I need to take your statement, Mr Lawrence." He put the bottle of water in front of John.

"Sure." John unscrewed the bottle and took a swig. The water was cold. He told the story again while Moreton took short-hand notes. Occasionally he would interrupt the flow and ask a question.

"Where did the van come from?"

"Dunno. Didn't see it until it pulled into the driveway."

"Into?"

"Across, but angled in."

He gave a description of the second man with Betty. Tall, twenty-something, dirty blond hair, shoulder length. Skinny, wearing a black hoodie. No, the hood was down. Jeans. Didn't notice the shoes.

"He say anything?"

John thought. "Don't think so."

"The one who shot Mr Mallard? He say anything?"

"No."

"Any idea why he fired?"

"No." Thinking back, replaying it, the guy seemed keen, almost grinning, when he used the gun. "He could have just pushed him out of the way. Ken's an old guy."

"What about the driver?"

"Didn't see him clearly, not till I caught up with the van at Ross Street. Twenties maybe, average build. Jeans, green T-shirt. Average height. No tatts that I noticed."

"He say anything?"

"Someone shouted just before the van drove off. Not sure who, or what they shouted." John opened the bottle and took another sip of water. "Dark hair. The driver had dark hair."

"Okay."

It took two hours to finish the rest of the statement, Moreton going over the details more than once. Finally he put his pen away and closed his notepad.

John was about to ask if he could go now when there was a knock, and the door was pushed open by a woman.

"How's it going?" she said.

"Just finishing up. Mr Lawrence, this is DI Walker," Moreton said, as the woman put a folder on the table and pulled up a chair next to Moreton.

John nodded to her and waited. She didn't look much like a senior cop, dressed in T-shirt and jeans. Her black-rimmed glasses were perched above a spray of freckles across her nose, and her red hair was long and worn in a plait down her back. Somewhere in her forties, John guessed.

Walker peered up from the file and said, "We got your file, John. Hot off the printer. It's interesting."

"Previous?" said Moreton.

Walker slid the file across to him. "No. Army, Sergeant John Lawrence. Left the ADF in 2005. Injured in Afghanistan."

Moreton looked up from the file to John's scarred arm, then went back into the file.

"Not much else in there," said Walker. "Just basic records, when he joined, when he left. Nothing about what he did in between. Most of it is sealed."

"What does that mean?" Moreton asked.

"It means they don't want us to know. Probably something heavy, special forces, counter-terrorism, some secret shit like that." She looked John in the eye. "Means he's the real deal. Am I right, Mr Lawrence?"

John said nothing.

Moreton flipped through the pages in the file then closed it and slid it back to Walker. "So, Mr SAS? A dangerous man. Just happens to be around when his mum gets kidnapped. One dead, two seriously wounded."

"Yes," said Walker. "The only kidnapper you got anywhere near didn't fare too well."

John shrugged. "That was an accident."

"Still, a pancaked head always impresses," said Walker. "I understand your mother used to be a bit famous."

Moreton looked at Walker then at John.

"She was a war photographer, a photojournalist," John

said.

"Quite famous apparently," Walker said to Moreton. "Probably before your time. Vietnam, Lebanon, Rwanda. You can Google her. I just did." She turned her attention back to John. "The question is, Mr Lawrence, why is someone trying to kidnap your mother?"

"No idea. I've told your mate here all I know, and I want to go now," said John. "I want to see my mother, and I find out how Ken is doing."

Moreton looked at him. "Just got to get someone to type this up, and get your signature. Won't take long."

"Surely I can come in tomorrow and do that."

"Better to do it now."

"Look I live in Camperdown, it's only ten minutes away. Give me a call – I'll come back anytime and sign it."

"These are very serious matters, Mr Lawrence," Walker said.

"We appreciate your cooperation but we're going to need you to stay a bit longer," Moreton added.

"Look I'm cold and tired, and I want to see my mother. Unless you arrest me I'm leaving now."

Moreton stood up. "You're involved in the death of one man and the shooting of another two. You're not leaving till we say so."

John stood up, slowly, and smoothly, not wanting to give Moreton an excuse to overreact. He was a head taller than the policeman, his torso bare, melted flesh scarring up his left arm and shoulder. As he moved, goose flesh slid over hard, lean muscles that didn't need protein shakes or steroids. "Unless you charge me, I'm going out that door."

Walker let out something that might have been a laugh. "Alright, Mr Lawrence, go and see how your mother is, but make sure you're in here tomorrow morning." She looked at

140

her watch. It was just after two. "Harry, get Dave to type up that statement."

It was nearly three by the time John got to Royal Prince Alfred Hospital. He had the taxi drop him at Camperdown so he could grab a shower and some clean clothes, before walking up the hill to the hospital. He was in a hurry but he didn't want to be walking around half naked.

There were a couple of young journalists and photographers hanging around outside the main entrance, providing a bit of distraction for the desperate patients who had shuffled out into the forecourt in their gowns and slippers for a smoke. The smokers sat around under the giant fig trees that lined the road, some on their own, some in small groups, talking quietly. One man even had a drip on a wheeled stand beside him as he sat on the old sandstone wall sucking on his cigarette. Billy was there too. Sitting with the smokers, watching the cops and the media.

"You okay?" John asked.

"Yeah."

"Did you hear anything about Ken?"

"Ambulance took him." Billy looked down at the bitumen paving beneath his badly scuffed shoes. "He was alive then, when they took him. I walked over here but nobody'll tell me how he is. Cops won't even let me in. Then someone said your mum was here too. Thought I'd wait for you."

John squeezed the boy's shoulder "Thanks, mate."

"I did what you said with the T-shirt, kept pushing on it, tried to stop the bleeding. But there was blood everywhere. He looked pretty bad. Grey almost."

"What did the ambos say?"

"Not much. Said I done the right thing. Said he'd have

died otherwise. That's all really."

"Shit." John shook his head. "He was a nice old bloke."

"They said he might make it."

"Yeah." John turned and looked at the people milling around the front entry to the hospital. "Jesus, yeah. Old bloke, but strong, single wound, good response time." He turned back to the boy. "Listen, Billy, you did really well. Whatever happens to Ken, you did the best that could be done for him. No one could have done anything else. Okay? You remember that, because you will wonder, Could I have done more? And the answer is you did everything that could have been done. I've seen this shit before and the only thing that makes a difference is to stop the bleeding and get transport fast. You did that. You did the best things that could be done in a shit situation. Okay?" Billy just looked at him and John realised he was freaking the kid out. "Okay. You did well, Billy. I'm proud of you. Let's go find my mum."

John walked straight past the journalists with his arm around Billy's shoulders. He didn't stop, he didn't make eye contact. A young woman turned to one of the cops and spoke briefly to him. The cop nodded, but by the time the woman turned back John and Billy were on their way through the doors.

They found Betty in an intensive care ward just off the Accident and Emergency department. There was a young constable at the door, and John had to show identification before she would let them in. Betty was unconscious, looking very small and frail in the big hospital bed. An oxygen mask covered her face and a big mesh bandage was wrapped around her head. Leads trailed from beneath her gown to a vital signs monitor, and a cannula in her hand connected her to a drip bag. A young nurse was beside her, noting down observations on her chart.

142

"How is she?" John asked bending over and stroking his mother's cheek. "I'm her son."

"Oh, good. I'm glad you're here. She's stable at the moment but she has suffered head trauma. Skull fracture. Her chest too, but no ribs broken."

"Christ."

"They've done brain scans and they're talking about putting her in an induced coma."

John felt numb.

"They'll need you to fill in some forms. I'll let you know when they're ready."

"Shit," said Billy, when the nurse left. "What happened? They said there was a crash."

"Yeah, she was in the back of a van when it hit a power pole. She would have been thrown around."

"What about the men?"

"Shot another bloke, the bus driver, then they ran off. Don't think the cops have caught them. What about you? Are you okay? What did the cops ask?"

"Just what I saw. What the two guys looked like, did I know you. That sort of stuff. Didn't take long really." He looked up at John. "Ken had already gone in the ambulance by then."

"You were on your own?"

"There were some others from the village and that. Wanting to know what was going on."

A young woman appeared at the door to the ward, said something to the constable and came inside. She was in her early twenties, thin and pale. She looked uncertain, pausing and turning back towards the constable for confirmation after a couple of steps. The young constable nodded to her.

"Excuse me," the young woman said to John, "is this Mrs Lawrence?"

"Yes," said John. "Who are you?" Wondering if she might be a journalist, until he noticed her red eyes.

"Sorry, I just ... I'm Lucy Mallard. My grandfather—"

"You're Ken's granddaughter? How is he?"

The young woman looked as if she was about to cry.

"Sorry. I'm John, John Lawrence." He nodded towards the bed. "I'm her son." John pushed a chair across to her. "Here, sit down. This is Billy. We were going to try to find out how Ken was doing, but you've found us first."

Lucy Mallard tried to smile. "Thank you. I don't really know how he is. They said the operation was a success but ... I'm so worried about him. He's not awake yet, so I wanted to come and see Mrs Lawrence. To see— How is she?"

"Like you, we don't know a lot. She's got a fractured skull. They haven't said what the extent of brain injury might be. Not yet."

"I was hoping she would be awake. I want to find out what happened."

"We were both there," John said. "It was pretty quick. Your grandfather was brave. Bloody brave, taking on two armed men."

"The police said it was a kidnapping. Is that true? They said a young boy kept him alive, till the ambulance came. Was that you?" She looked at Billy.

Billy shrugged.

"Yeah, it was Billy," said John. "He stayed with Ken while I went after Mum. He stopped the bleeding till the ambulance came."

Billy was standing beside the bed in his slightly too small second-hand school uniform, looking uncomfortable and embarrassed.

"Thank you," Lucy Mallard said.

"Just did what John said to," Billy mumbled.

144

"You saved his life," she replied.

John told her what had happened that morning. Describing the events again, he recognised the process that was turning the events of the day into a story. With each retelling it was becoming neater, less confused, more of a self-contained package. The story about Mum's kidnapping. Each time he told it, it became less like the confused, adrenalin-charged reality. "I'm sorry I didn't get there earlier, before they shot Ken."

"Then you would have been shot," said Lucy.

"Possibly," said John. "No way of knowing." The clowns might have backed off if he'd got there sooner. Come at them hard and fast before they got to the van. It might have changed things.

"They would have just shot you both," said Billy.

Later in the afternoon, after Lucy Mallard had gone, John took Billy home. The boy wasn't keen to leave but John wanted him to go and get something to eat and to rest. "I need to get some things for Mum and get back to the hospital," he said.

The story was all over the six o'clock news, that was how Large found out.

"For fuck sake," he spluttered through his first mouthful of stir-fried beef and basil.

"What's wrong, honey?" said Darlene, carrying her own dinner in from the kitchen, plate in one hand, glass of cold chardonnay in the other.

Large pointed at the screen, chewing and swallowing his mouthful. He took a drink from his beer bottle before he spoke. "The news. Some idiots tried to kidnap an old lady from a retirement village."

145

"Why would they do that?" Darlene put her glass down on a side table and settled back into her recliner. "Is she rich or something?"

"That's what I'd like to know."

The news coverage showed lots of footage of the front of the retirement village and a white van that had crashed in Forest Lodge. There was plenty of blue and white police tape and the little yellow plastic evidence tags the cops use when they are photographing crime scenes. The journalist spoke directly to the camera in front of the van, then the scene cut to a senior uniform cop, rumbling on in a series of clichés: *shocking crime ... one man dead ... shocking circumstances ... can't confirm ... community outrage.* Basically saying fuck all except that there was a kidnap attempt, one man had been killed and two others wounded.

That was all Large knew until the next morning. By then the news bulletins had a name for the dead man. It was Brain. It sounded like Jimmy had run out on him when some bystander decided to intervene. Panicked. And now the big Serb was dead. The gruesome details were all over the Saturday papers, together with photos of Brain's body under a blanket.

Jimmy showed up at nine thirty, just as Darlene was getting ready to leave for her sister's place. Large had to get Jimmy to move his Commodore out of the driveway so Darlene could back out. It gave him a chance to calm Jimmy down a bit, get him to shut up until Darlene had gone. There was no point getting her fired up too.

"See you on Thursday then." Large leaned through the window and gave Darlene a kiss. Sharon jumped across Darlene's lap and licked Large's face. "Yeah, you too," he said.

"Don't forget the food in the freezer," Darlene said,

putting her sunglasses on, and reversing out of the driveway.

Large and Jimmy walked back to the house side by side. "Okay," Large said. "Tell me. Why the fuck did you start shooting?" Leaving out the bigger question of why the fuck they thought kidnapping the old woman was a good option.

Jimmy wasn't happy. "This old cunt wouldn't back off. Okay, Brain shouldn't have shot him, but what was he meant to do? What's the point of having a gun? The old prick grabbed his arm, didn't he? Brain's got his gun out, waving it around. What sort of fuckwit grabs his arm? He's just asking for it. What was Brain meant to do? Say sorry, old mate, do you mind taking your fucking hands off my fucking arm. He's got a Glock in his other hand what's he going to do? Brain is ... Brain was ..."

"He wasn't one to back down," said Large.

"No, he wasn't. Then this other fucking hero shows up. Where did he come from?" They were in the study now. Jimmy pacing back and forth, working himself up. "Why did he stick his beak in, be a fucking hero?" Large thought Jimmy might start crying, but instead he started ranting again.

"So Brain shot the old cunt, and so he should have. The old guy had it coming. No fucking business getting all heroic. And the other guy came out of nowhere. Blindsided Brain, put him down on the ground, shoves his head under the wheel. I'm shouting at Matt to put his foot down. To get the fuck out of Dodge." Jimmy stopped pacing and looked at Large, sitting behind the desk. "Crushed his whole head, they said. That must have looked awful. Can you imagine? His brains would be all over the road. I'm glad I didn't see that. Bloody hell, no. And his face, imagine. Fucking tyre tracks, Jesus. The poor bastard." Jimmy threw himself down in the leather lounge. "That prick is gonna pay. Fucking Serbs know all about revenge."

"You're not a Serb," said Large.

"No, but Brain was and I swear to god I'm going to do that big cunt. Do him slowly, with a knife. Cut him till he's begging. Leave him hanging somewhere, let him bleed out."

Large tried very hard to keep his temper under control while Jimmy ranted. This whole thing was a fucking disaster. He was tempted to take his money and pull out. Hit the road. Spend the rest of his life getting massages and blow jobs somewhere warm. But he knew it wasn't that simple. There was Darlene, there was Pike, and there were twenty-four Glocks arriving in three weeks. No, retirement needed to be a controlled withdrawal, not a fucking rout. Not unless the jacks were on him. And they weren't, not yet.

He had liked Brain. Not the smartest bloke, but funny, always ready for a laugh. Could tell a good story. No front to him either, he was all out there to see. No hidden agendas. Still, it must have been quick. Messy, but quick. No open casket for his family.

"Who was this guy, the one that killed Brain?" Large asked.

"Dunno who he was or where he come from. Brain was waving his Glock around but the guy just ran up and tackled him."

"Well, now he's another cunt we've got to settle with."

"We don't know who he is," said Jimmy.

"We'll find out." Large stood up and walked over to the window. There were bees flying around the bush outside. They were all over the little white flowers, busily poking their faces into the flowers. Darlene would know the name of the bush, she was into all that stuff.

Large turned his back on the window. "Right, first off, you and Matt need to disappear for a while. Get out of town. Lots of people saw you, someone will ID you. And cut your hair, do it yourself, don't go to a fucking barber. And change the way you dress."

"Yeah, okay," said Jimmy.

"Have you got somewhere you can go?"

"I've got an aunty down in Thirroul. She's always saying I should come and stay, you know, have a holiday by the beach."

"Okay. Go there, and take Matt with you. Stay out of sight. Call me when you get there. Get a new phone too, ditch the old one. Now piss off, I've got some thinking to do."

TWELVE

We Didn't Talk About it Much

John was at the hospital early on Saturday morning. There was a different cop on the door so John had to show his ID again to get in. His mother was still unconscious. He found a nurse but she said he'd have to wait till the doctors were available. John sat by Betty's bed, reading the paper, occasionally holding her hand, squeezing it, stroking it. All he could do was wait. He had to be at Leichhardt Police Station at nine so after an hour he kissed Betty's hand and left the hospital.

At Leichhardt, John was ushered into an office where he was greeted by Moreton and Walker. "How's your mother?" Moreton asked, passing across the typed statement for John to read through.

"In a coma, still. Fractured skull, chest badly bruised but no bones broken. I haven't had a chance to talk to the doctors yet."

"This won't take long," Moreton said.

John just looked at him and nodded. He read through the statement. The events it described were washed clean of emotion, reduced to a sequence of facts. While John read,

Walker fiddled with her phone, tapping the screen a few times then reading some messages.

John signed the statement and passed it back to Moreton. Walker looked up at him, but a chime from the phone had her tapping at the screen again. When she was satisfied, she left it face down on the desk.

"How is the investigation going?" John asked, directing the question to Walker. "Do you know—?"

Walker's phone dinged again and she picked it up. John waited.

"Go on," she said scrolling through something on the screen. "I'm listening." She began typing something on the tiny keyboard.

John nodded. "No, it's okay. I'll wait."

She finished typing and put the phone down again. "Sorry, bloody meetings, trying to get everyone in one place at the same time. Herding cats."

John nodded again. "I want to know who tried to kidnap my mother, and why. I want to know who the guy was that died." He looked at Moreton and back to Walker. "I want to know what is going on."

"Yes, of course you do," said Walker. "We know who the dead man is but not why he was trying to kidnap your mother."

"Who was he?" John said.

"His name was Branco Delic," said Moreton. "Know him?"

"No."

"Delic, Branko Delic." Moreton repeated. "Known as Brain, apparently."

"You're kidding," said John.

"No. I'm not. His street name was Brain."

"Christ."

151

"He was twenty-six," said Walker. "Lived in Panania. Been in and out of the system ever since he landed on our sunny shores."

"Where's he from?" said John.

"Refugee." Moreton read from the file: "Bosnian Serb, arrived in ninety-six, ten years old. Came with his sister and mother. Father was already dead. Did eighteen months for assault ..." He flipped a couple of pages. "That was in 2007, nothing since. Seems to be associated with small-scale drug distribution."

"Nothing as ambitious as kidnapping," Walker said. "It won't be long before we know who the others are. We're waiting on forensics from the van, and ballistics. We may get some DNA from the vehicle too, but it's more likely that we'll get something from Delic's known associates before that comes through. The witness descriptions haven't had any hits from the files, but if we don't get any leads from the intel we may try for some photofits. Has Dave Timmins spoken to you about that? He's supposed to be setting that up."

"No," said John.

"Okay, maybe we can do that this morning while you're here, while the impressions are fresh." Her phone started vibrating. She read the screen, sighed, then turned off the phone and put it in a pocket. "Yeah, so, photofit next."

John looked from her to Moreton. "Why though? What's the motive?"

"Yes," said Walker. "Motive has been underlined several times with lots of question marks on the white board."

"Little old lady," said Moreton. "Minding her own business, in her apartment. Two blokes walk in on her, then wham-bam: kidnapping, guns, car chase, dramatic rescue."

"Ordinary little old lady," said Walker.

"Except that her son is ex-special forces," said Walker.

"And the little old lady used to frequent the most violent shit-holes that the second half of the twentieth century had to offer."

"So we are open to the possibility that the motive might be out of the ordinary too," added Walker. "Like the backgrounds of the participants."

"Victims," John said. "We're the victims here. And I have no idea what it was about."

"How long has your mother lived at Forest Court?" said Walker.

"Not long, a couple of months."

"She came straight from Paris?"

"She'd been there for years. At the end of last year she had an accident, broke her leg. I wanted her to come to Sydney so I could look after her, but I think she's found it a bit difficult. Getting used to a new place, after so long away."

"A retirement village? After Paris?" Walker didn't add *What did you expect*, but John heard it.

"So, was she lonely?" asked Moreton.

"Don't think so. It was a bit hard at first, not much in common with the other residents, but she made a couple of friends. Ken Mallard was one."

"Can you think of anything? Anything that might explain yesterday's events?"

"No, I can't."

"You sure? Little old ladies don't get kidnapped every day. Not around here. There must be some reason for it," said Moreton.

"Why is she at the village, why not have her at your home?" asked Walker.

"My place is a mess, I'm still renovating. There are only three habitable rooms, including the kitchen and laundry. It wouldn't have worked."

"Especially after being apart for – how many years?"

"A lot. I was born in Paris but I've spent most of my life in Australia. Mum sent me to school here. My friends are here."

"What do you know about your mother's work, her career?"

"I know where she worked. Who for. Not much detail, we didn't talk about it much."

"I've seen some of her photos online," said Moreton. "She was good. Covers of *Time* magazine and *Life*, high-profile stuff."

"She was in Vietnam?" asked Walker.

"Yeah, that's where she started. And Cambodia, Lebanon, Bangladesh, Biafra and Rwanda. Sarajevo, that was her last, she was getting on a bit by then."

"She was a bit of a legend in her day," said Moreton.

"Maybe," said John. "She was very dedicated. She would have been a pain in the arse for the media managers but probably not for the grunts. They would have got her."

"You said Sarajevo was her last assignment?" said Walker.

"Yeah. She retired after that."

"It was a siege wasn't it? Was she there long?"

"I don't think so. There was some problem. Her fixer got killed. Mum didn't talk about it much. Never went back."

Walker and Moreton exchanged a glance. Moreton said, "This Delic, the guy you killed, he's from Bosnia. Came here as a kid after the war. His father was killed in Sarajevo."

John looked at him. "So?"

"Just wondering if there might be a connection."

"I have no idea, but there were a lot of people killed in Sarajevo. You'll have to ask Mum. When she wakes up."

"Thanks for your time," said Walker. She handed him a

business card. "If you remember anything about yesterday or your mother's work that might be relevant let me know. I'll take you around now, and see if we can get this photofit organised." As they stood she added, "That kid, Billy Sheehan?"

"Billy? What about him?"

"Just, how does he fit?"

"Mostly he doesn't fit. Bit of a loner. Bad home situation."

"Yes, we know his family. His mother has a few convictions. Drugs. Tom seems to be keen to carry on the family tradition."

"I can imagine."

"So what's the story with you and Billy? You signing on as a Big Brother?"

John looked at her, trying to gauge her expression. "No. Billy just helps me out with some of the renovation work on weekends. He's not too much of a nuisance. Turned up for a sticky beak one day. Curious because my place used to be owned by his grandmother. I think he's looking for a bit of relief from his dysfunctional family. Mum likes him too."

John went back to the hospital when he finally got away from the police station. During the afternoon, Betty opened her eyes. Only for a little while but the doctors said it was a good sign. It meant she was starting to come out of the coma.

The registrar reckoned that Betty would be okay. "There's no brain swelling," she said, "that was our main concern, so we don't need to keep her in an induced coma. The fracture is stable, not depressed at all. She's started to wake up now. Those are all good indications."

"What about her chest injuries?"

"Nothing broken, just deep bruising. She'll be sore, but she'll recover."

John waited until visiting hours had ended but Betty didn't open her eyes again. He walked up to King Street to pick up something to take home for dinner and for something to drink. With a plastic bag full of Thai food in one hand and a six pack of beer in the other, he walked south along the winding Victorian shopping strip.

There were a lot of people out and the passing parade was entertaining to watch. A lot of skin and a lot of ink on display. Piercings were popular too. The crowd was mainly young, students, and plenty of freaks, representatives of the various urban tribes he had no names for. Newtown was close to the university and was renowned for grunge and alternative lifestyles. The few times that John had been here when he was in his late teens, his main impressions had been of dog shit and broken glass. It was a land of workers and junkies in those days. Nowadays it seemed to have cleaned up its act a bit, but he was glad to see it still had a bit of edge, that it hadn't become too middle class.

A lot of the students seemed to be having their parents take them out for dinner, to get a solid feed into them, knowing that they would probably only eat cereal or pot noodles for the rest of the week.

Back at Camperdown, John found Billy waiting on the front veranda. It was Saturday – he hoped the kid hadn't been waiting all day. He should give him a key.

"How long have you been here?" he said as he opened the door.

Billy shrugged. "Couple of hours. Came by this morning, wasn't sure if you'd be working. Went up the hospital when you weren't here. Wanted to find out how your mum and Ken

156

were. Bastard cop wouldn't let me in."

"He was just doing his job. You should have rung me."

"Didn't want to worry you."

"Mum's not come 'round yet. Docs reckon she's okay, though. Showing some good signs. I didn't see Ken. Have you eaten?"

Billy shook his head.

Inside John opened a beer for himself while Billy filled a glass with ice from the door dispenser on the new fridge and poured orange juice over the top of it. John divided his pad kapao between two plates, and they sat down side by side at the kitchen bench.

While they ate, John opened his computer and typed *Branko Delic* into the search engine. There were lots of hits but the only Australian result was a Facebook page. The young man who'd had his head flattened on the pavement outside Forest Court stared back at him, smiling. A big, dopey smile. Delic didn't look like a kidnapper in the photos, he just looked like your usual young Australian shithead. There were lots of photos of Delic giving the finger to the camera, arms around his mates' necks. Mouths open in the middle of stupid faces. In most of them he looked drunk or stoned. Not many women featured in the photos and those who did were notable for the amount of teeth and cleavage they were showing. The men favoured singlets in black and shaving the sides of their heads. Their bulging shoulders and upper arms were steroid pumped and decorated with tattoos.

Delic listed his employer as a smash repair workshop in Moorebank and his interests as fast cars and tight women. Jesus what an arsehole. He was about to close the computer when Billy said, "That's him. The other one." He leaned over and put a greasy finger on a face in the background of one of the photos. It was the skinny blond man who had shot the bus

157

driver. The photo had caught him looking past the camera at something. Delic and another idiot were in the foreground, leering at the camera, but the other one, the passenger, was staring intently at something. It was definitely him.

"Yeah, that's him. Well spotted."

They checked through Delic's friends, but the guy wasn't among them. Only a few of their pages allowed public access to their photos, and none of those that did featured the skinny blond man. John went back to Delic's page and saved a copy of the photo on his desktop.

THIRTEEN

OP

John didn't sleep well that night. He lay awake listening to the city's night noises and thinking about his mother. About Delic, and Sarajevo. And about his father. He'd have to do something about Jorge's furniture soon.

When the currawongs and butcher birds started singing in the park he sat up in bed and opened his laptop to look at the photo he had saved. It was definitely the same bloke, thin face and deep-set eyes, long curly blond hair. Acne scars. He reached over to where his jeans were folded on a chair and retrieved Walker's card from his wallet. He was about to email the photo to her but decided to call first, in case there was anything new she could tell him. It was still dark out, so he read a couple of online newspapers. When the sky became light he decided that the gym at Broadway should be open by the time he got there. He dressed quickly, threw a small towel and his wallet into a backpack, and set out running, up the hill towards the hospital and the university. There were other gyms closer but he preferred this one. It was old school, wooden floors, smelly, more free weights than machines. And, importantly, no video. He liked it a lot.

After an hour on the weights he was sore and sweaty. He walked home along Parramatta Road, passing a police random breath testing road block. Set up to catch morning-after drunk drivers, John presumed. Four cars and a motorbike. He hoped the cops were putting that much effort into finding the kidnappers.

After he'd had a shower, he walked down to the coffee shop beside the park and ordered a flat white and a bacon and egg roll. He sat at a table on the footpath and watched the sun light up the grass and the trees. The park was full of people out for a walk or a jog. Lots of dogs, most of them running around loose, chasing balls, sniffing each other. Some of the little ones doing a bit of half-hearted yapping. Later there would be kids playing rugby on the oval, and families picnicking on the grass.

At eight o'clock, he called Walker's mobile.

"Walker." She answered after two rings, sounding impatient.

"It's John Lawrence." There was a short pause.

"Mr Lawrence, what can I do for you?" Her tone was curious now.

"I was just looking at Facebook last night. I found Delic's page. Branko Delic."

"Yes, we've seen it Mr Lawrence."

"Yeah, of course you have. Thing is, there's a photo on there of the other guy. The skinny one."

"The one that shot the bus driver?"

"Yeah, that one. It's definitely him. I can send you the photo. Email it."

"Yes, do that please. That would be very useful." She paused then continued. "Mr Lawrence, why are you checking out Delic?"

"It's just what you do, these days, isn't it? Google people."

160

He wanted to know why they had tried to kidnap his mother, what the risk was. He wanted to know who else he might have to kill.

"Don't, John. It won't end well. Let us do the investigating, we're good at it."

"Of course, just trying to help. But she's my mother. I'm going to look out for her."

"It's not your job, John. Just send us the photo. It's a good find but leave the investigating to us. You look after her. That's what she needs."

John hung up. They could do the investigating but he wasn't going to trust them to do the protecting.

Back at his house he emailed the photo to Walker, then thought about what to do next. Before he went back up to the hospital he should go over to Forest Court to check on his mother's apartment. He hadn't been back there yet and he had no idea what state the kidnappers and the police had left it in. He'd probably have to do some cleaning too.

Large watched the white Toyota utility crawl along the street towards the retirement village. When it reached the gates it swung out across the road and did a three-point turn to park next to the driveway. The driver stood by the door, scanning up and down the street before he disappeared through the gates. Large had seen him before. On the TV news, getting into the back of a police car. He could be the one who did for Brain. Jimmy said the killer was tall and this guy was well over six feet. He must live nearby or maybe he's visiting someone? Could have a parent here or something. That would explain why he was around to stick his nose in on Brain and Jimmy.

Large was watching the street from a borrowed Volkswagen

161

campervan, parked behind a small Suzuki hatchback, fifty metres from the retirement village. From there he could see the entrance and had a clear view up and down the street. He had arrived just before eight thirty and planned on spending the whole day here if necessary. Something was going on at this place and he wanted to know what it was. He had made himself comfortable in the back of the van and had the curtains arranged so that there were gaps where he needed them, but they still kept most of the interior screened. It was busy enough that a strange van wouldn't be noticed. This part of Sydney was full of backpackers and young travellers. People were used to seeing campervans and big old station wagons full of bedding parked in the street for long periods.

The police and media were long gone, taking their vehicles and blue and white tape with them. Now it was just the locals. Before the ute had shown up there hadn't been much to see, just a steady stream of pedestrians. Occasionally cars came and went through the gates, and a taxi arrived to pick up two old women who were waiting on the footpath just outside.

At ten, Large poured himself a small cup of coffee from his thermos. Just a small one, he had to strike a balance between staying awake and spending all day pissing into the fruit juice bottle he had brought along for that purpose. He had a small radio with an earpiece, and was listening to a classic hits station. Anything to stay awake. He had made himself some sandwiches too, sliced sausage and tomato sauce, but he'd save those for later.

Large was finishing off his coffee when the man from the ute came back out. He stood on the footpath watching the street again for a full minute before he got back in the ute. Large watched it pull out and drive away from him. It made a U-turn at the corner then came slowly back past the village

162

again. Large sat well back from the side curtains as it went past. Careful bastard, he thought, as he pulled out his phone and dialled Frank Martel's number.

"Yeah?" Frank answered after two rings.

"Hello, Frank, it's Phil Waters. How are you?"

"Large? I'm good mate, how're you going?" said Frank.

Large had known Frank Martel for years. They used to play cricket together in the district team. Those were good times. Nowadays Frank had given up being a fast left-arm bowler and was something high up in the Roads and Traffic Department. He was a very useful friend. "I'm fighting fit, Frank. Top form. Listen I'm sorry to interrupt you on your Sunday."

"No worries, I'm just trying to decide if I can put off mowing the grass for another week. What can I do for you?"

"Can you check out a rego for me? Usual rate."

"Sure thing."

Large read out the registration number. "White Hilux ute. Not very new."

"No worries. I'll call you back. It'll be tomorrow morning, after I get into the office," said Frank.

"Thanks, mate." Large put the phone away and settled back with the radio on again, to see who else might turn up.

The street was shady, lined with big gum trees, but still the van heated up quickly as the sun got higher. Large cracked all of the windows he could, trying to get a bit of air through the back part of the van. He took off his sweatshirt, but even in T-shirt and shorts he was uncomfortably sweaty by eleven thirty. Every now and again a loud ding or clunk surprised him when a twig or gumnut fell out of the tree onto the roof of the van. Bloody gum trees were always dropping some

163

shit. Large had cut down the two big gum trees at his place – first thing he did when he bought it. Replaced them with three silver birches. Much nicer trees. Hopefully the gum tree above him now wouldn't drop a big branch on the van – he had to get it back to Darlene's brother in one piece.

When the weekend sports show started on the radio, Large decided he needed some fresh air. He climbed out of the van and crossed the street. There had been no more cars visiting the village but a few more people had gone out on foot, mostly heading towards Glebe Point Road. He pulled out his keys and waited for someone to come out. It didn't take long. A small, hunched-over woman with a walking stick came through the gate.

"Excuse me," said Large. "I don't suppose you live here?"

The woman looked uncertainly up at him, a big sweaty man in shorts and a T-shirt. "Yes, I do," she said.

Large held out the key ring. "It's just that I was walking past and I saw a young man drop these keys. He went in here, but I don't know which unit he is in, what button to press. He was a youngish man, tall, fit looking. Some scars on his arm."

The woman smiled. "Oh, that will be Betty's son," she said. "Betty Lawrence, she is. Number twelve. Her son is called John. Only the one son, I believe."

"That's great." Large beamed a big smile at her. "Thank you." He made to turn toward the gate.

"Terrible what happened on Friday," the woman said. "Poor Betty and Ken. They're both still in hospital apparently." She peered up at Large. "We're not even safe in our own homes anymore. Lucky her son was there to stop them. He's a nice young man, John is, very polite. Used to be in the army, that's what Rosemary Bennet said. He should be able to look out for Betty. I hope he stays close by. I'll feel safer with him around the place."

Large thanked the woman again and waited just inside the gate for her to hobble slowly out of sight down the road. When she was gone Large pocketed his keys and strolled back to the van. John Lawrence. Ex-army. That was good to know.

He ate the sandwiches and finished off the coffee for lunch. The afternoon dragged by, stuffy and hot in the back of the van. He listened to a match between the Sharks and the Tigers, while old people and families came and went, but none of them seemed out of the ordinary. When the game finished he thought stuff it, and started to pack up. He hadn't learned anything new during the afternoon except how crap the Sharks were this season and how unpleasant it was to piss into a juice bottle in an overheated campervan.

John watched his mother's eyes flick back and forth, following the nurse as she moved around the bed to pull back the screen curtains. Betty hadn't spoken yet but she had squeezed his hand a couple of times. She was coming good and John was relieved. He was sitting beside Betty's bed in a blue vinyl armchair, reading the online version of *Le Monde* aloud. It was impossible to tell if Betty was listening at all but when he read a story about the French finance minister being accused of sexually assaulting a junior clerk, she squeezed his hand so hard he was worried she was having a fit. When Betty had first started to wake, the nurses had brought some wide fabric straps to secure her arms. "Just in case. They're often confused when they come out of the coma, sometimes they flail about with their arms, it can be distressing and they can pull out their tubes."

"How long will it take? To wake up?" John had asked.

"It's not like sleep. She's not just waking up. It takes a while for the brain to recover from the trauma. Everyone is different, we'll just have to wait and see." The nurse's name was Siobhan. She took the chart from the end of the bed and started filling it in. "You're doing exactly the right thing, reading to her, talking. She's been a lot more responsive since you've been here today."

John was running out of new articles to read to Betty, when DI Walker appeared at the door.

She had a quick word with the constable outside in the corridor then came into the room and stood watching Betty from the end of the bed. "How is she? We heard she was coming around."

"She is. Slowly though."

"We really need to talk to her."

"Yeah. Me too."

"Any estimate on when?"

"Not really. Could be a day or two, if we're lucky. Everyone's different, that's what they keep saying."

"Helpful."

John shrugged. "I'm just glad she's coming around."

"Of course." Walker nodded. "What are you reading to her?"

"*Le Monde*. I'm down to the sports section now. Getting desperate, two Frenchmen have made the quarter-finals of some tennis tournament in Dubai." He looked at his mother's pale face, head bandaged in white gauze, and with an oxygen tube beneath her nose. "I thought a bit of Francais might help. Something a bit familiar, but she hates sport."

"You should probably stop punishing her then; she's been through enough pain already."

John laughed. "Yeah, you're right." He reached down to

a bag on the floor beside the bedside table and pulled out a stack of Betty's portfolios. "I brought these too. Thought they might, I don't know, stimulate her? Get a response at least." He opened one of the heavy black folders and showed it to Walker. "1995, Sarajevo."

Walker fetched a chair from beneath the window and pulled it up next to John, watching him flip through the pages of the portfolio. The images were a strange mix of modern and medieval. Full of the haunted, gaunt faces of a trapped civilian population trying to live under the guns. Of blood stains on flag stones, and the deadly radial symmetry of scars left by fragmentation shells on ancient stone.

"When I was a teenager, I thought something terrible would happen to Mum. In Beirut, or Palestine, or Africa maybe – but not here, not Sydney." He had brought her home so she'd be safe, not so some trigger-happy arseholes could kidnap her.

"You said Sarajevo was her last job, didn't you?"

"Her last war. She did a bit of work after that, but only in France. Maybe a bit in Germany and Britain."

"It was nasty."

John gave a grunt. "Looks like it, but they're all nasty." The murderous civil wars that tore Yugoslavia apart had kicked off just after he had joined up. There had been a lot of chat about them during training, mainly to do with tactics and weapons. "She won an award for Sarajevo," he said, passing the portfolio to Walker.

On one page was a certificate: *News Photo of the Year 1994, awarded to Betty Lawrence*. On the other page was a photograph of a body lying in a street. Bright red blood pooling in the gaps between the paving stones. In the background, a group of seven people crouched against a wall, staring at the body. The people were well dressed, they looked like they were on the way to work. Except for the fear on their faces.

"Sniper," said John.

"She must have been standing in the open to take that shot."

"Yes. She was lucky."

"She's a risk taker," said Walker.

"Mum would say that the woman deserved to have her death acknowledged, recognised."

"They all do, all the victims."

"Luck always runs out," John said, turning to his mother. She was looking straight at him, her blue eyes were wet and there were tears on her cheeks.

Betty's eyes flicked between them as Walker passed back the portfolio and said, "Alright, I'll leave you to it. We'll keep in touch with the hospital and we'll keep a uniform on the door here for the moment. At least until we find out what all this was about." She paused at the door and turned back. "Thanks for emailing that photo, by the way. Harry has sent it out on the system. We should hear tomorrow if anyone can put a name to the face."

"Glad to do something useful."

"Look after your mum. That's useful."

Sarajevo was bad.

Betty shouldn't have gone. She was too old, too weary. Too wary, perhaps. But it was a big story – for a while it was the only story. And it was Europe, it was home. So she called up Hubert Foss, updated her accreditations and a week later she was on a French UN-flagged C-130 spiralling into Sarajevo. And taking fire.

"Bosnian Serbs. Call themselves militia, just gangsters really." The man next to her was a Canadian journalist called

168

Pete something. Big guy, Canadians always seemed to be huge. "This your first time?" The plane twisted and turned on its descent, trying to make it a bit harder for the bored gunmen on the mountains to hit it. She knew he was wondering what a woman her age was doing flying into a siege.

"It's my first time for this war. Not for Sarajevo," she said. "I was here for the winter Olympics in eighty-four."

"You'll notice the changes then," he said, bracing himself as the plane lurched again, and Betty became unpleasantly aware of her stomach.

"So I hear," she said when the plane steadied. "How many trips have you done?"

"This is my fourth time."

Betty nodded. "You're hooked."

"Yeah, I am. It's the story for the end of the century isn't it? A modern European city being reduced to rubble by primal ethnic hatred."

Betty had spent two weeks in the city trying to understand the war. Trying to work out how to convey the brutal intimacy of the siege. Sarajevo had been transformed by the deadly geometries of the fields of fire. There were some places where children played in relative safety, while just a football's bounce away was the hunting ground of the snipers. Every day people took their lives in their hands just going to and from work. Waiting for the shots, counting off the seconds, hoping they could cross to safety before the sniper reloaded. Then there was the ever present risk of being in any open area. The threat of mortar fire, called in by some hidden spotter who had decided that enough people had gathered in one place to make a target worth a expending few rounds on.

Betty photographed the many sniper alleys, capturing terrified women dressed for the office or the market, running for their lives. She photographed desperate people trapped in a ruined claustrophobic city, being terrorised and killed by people they knew, people who had recently lived beside them, but who one day had left the city to camp in the mountains and try to destroy them. It was incomprehensible, and although her photographs were as good as usual, Betty never felt that she understood the conflict, never felt that she had captured the truth of it.

Her fixer, the young woman who drove her around and translated for her, was called Aida. Beautiful eyes, she had. Shorter than Betty but dark, with black spiky hair and a leather jacket that Betty never saw her out of. Aida drove them around Sarajevo like a rally driver in her beaten-up VW Golf, complete with bullet holes in the fenders and rear doors.

The trip to Sarajevo had ended badly. She and Aida had been to a site overlooking the river to interview one of the defence commanders. On the way back they had to take a detour because of the shelling. Turning down a side street, a kid on an old dragster type of bike came out of an alley just in front of them. Aida jammed on the brakes and the car skidded across the cobbles and stalled. The kid looked back over his shoulder at them, grinning as he rode into an exploding mortar round. Boy and bike were launched into the air, landing twenty metres down the road. Betty and Aida watched him land, then Betty started to get out of the car but Aida grabbed her arm. "No! It's too late." She let go of Betty and tried to get the car started. But Betty was out of the car and running for the boy. Aida screamed something, getting out too, watching Betty. She was standing by the car door, still shouting at Betty when the second shell landed two metres in front of her. The explosion threw Betty headlong onto the pavement stones. It tore Aida into shreds of bloody rags and black leather.

FOURTEEN

Business

Frank Martel rang Large with the address just after 9am. By nine forty-five, Large was back in the campervan, watching Lawrence's house. It looked like a shit-hole to Large, squeezed between a new warehouse conversion and row of trendy terraces. A rotten tooth in a none-too-pleasant smile. Large would have demolished it, if it was up to him, replaced it with something nice and modern, but it looked as if Lawrence was trying to rebuild the dump.

By midday, Large was struggling to stay awake. There had been no sign of Lawrence or anyone else. No sign of life at all. Large decided to take a walk, check out the back of the house. Broughton Street was quiet: it had been closed off at one end by the local council in an attempt to stop rat-running. Just past the closed-off end of the street was a large park with shady fig trees and a sports oval showing signs of wear from a weekend of football matches. He walked down to the park, turned right then right again into a lane that ran behind the houses. It was narrow and lined with tall timber fences. Most of the fences had roller shutter doors, allowing remote-controlled access to the off-street parking that would

171

add another $30 000 to their already inflated values. The back of Lawrence's house didn't have a roller shutter, it had an old timber gate. Unlocked. Large lifted the drop bolt and let himself in. The backyard was featureless, just mown grass from fence to fence and an old concrete path from the back of the house to a non-existent Hills Hoist clothes line. Along the southern fence line there was a stack of flooring timber covered with a blue poly-tarp. Steps led up to a small back veranda. Large went up them as quietly as he could and peered through the windows into the kitchen. It had new benches but the floor was just raw timber. It all looked pretty makeshift, as though Lawrence was camping in the house while he rebuilt it around him.

Large was getting a bad feeling about this guy. This was someone who planned, who was ambitious and willing to make sacrifices. Nothing about what he had seen of him spoke of stupidity and recklessness. He had gone after Jimmy and Brain, two armed men, without hesitating, knowing exactly what he was doing. And the way he had watched the street outside the retirement village, looking for surveillance. No, this prick was dangerous.

Large walked back to the campervan and drove to the Sailor's Retreat in Sans Souci. It was one of his favourite pubs. A good place for thinking, dark and quiet, the pokies hidden away in a small room, and the television screens turned off unless there was a game on. It was the sort of pub where no one bothered you. He ordered a steak and took his schooner of Reschs and the buzzer for the food order out the back to the lounge. At this time of day there were few people around and most of those were on the pokies or in the front bar. Large gave the only couple in the lounge a wide berth, and sat at a table in the corner.

John Lawrence was definitely a threat. It was probably

him and his mother who had brought the machine guns in. He wasn't sure exactly what they were up to or how they had worked it, but it didn't really matter. Lawrence just had to be removed from the equation before he did any more harm. Even if Large couldn't get hold of the guns and money in the suitcase, it might be safer all round just to knock Lawrence rather than to try to deal with him. Not to mention whoever he might be fronting for. No telling who that might be. As he'd said to Dennis, any number of cunts. But if Lawrence were to just disappear, then things could get back to normal. The suitcase might turn up but if it didn't, the main thing was to remove Lawrence.

How to do it was the question. Killing someone unsuspecting is easy, but this guy didn't look unsuspecting. He always looked on edge, always watching.

They could try lifting him off the street, take him back to the workshop, do it there. Get some answers then disappear him. It would mean surprising him somewhere quiet. Maybe near the retirement village – seemed like he visited his mother a lot. It would need three people: two with guns to take him and one driving. Jimmy and Matt? They'd fucked up with the old woman. Could he trust them? Did he really need to question Lawrence? Why not just kill the prick? Do it in the street, send a message to whoever. Motorbike and a sawn-off. Close range, make a mess of him. Pull up beside him when he's getting out of his ute. One barrel to put him down, one to finish him. Simple, don't try to get too fancy. Large finished off his drink and looked around the lounge. It was after three now, and the bar was empty except for him. He'd do the job himself, he had a sawn-off, all he needed was a bike, something quiet but fast.

* * *

173

John chose an internet café above a gift shop in Newtown. He bought a bottle of water and an hour of credit from the bored-looking Chinese guy at the counter. The place was nearly empty, just a couple of young women next to each other at the front. Backpackers, he presumed. John settled down at a computer with a view of the stairs that led down to the street and the door to the toilet. He read a couple of online news services until one fifteen. Then he opened up an obscure restaurant review blog and left a comment on the latest post, mentioning how good the smoked trout had been last time he had been to whatever the restaurant was. Ten minutes later the next comment appeared. John used the name on that comment to set up a new email account. He logged out, waited five minutes and logged back in. There was a message from Smokey in the drafts folder.

~that you bastard

John opened the message and typed 'yeah' before re-saving the draft message and logging off. He waited another two minutes before logging back on and checking the draft message.

~long time
it is
~you ok
yeah but i need a favour
~what
gat 9 compact
~trouble
risk management
~usp ok
clean
~yeah
how much
~5k

kidding
~what it costs
how soon
~where
syd
~thursday
ok 3k
~fuck off
3.5
~4
ok
~cunt
love you 2

Pike came for him as he came out of the pub. Large paused on the footpath, putting his sunglasses on against the bright afternoon sunlight. A black van pulled into the kerb, its side door sliding open before it had stopped. At the same time both his arms were grabbed and he was thrust towards the door. Large managed to get his feet onto the door sill, tried to use his legs to throw his body backwards, but one of the men kidney punched him. Large twisted with the pain and felt his legs collapse. They flipped him onto his face, driving him into the hard metal corrugations on the floor. The impact pushed the sunglasses into his face, snapping them in two. Blood filled his nose and his mouth. He was dazed and in pain. When he managed to focus his eyes, all he could see was a small stainless steel screw lying in one of the floor channels. The van began to move. Large knew he had to get out. He gave a roar and pushed himself back and up. Three sets of boots immediately started kicking at his head and ribs. His arms were pulled back behind him and he felt cold metal on his neck. "Stop wriggling, Mr Piggy, or this ends now." It was Pike. Large was definitely going to have to kill the cunt. He lay still, trying to stay calm, trying to think. They threw a blue poly tarp over him and Large lay in the weird blue gloom with the metal ribs of the floor biting into his knees and elbows. Every bump added to his pain and anger. At first he thought he could tell the direction they were travelling, but after a couple of turns he had no idea. Eventually they got onto a fast road with no turns or stops, one of the motorways, Large guessed. Heading out of town.

Pike and his men didn't talk much. They knew where they were going and what they were doing. They had probably done it before.

The van veered left off the motorway, and slowed. They were on a winding road now, going up and down hills, the driver having to change gears frequently. Large lost track of time until the van turned sharply and bumped up a short ramp. It got darker under the tarp just before the van stopped. He heard and felt the side door sliding open. Hands grabbed him and the tarp and dragged him out. He landed hard on a concrete floor, but they continued to drag him away from the van. The tarp came off and he blinked in the harsh flat light of overhead fluorescents. It was some kind of warehouse. There was a smell, not strong, but familiar. It took him a moment to realise it was the smell of fresh meat. A butchery. The concrete floor was painted white. There were large floor-mounted machines around the walls, and above him were steel rails with hooks for the carcasses.

Large tried to stand up, but a kick to his knee quickly put him back on the floor. He lay on his back and looked up at the four men standing around him. Pike, the two tattooed wonders who had come to his house and a skinny one with a goatee. Probably the driver. No one said anything for a moment, then Pike spoke. "I hear you've been telling tales about me."

Mick Cole must have said something. Whatever he'd said, it obviously hadn't been well received. Large lay still, watching Pike. His nose was blocked with dried blood and his mouth was dry.

"Nothing to say now, Mr Piggy?" said Pike. "You were pretty cocky at your place and pretty talkative to Cole." Pike nodded to one of the tattoo twins and Large felt another kick to his ribs. He gasped with the pain that tore through his side as ribs broke.

"I didn't—" Blood filled Large's mouth. He gagged and rolled onto his side, spitting blood and mucus onto the floor. He tried again. "I didn't know the guy was connected. I checked – no one I asked knew him."

"I know," said Pike. "If I thought you'd done it knowing he was with my sister, you'd be dead by now." He started to walk, circling around Large. "The problem is that you did beat him up. He may be a fuckwit but he's my sister's fuckwit. And you put a gun on me. That was a big mistake." Pike swung a kick at him. Large tried to grab the foot, but Pike was too fast. He landed the kick to Large's ribs, danced out of range of his flailing arms, then came back in, planting a stomping kick on his upturned face.

Large's head felt as if it had exploded with lights and pain. Then someone kicked him in the balls. He vomited, retching uncontrollably, writhing on the floor. He tried to curl into a ball to protect himself from the storm of blows that fell on him from all sides. He couldn't see, couldn't breathe. His eyes were full of blood but he didn't pass out. He felt it all.

Eventually the kicking stopped. Large sobbed and choked on his own blood. All that was left was pain and hatred. Someone played a water hose over him, running the stream up and down his body. The water cleared the blood from his eyes. He watched water and blood flow across the floor and circle a grated drain before disappearing. When the hose was turned off, cold added itself to the list of his pains.

Pike stepped back into Large's field of vision, staring down, his head haloed by a fluorescent light tube. "That's the entertainment over with, now down to business." He smiled and waited but Large had nothing to say. "Alright," Pike went on, "you owe me fifty K for beating up the fuckwit boyfriend." He squatted down beside Large's head. "But for putting a gun on me," he said softly, "I'm going to take your trigger finger." He stood up again and moved over to a big electric bandsaw. It shuddered to life when Pike pressed the power button, then settled into a well-balanced high-pitched hum. Pike picked a large beef bone out of a bucket beside the machine and held it up for Large to see. When he put the bone to the blade, the saw's hum changed to an angry scream as it ripped through the length of the bone.

Pike dropped the bones back into the bucket. "I bet you wish you'd pulled that trigger now, hey?" he said.

Large didn't move, didn't respond, just lay shivering on the concrete floor. He focused on the pain, exploring it, analysing it. Owning it.

Pike looked disappointed. "Get the fat cunt up here. Joe, you hold his legs."

Three of them picked Large up off the floor and dumped him face down on a long metal trolley. Large tried to move but their fingers dug into his flesh, holding him fast. He concentrated on breathing, keeping it shallow, keeping it steady. In, then out. Nice and smooth, trying to avoid the stabbing spasms that movement sent slashing through his body. They wheeled him over to the saw.

"Nothing to say?" said Pike. "I'm disappointed. You're

usually so talkative." He grabbed Large's right hand by the wrist and straightened out his index finger. "I'd curl those other fingers up if I was you. Don't want to lose more than you need to." He moved Large's hand toward the thin metal blade that was turning so fast it was just a blur.

Large twisted and tried to pull his arm back. A punch to his ribs sent pain screaming from his chest to his core. Pike held Large's wrist in one hand and his finger in the other and began sliding them toward the blade.

"Wait, just wait!" Large screamed.

Pike turned his head. "I don't think so."

"You said business—" A coughing fit wracked Large, unleashing new dimensions of pain. When the spasms subsided he spat blood and a tooth onto the metal trolley.

Pike waited patiently, tightening his grip. "Yeah, business. Fifty K, and the finger. Weren't you listening?"

"Guns." Large's voice was a faint croak. "Machine guns."

Pike bent down beside Large's head. "What are you talking about, fat man?"

"Machine guns, I can get them."

"Of course you can. The usual homemade pieces of shit, no doubt. No thanks."

Large was racked by coughs again. He focused on the pain until it merged with the background scream of his body. "No. Imported." He tried to get his breathing steady again. "Submachine guns."

"You want to use them to pay the debt?"

"Yeah, you said business ..."

"I thought you had a deal with Cole. It's the only thing the old fart's any use for."

"That's for the Glocks," Large gasped between breaths. Smooth and shallow. "This is different."

"How many?"

Large tried to remember what Dennis had said. "Four. Maybe five."

"Five?" Pike thought about it for a moment. He let go of Large's hand. "Five submachine guns will do for the finger, but I still want the fifty K. And I'll need to see these guns."

Large pulled his hand away from the saw blade.

"They better be what you say or you're dead," Pike said.

Betty couldn't work out why her toes hurt. Something was pressing on them.

She was in a pale blue room and there were mauve curtains hanging from the ceiling. And a television on the ceiling too, but the screen was dark. Outside, through the open door, she could see people moving past in a corridor, and could hear voices, parts of conversations she couldn't understand, footsteps going back and forth. There were a pair of feet visible, black boots, blue trousers; someone was sitting just outside. The back of her hand itched. There was something stuck to it, tubes, more tubes on her face. A machine next to her pinged softly. She watched the red numbers changing for a while, wondering what they meant. She was in hospital again. The sheets were tucked so tightly across her feet that they were pressing on her toes. She twisted her legs and tried to sit up but only seemed to slide further down the bed.

"Mum?"

Betty turned her head to the voice, to John. He was sitting beside her with a magazine in his lap, but he wasn't looking at it.

"It's alright, John." Was that croak her voice? Was it alright? Her throat was very sore. She needed something to drink.

A nurse started to talk to her, a young Asian woman, very pretty, with gold earrings. She was taking tubes and a mask off Betty's face. A man in a blue tunic leaned her forwards and rearranged the pillows behind her then helped her to sit up. He was strong. There was a woman in glasses with a stethoscope around her neck leaning in too. Behind them all she could see John standing at the foot of the bed. He was grinning and talking to a policewoman, but he kept looking at her. Betty smiled back. She tried to ask a question but the words wouldn't come out.

"Give her some water," John said.

Someone put a cup in front of her with a straw. She took it into her mouth and sucked in cool, stale-tasting water. After a second sip she pushed the cup away. John was still there but the policewoman had gone. "What did I do?" Betty asked.

They barely stopped the van when they dumped Large in the driveway of his house, just slid the door open and pushed him out onto the concrete driveway. He stumbled, trying to stay upright, but fell onto his hands and knees. He couldn't get up again so he stayed there, resting his head on the concrete, feeling the grit of the worn surface press into his forehead. There was no part of him that didn't hurt, that wasn't screaming for attention. But he was alive. Pike would come to regret that. And he still had all his fingers. Promising the guns had bought some time, but he'd have to deliver. Revenge could wait. There would be opportunities – Pike was too sure of himself, too arrogant. Large could wait. Pike would make a lot of enemies, and Large was going to be top of the list.

He crawled to the letterbox and pulled himself up to

stand, trying to shut out the jabbing pain from his broken ribs. He walked very slowly to the house and let himself inside, calling out to Darlene before he remembered that she was still down in Berry. He'd have to look after himself but at least he wouldn't have to put up with hysterics and endless fucking questions. He got his Sig from the hall table and took it and a bottle of vodka into the bathroom. He threw back two hefty slugs with a handful of paracetamol, and sat in the shower stall with hot water pounding on him. He didn't bother to undress, just leaned back against the tiles and enjoyed the warmth while he waited for the drugs to kick in. When the water started to run cold he stripped off his clothes and got slowly into bed, leaving the Sig on the bedside table. He was going to make sure he always had a gun within reach from now on.

FIFTEEN

Is This Normal?

In the morning, Large was so stiff he could hardly move. He was pissing blood and his face was horrible: eyes blackened and swollen to tiny slits. He daren't touch his nose; it was twice its normal size and looked as if any adjustment would be painful. He needed a doctor but he called Jimmy instead. The dickhead must have been enjoying the beach life, the amount he complained about having to come back. "Just get back here and bring Matt."

"For fuck's sake, what happened?" Jimmy said when they arrived just after 11am. Matt stared, not saying anything.

They helped Large into the car and drove him to the emergency department at Sutherland Hospital. Large told the triage nurse that he'd fallen down some stairs drunk. He didn't care that the nurses and doctors didn't believe him. They set his nose, dressed the other wounds and sent him on his way with some serious painkillers. "Nothing we can do for the ribs. Just try not to breathe," said the young smartarse doctor who discharged him. Large would have happily broken a couple of his ribs, give the prick a bit of life experience.

When they got back to the house, Large went straight

back to bed while Matt went out for some some pizzas and a slab of beer.

"You stay here," Large told Jimmy. "Have you got your Glock?"

"In the car."

"It's no fucking use there, is it? Go and get it. I'm not taking risks anymore."

Large slept through the rest of the afternoon and night, waking up groggy and stiff on Wednesday morning. He forced himself out of the bed and into the pool, enjoying having his body supported by the water. He rested, leaning back against the side of the pool. Everything hurt.

Matt was frying bacon when Large made his way slowly and carefully to the kitchen. It smelled fantastic. "I'll have some of that, and a couple of eggs. Poached, and toast."

Matt grinned. "Glad you've got your appetite back."

Large just grunted and shuffled out to the lounge room.

"You sound a bit more like your old self." Jimmy was sitting on the lounge watching a music show – lots of coloured lights and facial hair. Large grunted in response and lowered himself carefully into his chair. He took the remote and switched to ABC News 24. *Let's see what else has been happening*, he thought, as the news came on.

They sat in silence watching the television and eating their breakfast. Matt didn't say much, but he knew his way around a frypan. Large had to chew carefully to avoid the gaps where teeth had been knocked out. He was going to have to see a dentist too. He sipped carefully at the mug of strong tea.

Jimmy was lying on the lounge, transfixed by the big screen. Some financial story about interest rates. "Wake up!" Large shouted, switching the television off.

"What?"

"We need to get hold of those machine guns."

"Yeah, I know, but how are we going to do it?"

"You and Matt are going to have to do it. I can't, not for a while anyway. Lawrence must have them stashed somewhere. Get the cunt. Make him give up the guns. Then kill him."

Jimmy brightened up. "Sure."

"One thing," said Large.

"What?"

"Don't fuck it up. Don't be a smartarse, just put a gun in his face, a bag over his head, hurt him till he talks. Then shoot him. Just keep it simple."

Betty was asleep, half reclining against a pile of pillows. She was still sleeping a lot through the day. They had moved her out of the intensive care unit and into a private room. The monitors were gone, and so was the big bandage on her head, leaving a small dressing for the cut on her forehead. Her skin was very pale. It looked thin, barely capable of covering her bones.

She could walk to the bathroom with some assistance now, but she still couldn't remember anything about the kidnapping. The police were frustrated. John had seen Moreton talking to the doctors, shaking his head, getting agitated. The doctors just shrugged. No one knew if the memory loss would be permanent, or how extensive it would be.

After the last brain scan, a doctor had asked John if his mother had been diagnosed with dementia before the kidnapping. "There are signs on the scans," she said, "early stages but definitely there."

Shit.

"We'll have to wait till she gets over the trauma completely, but it probably means she won't get back to where she was before. We'll refer her to a specialist. Try not to worry about it, let's just get her up and around first."

Try not to worry? Jesus. John was still trying to process all this when his mobile phone started bleating. It was Walker. Moreton had told her about the amnesia.

"Post Traumatic Amnesia? That's going to be a great help then," she said.

John didn't know what she expected him to say to that. "The last thing she remembers is having a cup of tea on Friday morning. Out on her terrace. Nothing after that, not till she woke up."

"She likely to come good? Get the memories back?"

"Possibly not. And if she does, there is no telling when. What did the doctors tell Moreton?"

"Yeah. Basically the same." He heard Walker sigh. "We got a name to go with face you identified. Jimmy Duggan? Mean anything to you?"

"No. Who is he?"

"Associate of Delic. Never been charged with anything. There's not much on him yet. But we will find him."

Well, get on with it, John thought. *Leave me and Mum alone.*

But Walker hadn't finished. "John, did you know your mother had a file?"

"A file?"

"ASIO file. Dates back to the seventies. Makes interesting reading. Seems she had some pretty unsavoury friends back in the day."

"What are you talking about?"

"Her associates were of interest. Palestinian terrorists."

John looked at his mother, propped up against a pile of pillows. "I've got to go," he said.

"John?"

"What?"

"The guard. I've got to pull them off after today. Haven't got the overtime budget."

He hung up on her.

John drove. He didn't know where he was going, he just needed to be moving. Whenever the traffic slowed or stopped he turned off and got onto back streets. It was slow going and often required backtracking, but the randomness of it suited his state of mind. His wandering route took him into parts of the suburbs he didn't know existed.

He needed to talk to his mother. She was still too fragile now, but eventually the questions would have to be asked. He knew his father had been killed in a terrorist attack, by an Algerian working for one of the Palestinian groups. Had his parents somehow been associates of the man who'd killed Jorge? It didn't make sense. Betty had always hated all that, all the idealists who gave no value to human life. So quick to kill and maim the innocent to advance their causes. Or just to get publicity. He couldn't believe that Betty would be associated with those people, but what about Jorge? He'd been an academic, a writer, an ideas man. John didn't know enough about him. ASIO could be wrong. It wouldn't be the first time they had fucked up. They would just be basing their reports on what the French told them. But he didn't really know much about Betty either, he supposed. Not when she was young. She must have been very determined, hot-headed even, leaving Sydney to go and look for her mother, and not coming back. She was impulsive and she was used to getting her way.

If they were mixed up with the Palestinians, it made more

sense that she hadn't spoken much about his father, about his death. It made some sense of her objections to him joining the army. Had he got those things from his father? What else might he have got in that little packet of genes? The ability to kill? Was that something you inherited? Had Jorge been a killer?

When he was a teenager he had tried to find out about Jorge. He looked up the newspapers from 1975, but all he found out was that Jorge had been shot by a terrorist during a confrontation with police. But he had been killed at his own home – what was the terrorist doing there? The papers didn't say Jorge was involved, but maybe it had been suppressed for some reason. Operational imperatives.

He kept driving, meandering his way through Petersham, Marrickville, Ashfield and eventually on to Bankstown. The houses got bigger and further apart as he moved west. The traffic changed too, more commercial vehicles, older cars. He stopped in Cabramatta for some lunch. A Vietnamese pork roll, which he ate sitting on a bench at a bus stop, sipping from a bottle of water while he watched the people on the street. An old Vietnamese couple walking on the other side of the road made him wonder if any of the people who had fled Vietnam and settled in western Sydney had been photographed by his mother during the war.

He binned the paper bag that was now soggy from the brown sauce in the pork roll and got back in the ute. Where to now? It was clouding over, but he didn't want to go back to RPA. Not yet. He didn't know what to say to his mother. He should find out something about dementia. Had there been signs that he had missed? Forgetfulness? She was a bit vague sometimes, but she was old. That's what old people were like.

He started driving again, heading out of Sydney, thinking

he might drive down to the Southern Highlands, Berrima. Go down through Kangaroo Valley to the coast. Have a swim in the ocean.

When he saw a sign to Moorebank he swung the wheel, waving an apology to the truck driver he cut across as he got off the Hume Highway. Moorebank was where Delic's smash-repair shop was. He pulled over and used the GPS system on his phone to find it.

PDW Smash Repairs was on a loop road between a foundry and a furniture removalist, in a small industrial estate that was squeezed onto a wedge of flat land between Heathcote Road and a creek.

John drove slowly past, then went right around the block before parking two hundred metres down the road outside a civil engineering contractor's yard. From there he had a good view of the street and the workshop. The front was made up of a concrete forecourt behind which was a single-storey workshop. There were two large roller shutters, and a small door on the left with a sign that said "Office" above it. The forecourt was filled with cars. Damaged cars, some being worked on, waiting to have the paint work finished. Through the big doors, John could see more cars inside, in various states of damage and disassembly. On the other side of the removalist's warehouse there was a laneway that led through to some scrappy parkland lining the creek.

John watched people coming and going in the street and around the various workshops. It was a busy area and no one paid him any attention. He didn't really know what he was looking for. He was curious though; why would someone from here try to kidnap Betty?

He couldn't see any cop surveillance – either they weren't there or he wasn't good enough to spot them. Both ideas were equally disturbing. On the bright side, though, if they weren't there he didn't have to worry about getting lifted and charged with obstructing an investigation or whatever they could charge him with. He was sure they'd find something if they thought he was getting in the way.

He decided to have a look around, so he left the ute parked in the street and walked past the removalist to the laneway. It was mostly gravel and weeds with a cracked concrete footpath down the middle. There were steel bollards at both ends to stop vehicles driving into the parkland. To stop stolen cars being dumped in the creek, probably. John followed a track worn through the long grass that led down to the line of trees marking the creek. Looking back up the slope he could see a single door in the back wall of the workshop. The door opened directly onto the park. Two men in blue coveralls were leaning against the wall smoking. John stayed in the trees, watching as they finished their cigarettes before they went back inside. Where the track met the creek, someone had placed large stepping stones in the muddy water. There were old tyres and a shopping trolley in the creek bed too. On the opposite bank the track continued up towards a street lined with single-storey houses.

It started to rain lightly as John walked back to the ute. He waited and watched the workshop through the rain-spattered windscreen. Just after four they started moving the vehicles from the forecourt into the workshop for the night. Pushing them on trolleys, squeezing them in. When they were finished all the floor space was occupied by cars. A group of young men came out of the workshop, laughing and shouting as they ran to a dark blue Nissan Skyline parked in the street. John thought he recognised two of them from Delic's Facebook page, but the blond guy wasn't there. Two older men followed them out of the workshop and began closing the roller shutters. John didn't recognise either of

190

them.

He started the ute and followed the Skyline as it pulled out. The car was easy to spot, with its fancy paint job and fat exhaust. With the chrome wheels and tinted windows, it looked as though the owner had made use of every one of the neighbourhood's car workshops to trick it out. When they turned right onto Heathcote Road he stayed in the left lane, letting a couple of cars slip between him and the Skyline. They crossed the Georges River and the railway line on a long, low bridge, then took an exit that brought them back around under the bridge beside the railway line. The Skyline pulled into a car park beside Liverpool station. John followed them in and drove past as they parked. He found a spot near the exit and waited, watching the young men run across the road in the rain. They went into a hotel that was painted bright blue and covered in posters advertising special deals: ten-dollar steaks and strippers on Wednesday and Thursday nights.

The apprentices were ordering drinks at the bar when John stepped into the beery gloom. This was their regular watering hole, judging from the way they were joking and laughing with the barmaid, giving and taking a bit of shit. They took their drinks and sat at a table close to the stage, where they'd have a very good view of the strippers. John bought a schooner and sat at a table at the other end of the bar. His view was of the apprentices and all the doors.

The young men were looking at something on a mobile phone, passing it around the table. From their laughter and general stupidity, John presumed it was porn, or maybe a cat.

The pub was filling up now, attracting workers who had knocked off for the day, and who were intent on working on their drinking and getting an eyeful of inflated mammaries before they went home to their families. The crowd was cheerful and noisy at this early stage, but the number of black-clad bouncers who had taken up positions at the doors meant that it wouldn't necessarily stay that way. John couldn't see the apprentices' table anymore. Not that it mattered – he wasn't going to learn anything useful here.

When the PA system fired up and the manager started to spruik the show, John finished his beer and left.

It was seven by the time he got back to the hospital. He left the ute back at Camperdown and walked up the hill through the light rain.

His mother was asleep. Billy was sitting next to her, flipping through a magazine.

"What are you doing here?" John asked.

"I came over after school. Tom was at home, arguing about something with mum." He shrugged. "You didn't tell me she was awake."

John sighed. "No, I didn't. Sorry. You're right, I should have called you."

"There was no cops, and no one knew where you were so I thought I'd better hang here. Keep an eye on her."

John felt like hugging the boy, but didn't. "Thanks, mate," he said. "I've got it now. You had anything to eat?"

Billy shook his head.

"Here, get yourself a burger on the way home." John held out twenty dollars.

"That's too much."

"No. It's not enough, but it'll have to do for the moment." He held the boy's shoulder briefly then pushed him gently towards the door. "And don't forget to do your homework."

"Already done it."

"Sure."

John was glad his mother was sleeping. He didn't know what to say to her yet. *Were you a terrorist? Was my father? Is that why they tried to kidnap you? What the fuck is going on, Mum?*

"Is this normal? Sleeping so much?" he asked the nurse who came around to check on Betty.

"She was awake this afternoon for a while, had something to eat. It takes time. She was speaking some other language—"

"French. Mum lived in France for most of her life."

The nurse nodded. "Yes. It could take a while for her to get back to normal. Try not to worry."

Try not to worry. John sat by his mother for a while, looking through a couple of magazines he had already read once. There was no point him being here. He'd come back in the morning, maybe she'd be awake then.

He was on his way out of the building, going through the lobby, when he stopped and went back to the enquiries desk. The young man on duty directed him to a ward on the east side of the fifth floor.

He found Ken Mallard sitting up in bed, fiddling with the remote control for his television. He was in a room with four beds, only three of them occupied. Ken smiled when he saw John. He turned the television off and dropped the remote onto the bed covers.

"John, how are you? I was just trying to find something worth watching."

"How're you doing, Ken?"

"Oh, I'm alright. Hurts like hell, and the drugs don't seem to make much difference. But you gotta put up with it. Can't stop breathing."

"No. You've got to do that."

"They reckon I'll be here for a while. How's Betty going? I wanted to go and visit her but they said I can't yet. Can't see why, it's only in the hospital. Surely Lucy could wheel me around there. But they say no."

"Mum's out of the coma now. But she's sleeping a lot. They say she might have dementia." He shrugged. "Might have had it before. They can't tell. Reckon there's no permanent damage from the crash. Just have to wait and see how she goes."

"Dementia, Jesus. She never seemed ... forgetful or anything to me. She was pretty sharp, I thought."

"Yeah," said John. "She could be sharp alright."

Ken smiled. "She has opinions. That's for sure."

John left when visiting time ended. It had stopped raining now and he stood underneath the fig trees, watching the bats fluttering around in the canopy, squeaking and chattering at each other.

Food, he thought, turning left and walking up the hill to King Street. He found a small, cheap-looking Thai restaurant and ordered massaman curry. The restaurant was brightly lit with fluorescent tubes and had yellow-painted walls. Above the counter there was a little Buddhist shrine and one of those strange golden cats, waving its paw at him. It was his kind of place. There were plenty of others eating alone: taxi drivers breaking their shifts, and students escaping their tiny apartments for half an hour for a feed before hitting the computer again. The food was good and it was quiet, not the sort of place that attracted big noisy groups.

After the curry, John wandered along King Street, watching the crowds who were starting to migrate from the restaurants to the pubs and bars. Past Newtown station he heard loud music coming from a pub and crossed the road to check it out. There was a four-piece band in the front bar

194

playing covers of eighties and nineties rock. He found a stool at the back of the bar and ordered a Jameson. When the band finished their sets, John kept drinking. Kept thinking about his parents.

SIXTEEN

Pure Home Grown

It was after 2am when John left the pub. There were still plenty of people about on King Street but the back streets were quiet as he started the walk home. Only the occasional car, and no other pedestrians.

His route meandered through Enmore in the general direction of Camperdown, along narrow streets lined with terrace houses and parked cars. He walked in the middle of the road because the footpaths were so narrow and uneven, half their width taken up by trees with low branches that he would have to duck under. It was a clear, still night, marked by the constant grind of the city in repose. Between Newtown and Stanmore the railway line was elevated on a brick retaining wall, a barrier across the street grid, forcing cars and pedestrians down the hill to the Liberty Road underpass. There was a bit of traffic on Kingston Road but he left it behind, turning up into an area of old industrial buildings and warehouses that were being converted to apartments. They weren't really conversions – the builders just kept the old brick facade and built a modern concrete structure inside it, jamming in as many apartments as possible. It was happening all over the Inner West, the planners made them keep the streetscape intact but they gutted the buildings and lost all the individual character. He'd been to a couple of display units when he was looking to buy a house. Once you were inside they were all the same – you could be anywhere.

He heard a car behind him and stepped onto the footpath to let it go past. The silver Commodore cruised along the street and turned right without signalling. Probably looking for a parking spot.

There were temporary fencing panels and waste skips all over the footpath, so John stepped back out onto the road again. Ahead of him the Commodore came back out of the side street and turned towards him, coming faster this time. John moved to the side of the road, watching the car approach. It was close to him when he saw the nose dip, the car braking suddenly. An arm with a gun came out of the passenger-side window.

John ran. There were two shots in quick succession, the sound of glass breaking. Shouts. He leaped onto a skip full of rubble and vaulted over the fence. The chain-mesh panels swayed under his weight, leaning into the building site. He dropped to the ground behind the skip. Three more shots ripped the night, one then two almost together, slamming into the metal side of the skip. John heard car doors opening and running feet. He ran down the ramp into the basement of the building. Harsh orange light from the street lights silhouetted him until he reached the bottom of the ramp, where it was pitch black. Two steps into the darkness, John hit something solid with his left knee and fell onto the concrete floor. More shots, hitting masonry and steel close to him. John lay stunned for a second, then the pain in his knee came. *Fuck*, he thought, getting himself up into a crouch, ignoring the pain. The thing he ran into felt like bags of sand or cement. Good cover, anyway. He turned away from the light, willing his eyesight to adjust to the gloom faster. From the street he could hear voices, a half-whispered argument. His eyes slowly adjusted to the dark, and he started to make out shapes. Columns, stacks of building materials. There were pallets of bricks scattered among the concrete columns. Plenty of cover and there should be a fire exit somewhere. He moved further away from the entrance, feeling his way carefully, trying not to put too much weight on his left knee. And trying not to make any noise on the gritty concrete floor. He couldn't see any sign of the fire exit.

"Come on, we've got the cunt now!" It was shouted from the street and followed by the metallic scraping of the fence being moved. The sound of footsteps and elongated shadows preceded two sets of legs down the ramp. John started feeling around him, looking for something he could use as a weapon. An M4 would be good, but all he found was a bucket containing short steel bars. Each was about forty centimetres long and a centimetre thick, some kind of concrete reinforcing. He tested their weight in his hands. They would be very useful if he could get close enough to use them without getting shot.

The two men were at the bottom of the ramp now, out of the light. John took two of the bars and moved further along the wall, squatting down behind a stack of framing timber. The resiny smell of the pine overpowered the smell of dust that pervaded the basement. He could feel his knee beginning to swell and stiffen, but he couldn't stretch it out. He had to stay crouched, ready to move. How many shots had they fired? How far was the nearest house? Surely someone would call the cops. All he could do for now was watch and wait.

"You go right, I'll go left."

"It's too fucking dark down here. We need a torch."

"Did you bring one?"

"No."

"Then shut the fuck up. He's in here somewhere, we'll find him."

John heard them start to move, feeling their way on both sides of the ramp. He could hear the footsteps of the one coming towards him. John pulled himself up behind a concrete column and tried to judge the distance. When he heard a soft thud and a grunt, the man bumping into something, John cocked his arm and threw one of the bars low and hard. He heard it clanking off the wall and onto the floor. Shooting erupted from both of the men, filling the basement with noise and muzzle flashes. The flashes gave John all the target he needed. This time he stepped away from the column and threw overarm, hard and fast. There was a thud and a low cry before the second bar clanked onto the concrete floor. It was followed by a muffled thump.

"Matt? Where is he? What's he doing? Matt?"

John started moving toward the one he had hit with the bar. He'd have to be quick, the other one was moving too. Pain shot through his knee, but he kept going, picking a route between the pallets. If he could get Matt's gun he was going to put a big hole in the other prick.

He didn't make it in time. The other one found Matt first, falling over him in the dark.

"Shit, Matt. Matt? Jesus, wake up for fuck's sake. What's happened?"

John crouched behind a column and waited. He could hear sirens in the distance now. About bloody time.

"Come on. Wake up, Matt, you stupid bastard." There was a thud that might have been a kick, and then some slaps followed by groaning and retching. "Come on. It's the fucking jacks. Let's go."

John watched the men emerge into the light on the ramp, the skinny one half dragging the one called Matt.

"My gun—"

"What?"

"My gun?"

"For fuck's sake. There's no time."

John leaned back against the column, listening to the sirens get louder.

This time the police kept him in overnight. Sally Walker turned up just before 5am. "Starting to make a habit of this, Mr Lawrence," she said. "Shootouts – you'll give the area a bad name."

"Is it still a shootout if only one side is shooting?"

"Good point. I'll have Harry check the manual. We'll get back to you."

John took her through it all; it was the third time he had told it. When he had finished his story she surprised him by asking how Betty was.

He shrugged, "Sleeping a lot."

"Memory?"

"No change. She's pretty old for all this."

"Makes it harder for us," Walker said. "But having some prick stick a gun in her face, and then the bang on the head ... It's going to take a toll."

John watched her read through a copy of his statement, making occasional notes in the margin. She was wearing a red tracksuit, and her hair was pulled back in a ponytail. John presumed she had been in bed when they called her. He wondered if she lived alone.

"It was definitely the other kidnapper again?"

"Yeah, the skinny blond one."

"Jimmy Duggan. And the name he used, it was Matt?"

John nodded.

"Okay." She wrote another note in the margin. "The one you hurt, was that the one who started shooting, the passenger?"

John thought, trying to visualise the scene, seeing again the dim figures in the car, lit suddenly by muzzle flashes. "Not sure. Don't think so, but it's just an impression."

"How badly did you hurt him? Where was he hit?" She looked up at him. "Should we be looking for him at a hospital?"

"Head, I think. He was out, unconscious, till the other one slapped him, shook him awake."

"But he walked out?"

"With some help."

She scribbled on the report again. "Interesting about the guns. We've got two guns from these guys. Both Glock 19s, both virtually new."

"Is that unusual?"

"It's definitely noteworthy. Did these guys have accents?"

"Accents?"

"Yeah, former Yugoslav for instance, Serb, Bosnian? Middle Eastern?"

"Australian."

"Pity."

"No, these two were pure home-grown bogan."

He got home at 8am and went straight to bed, pulling his blanket over his head to block out the light.

At ten he was woken by the sound of a garbage truck backing into the cul-de-sac, its reversing alarm beeping loudly. He could hear one of the runners dragging wheelie bins out into the road. John couldn't remember the last time he had put his bin out. He crawled out of bed, pulled on a pair of shorts and ran out to the veranda. The bin was so full that the lid wouldn't shut properly and it smelled pretty bad. He manoeuvred it down the steps and out onto the street. "Got room for one more?" he shouted to the runner.

"Yeah, no worries."

"Thanks." He watched while his bin was hooked up at the back of the truck and emptied into the foul-smelling hopper, nodding his appreciation to the runner before he took the bin back onto the veranda. He stood for a while watching the street before he went inside. It was a nice day, half over already. He needed to see his mother while she was awake, so he could ask her about the Algerian. And about his father. It was a conversation he wasn't looking forward to, but he had to know.

When he was sure there was nothing unusual on the street he went inside and showered and dressed. He walked down to Parramatta Road, to a convenience store with computers in the front window.

There was a short cryptic message from Smokey, a new line on their draft email. It just said '4 broadway' followed by a vehicle registration number. His chat with his mother was going to have to wait a bit longer.

He bought breakfast at the café by the park: a flat white and a bacon and egg roll to take away.

"Do you want sauce with the roll?" the young Irish woman serving him asked. She was new. Blonde hair and black eyebrows.

"Yeah. That home-made relish. Thanks." He took the coffee and the roll back to the ute and drove to Broadway shopping centre. The ramp from Bay Street took him straight up to the top level of the car park. He drove across to the down ramp and wound his way through the coloured-coded levels to level four: the baby-shit brown level.

The registration number Smokey had sent belonged to a red Hyundai Getz parked behind the lift well. John found an empty slot in the next row and waited, eating his roll and drinking his coffee while he watched the car park. He checked all the cars, and the few shoppers who came and went. He noted that whoever did deliveries for Smokey had parked the Getz in a blind spot, out of range of all the security cameras. When he had finished his breakfast and was satisfied there was no one watching the Getz, he took the paper bag and the empty coffee cup and put them in a rubbish bin by the mall entry. Then he turned and walked back to the Getz. The key was in a magnetic holder beneath the rear left wheel arch. Inside the boot was a bright green shopping bag full of groceries. On top were onions, a bunch of basil and some pasta. John took the bag and locked the Hyundai.

Driving out of the car park, he turned left, down towards Wentworth Park, then around onto Wattle Street, past the Fish Markets and up onto Anzac Bridge. He turned onto Victoria Road and kept going west through Drummoyne, only turning back through Five Dock and Parramatta Road when he was sure he wasn't being followed.

Back at Camperdown he found a plain grey plastic gun case, a box of fifty hollow point rounds and a cleaning kit underneath the groceries. Smokey had done well. John popped the box and took out the stubby black Heckler & Koch USP 9mm pistol. It was ridiculous how much better he felt with a weapon in his hand. He stripped the HK down, put it back together again, and loaded the two thirteen-round clips. One clip went into his sock, the other into the grip of the weapon. He worked the slide to put a round in the breach and checked the safety before tucking it into the back of his jeans. Now he was ready.

Betty's bed was empty when John got to the hospital. He looked around the room and was just about to check with the nurses when he heard the toilet flush. A moment later the bathroom door opened and his mother walked out, leaning on her stick but moving surprisingly freely.

"*Bonjour,*" she said. "Where have you been? I've been expecting you all day."

"Sorry. I had a sleep in. Late night last night."

Betty grunted and walked around the bed to a big blue vinyl armchair. "I can't stand being in that bloody bed anymore. They won't tell me when I can go home. I'm perfectly alright now. I shouldn't be taking up a hospital bed. There will be sick people who really need it."

"They know what they're doing, Mum. Have you seen a doctor today?"

"Some woman looked at me this morning. She said I'm fine. I know that, of course I am."

"You were in a coma a few days ago, Mum. There's still a risk of brain damage."

"I'm perfectly fine. I just want to get out of here."

"I saw Ken the other day. He's looking a lot better than the last time I saw him. Still in a fair bit of pain though. He asked after you."

"I should go and see him. Where is he? You can walk with me, can't you?"

John looked at her. "Sure, Mum. Why not?"

They found Ken sitting up in his bed with his reading glasses perched on the end of his nose. He had a newspaper folded on the table in front of him and a pen in his hand.

His face was pale but a smile lit it up when he saw Betty stumping into the room. "Ah, there you are. I wondered when you'd turn up."

John moved some magazines off a chair so Betty could sit down.

"How are you, my dear?" Betty asked, squeezing Ken's hand. "You look well for someone who has been shot."

"Do I? It's not something I'd recommend. I'm just glad to be able to sit up now. How is your head?"

"Oh, you know ... hard as a rock. Can't remember a damned thing, though. They tell me you tried to be a hero and got yourself shot for your trouble."

"Yes. Bloody fool, that I am. Didn't think he'd actually do it." He started to laugh but then winced in pain. "Next time I'll let them take you," he said through gritted teeth.

"There won't be a next time," said John.

"No," said Ken, his face relaxing as the pain eased. "Not for that bloke. The police told me what happened to him."

"It was an accident," said John. "Would have been better if he was alive so the cops could question him, then we might have some idea what it was all about."

Ken was watching Betty, whose attention had been taken by the view out the window. He turned to John, raising his eyebrows in a question.

John just shrugged. "So what are you up to, Ken?"

"Oh, just the crossword. Bit of a struggle, can't seem to concentrate long enough to get any out."

"Don't look at me," said Betty, turning away from the window. "I'm officially brain damaged."

"You were no use before you got banged on the head, so no change there," Ken said.

"Your room has a much nicer view than mine. I wonder if I can get a transfer up here."

They were interrupted by a nurse who wheeled in a little trolley loaded with sealed packets of bandages. "Sorry, I need to change Mr Mallard's dressings."

"Time I got Mum back to her own room anyway," said John. "Before she tries to move in. See you soon, Ken."

"I'll come back tomorrow," said Betty. "Annoy you some more."

"Please do," said Ken, as the nurse pulled the curtains around his bed.

On the way back, Betty insisted they take a detour to the ground floor café. "I really need a half-decent cup of coffee, and something to eat that has some flavour. Something not boiled to death."

John watched her devour a salad and a custard tart followed by a cup of coffee. He didn't understand how she suddenly had so much energy. Maybe she would pay for it later.

"The police have been asking if you remember anything about last Friday. About the kidnapping," he said.

Betty took a sip from her coffee and put the cup slowly back on the saucer. "I know it's stupid but there is nothing, just the hospital, just waking up. I'm sorry." She dabbed at her mouth with a paper napkin.

"It's okay, Mum. It's amnesia. Everyone understands. Nothing you can do about it." He reached across and held her hand. "They asked about Paris, too. About the terrorist. About Jorge."

"They're both dead." Betty was watching a young man helping a heavily pregnant woman into a seat at the next table. She didn't look at John.

"Did you know him, Mum? The Algerian?"

"Yes. We all did. They thought he was some kind of hero, a freedom fighter. But he killed your father."

"How did you know him?"

"He was Jorge's friend. I never liked him." She pulled her hand away from his and lifted it to her face. "That suitcase was his. Jorge was just looking after it."

"The suitcase? What suitcase?"

"The one with Jorge's things. In the storage place."

"What do you mean it was his? The Algerian's? My father was looking after a suitcase for him?"

"Yes. I thought the police took it."

Oh shit, thought John.

Betty drank the rest of the coffee. "I'm tired. I want to go back to my room now."

When John had gone, Betty lay in her bed looking out the window, remembering Paris, remembering 1975. She had just returned from Beirut. That once beautiful city was being flooded with weapons and hatred. She had been away nearly a month, trying to cover the war developing between the Phalange and the Palestinians, trying to distil on film the brutal fighting between the militias and the growing toll on civilians on both sides.

She had spent the month trying not to get shot or blown to pieces. Always on edge, always wondering who she could trust. Then when she arrived back at Orly, Hubert met her with the news that Amin and his family had been killed. He was her Beirut driver and fixer. She had said goodbye to him only the day before. A bear of a man, Amin had started out as a taxi driver, but as the conflict developed he had spent less time picking up fares in his old Mercedes and more time hooking journalists up with members of the Maronite factions. He must have finally pissed someone off enough to take the trouble to wire some Semtex beneath his car. It went off when he was taking Sana and the children to school. Betty had known Amin since her first visit to Beirut in 1973. He was a loud man, always telling stories, always laughing at his own jokes. A deep laugh like distant artillery.

Hubert dropped her off at the apartment. "Get some sleep. I'll call you in the morning."

The apartment was empty except for a large brown suitcase in the middle of the living room floor. Betty stepped around it on the way to the bedroom, wondering what it meant. Had someone arrived? Or was someone leaving? She was too tired to think about it either way. She felt numb. She closed the curtains and crawled into bed, pulling the covers over her head.

When she woke in the late afternoon, she realised how hungry she was. Jorge was in the kitchen preparing rôti de porc. He always made a nice meal for her when she came back from her assignments. Her "little excursions".

She asked him about the suitcase. "Are you leaving me?" She smiled, rubbing her hand down his broad back, lingering over his buttocks.

He turned and kissed her. Softly, slowly. "*Bien entendu*, but before I go, I am cooking you dinner." He grinned at her. "It is Rashid's. He asked me to look after it for a couple of days." Jorge wiped his hands on a towel draped over his shoulder. "I will put it in my study."

"What's in it?"

"I didn't ask."

Rashid was one of Jorge's friends. An Algerian. Betty didn't know him that well, she saw him at the parties where all their fashionably left-wing friends talked romantically about revolution and imperialism. Betty was pretty certain that she and Rashid were the only ones who had seen the places the others were always talking about. Betty wasn't a

208

romantic, she had seen the torn bodies and heard the women crying. Neither was Rashid, he was always deadly serious. Even at parties, he'd be in a quiet corner talking with his small group of followers. Young men attracted to the mystery and secrecy, the sense of danger. Young women attracted by strength and beauty. Rashid was beautiful: brown eyes, curly black hair, a slim, hard body. And a brilliant smile, when he chose to use it. The men and the women who sat around him lived for that smile, worked hard trying to earn it.

Betty couldn't believe that Jorge hadn't asked what was in the suitcase. "Don't you care? You know he's tied up with the Palestinians and those fucking Germans? Don't you?"

"You don't know that."

"Yes, I bloody well do." Betty turned on her heel and walked through to the living room.

Jorge followed her, wiping his hands on a towel. "He's just—"

"Why do you think he wants us to look after this? He doesn't feel safe. Whatever's in here," she kicked the suitcase and it fell onto its side with a solid thump, "he doesn't want to get caught with it."

"He said just a couple of days—"

"Do you fancy the *flics* coming and finding it here? I certainly do not," Betty shouted. "I will not have that terrorist storing his bombs here."

"It's not a bomb."

"How do you know?"

"He's not a terrorist."

Betty just looked at him. "What is it that you think he does? Him and his creepy German friends?"

"He said he didn't have room ... It's not a bomb."

"You don't know that."

Jorge held up his hands. "*Calmes toi.*"

"I am calm. Call Rashid, or I'll call the *flics*."

"No. You can't do that, he's a friend."

"Your friend, maybe."

In the end she didn't have to call the police. The suitcase wasn't even locked. She just undid the big thick belt and snapped the locks open, not sure what she expected to see. She just knew she didn't trust Rashid.

Jorge went white when he saw the machine guns.

"Call Rashid," Betty said quietly. "Make him take it away." Then she left. Went out the door without a second look, without another word. That was the last time they spoke.

She had walked for a long time, thinking, trying to be less furious. Wondering if she should leave Jorge. How could he be so stupid, so gullible? She didn't go back. She spent the night with Marie Gabriac at her apartment in the Butte-aux-Cailles. If only she had stayed at home with Jorge. He might have lived.

Next day, the police told her what had happened. The DST were following Rashid. Maybe he spotted them, they weren't sure. When Jorge opened the door there seemed to be an argument, then Rashid started shooting. He shot Jorge first, and two of the cops in the street, before they killed him.

Betty never stayed in that apartment again. When the police were finished with it, the concierge put everything in storage. Betty had been two months gone with John then. She didn't mention the suitcase and neither did the police. She just presumed they had taken it.

John slid the passenger seat forwards and looked at the suitcase. He had jammed it in behind the seats when he took Betty to the doctor's surgery after she'd felt faint at the storage unit. With everything that had happened since then, he'd forgotten about it. And how heavy it was. He'd assumed it was full of books when he pulled it out of the storage unit, but after his mother's revelations, the weight worried him. He carried it inside the house and put it carefully on a table. The suitcase was old, made well before suitcases came with wheels. The big steel clasps were spotted with rust and the leather patches at the corners looked mildewy. A thick strap was wrapped like a big belt around it, running through the handle. The leather was dry, cracking and creaking when he undid the strap. The clasps were rusty and stiff but they weren't locked. The left one opened easily but the one on the right required the insertion of a screwdriver blade under the hasp.

Under the lid of the suitcase was a dark grey blanket, stained with what smelled like machine oil. When he lifted the blanket off, John understood.

He was looking at shiny black machine pistols. Five of them. Small things, with wooden pistol grips and curved box magazines. They had steel shoulder stocks folded forwards over their muzzles. He recognised the type. Škorpions, Eastern European; Czech, maybe. Indonesian special forces had used them too, may still do for all he knew. They were small calibre, but they were easy to conceal and very effective at close range. Good terrorist weapons.

John got some rubber gloves from the kitchen; he didn't want his prints on these guns. He picked up the top one – it was definitely real, not a replica. The safety was on, the breech clear but the magazine was full. Metal jacketed .32 ACP rounds. Wrapped in another blanket were five more magazines, all full, and six boxes of ammunition. He laid the guns and the magazines in the lid of the suitcase and lifted another blanket. "Jesus," he muttered. The bottom of the suitcase was lined with bundles of US dollars in neat paper wrappers. Three bundles deep, twenty-dollar notes. He had no idea how much it was but it looked like a lot. In two cloth drawstring bags he found gold coins: Krugerrands. He didn't know what they were worth either. *This just keeps getting better and better*, he thought. The suitcase was a terrorist kit, just add crazy and stand back.

SEVENTEEN

Blue Shoes

Large slammed his mobile phone on the desk. He'd had to call Jimmy to find out what had happened, the prick hadn't had the balls to call him. Useless bastards, the two of them. He was going to have to get hold of the guns himself. There was no choice, Pike wasn't going to accept any excuses, and Large had no intention of losing any fingers. He had considered the possibility of taking out Pike, but that would lead to a war with the Chiefs, and there was only one way that would turn out. No, he had to get the guns. And kill Lawrence. Revenge on Pike would be more complicated. It would have to wait.

He opened the bottom drawer of the desk and pulled out a bottle, his Sig and a fat black tube. He took a swig from the bottle of Mount Gay rum and screwed the suppressor onto the muzzle of the gun. It doubled the size of the weapon, but meant he could fire it almost anywhere without drawing attention. The next time he saw Lawrence, he wasn't going to fuck around, he was going to shoot first. From the shelf behind the desk he took a red and white Australia Post mailing tube. It had a red plastic cap on one end and a notch cut into

213

the cardboard at the other. The silenced Sig slid neatly into the tube, leaving the grip and trigger guard free. He put the rig and a box of ammunition into a sports bag.

On his way to the front door, Sharon got under his feet, scrabbling around on the polished floor, wanting to go out and chase the Davidsons' cat. "Piss off, you stupid fucking dog," he said as he shovelled it aside with his foot.

"You going out, love?" Darlene called from the kitchen.

"Yeah."

"Where are you going?"

"Hunting," he shouted back, but was drowned out by Sharon barking from the back of the lounge at the cat as it crossed the front lawn.

"Can you pick up some milk?"

"No."

John had just pulled the door closed behind him when a cab pulled up and Annette Morgan got out. Shit. It was a fortnight since she was last here. A fortnight since he had made a fool of himself with her. He had completely forgotten that she would be coming back today. After the last time, he wouldn't have been surprised if she hadn't come back. But here she was crossing the road, waving and smiling, looking good, in a white T-shirt and short pink skirt. John smiled back.

"Hi. How are you?"

"I'm well." She surprised him by coming in close and giving him a peck on the cheek. "How is your mum? I thought about calling but decided you probably had enough on your plate."

"Yeah it's been ... complicated."

214

Annette gave him a sympathetic look and squeezed his arm.

He looked down at her hand, resting on his forearm, suddenly very conscious of the HK tucked in the back of his jeans. "I'm sorry," he said, "I've totally forgotten you were coming today. I'm just about to go to see Mum at the hospital. Not sure how long that will take." There was a lot he had to talk to her about.

"That's okay," Annette said, taking her hand off his arm. "I'll be fine here on my own."

"I'll let you in and get you set up before I head off," he said, unlocking the front door and holding it open for her.

"Give your mum my regards. Tell her we need her to get better in time for the exhibition opening."

John smiled. "Sure. I'll tell her you're in town. That will get her attention. She likes the idea of having her own exhibition."

"And maybe you and I can get something to eat later? I don't have to go back to Canberra till tomorrow."

Betty wanted a cup of coffee, a decent one. The coffee in the hospital was horrible, over-brewed muck. And all she'd had for breakfast was some limp toast that came with butter and jam in those stupid little plastic containers. It was always a struggle to get them open. She knew there were lots of cafés close by in Newtown. John had taken her there when they had gone to the movies, to see that young Audrey Tatou. What was the name of the film? She couldn't find the words. They were just there. She could feel their shape, as if they were pushing against her brain through a membrane, but she couldn't see them.

Anyway, after the movie they had gone to a café. She'd had cake, a very nice orange cake. At least Sydney had decent cafés now. Not as good as Paris, but so much better than when she was young. Sydney was changing, she supposed, but it was so far away. So far from everything she knew, everything she loved. It felt as if her life had never happened. Here she was back again. Despite her successes, despite all the things she'd seen and done, here she was back again.

After the nurses had been around to take her blood pressure and change the dressing on her head, Betty climbed gingerly out of bed. She was stiff and sore but was certain she would feel better if she kept moving. Lying in bed was just making her stiffer. She looked a fright in the bathroom mirror, with no make-up and a bandage on her forehead. Still, it felt good to be wearing proper clothes again. She found her handbag and her walking stick in the little closet beside the bed and set off.

At the lifts, Betty joined the waiting crowd of nurses and visitors, listening to a conversation between two male nurses about a television show she had never heard of. When the lift came it seemed to be full but everyone squeezed up and the nurses made space for her between them. On the ground floor she walked out through the bustling lobby, past the café that she had been to with John the day before.

On the street it was cool but sunny. The road was busy and there were a lot of people walking about. Betty watched them for a while, then turned left and followed a group of students up the hill towards Newtown.

John arrived at the hospital with a bag of croissants and two cups of coffee jammed into a cardboard tray. He was going to have to ask his mother some hard questions and he wanted her in a good mood first. He needed to know about the guns and the Algerian. He needed to know if his mother and father had been terrorists too.

The hospital room was empty. So was the bathroom. He left the coffees and the croissants on the table and went back out to the nurses' station.

"She was there half an hour ago when I changed her dressing," said the pretty English nurse. "She can't have gone far." John went to the lift lobby while the nurses began checking the other rooms in the ward. The only people at the lifts were a man and his daughter, the little girl holding a string attached to a huge shiny orange balloon shaped like a fish.

Back in the ward, the English nurse looked worried. She shook her head, "She's not here. Not on the ward."

John didn't wait for a lift. He took the stairs two at a time down to street level. She wasn't in the lobby or the café. The smokers out in the forecourt shook their heads and shrugged – they hadn't seen her. John walked out to the street and scanned up and down, then he crossed the road and checked again. Nothing.

He went back up to the hospital room and examined it, moving through it quickly, just looking, not touching anything. There was no sign of a struggle. The bed clothes were pulled up and her nightdress was folded on the pillow. Her stick and her bag were missing along with the clothes he had brought in for her: a white top and blue slacks.

He called Walker. "My mother has disappeared," he said. "There are clothes missing. She might have just gone out on her own."

"Or she might not," said Walker.

"I'm going to Forest Court now," he said, "to see if she's gone there."

"How would she get that far?"

"I don't know. Taxi? She was walking all over the bloody hospital yesterday."

The house looked shut up when Large got to Camperdown. Same as last time he was there. He parked across the road and watched for a while, listening to the radio. Some guy talking about rising sea levels. Sounded like Bangladesh was fucked, and the Maldives would be even worse off. They'll all be arriving by boat soon, Large thought. After ten minutes watching and seeing no signs of life, he got out of the car carefully and crossed the road to the house. He was carrying the Australia Post tube in two hands as if he was making a delivery.

Large was about to ring the bell, his left hand reaching out for the button, his right still holding the Sig, when the door began to open. He didn't hesitate. He fired through the end of the tube. Three shots, into the door, above and to the left of the handle. The only sound the gun made was a popping click, followed by the shells ringing as they bounced on the concrete pavement.

The door stopped moving with the first shot. Large shouldered it open, pushing aside the body on the floor, stepping over it to check the hall and the front room. They were empty.

The dead woman's white T-shirt was soaked with blood. Small splinters of timber from the door protruded from the wounds in the centre of her chest. Large had no idea who she was, but he wished it had been Lawrence.

* * *

218

Betty was tired and her legs were sore by the time she found the small café on King Street. She sat at a table in the window and watched the people on the street go past while she waited for her coffee and croissant. They were mainly young people, students maybe, and staff from the hospital. Some were even still wearing blue theatre gowns, or had stethoscopes around their necks.

Betty had never been to university. It was something she regretted now. Too late, of course. She envied the young people. They were totally unaware of the freedom they had. Oblivious to the fact that age narrows your choices, the accretions of past decisions making it so much harder to change direction. She finished her coffee and picked up the last of the flakes of pastry, licking the end of her index finger and dabbing at the plate until they were all gone. It wasn't too bad, better than she had hoped.

Back out on King Street, she was surprised how many restaurants there were. None of them were French, of course. Australians seemed to have no interest in France these days; everything seemed to be Asian. Or Italian. Even the English seemed to be out of favour.

There were a few clothes shops scattered between the restaurants, though none of them looked like the sort of place that would have anything that suited Betty. They were all full of T-shirts and pre-torn jeans. She did see some pretty blue shoes with nice low heels. A young girl with hair dyed bright blue helped her try them on, which was just as well because it was a struggle for Betty to reach her feet these days. She was so stiff. The shoes were a good fit and the girl agreed that they suited her, so she bought them. Why not? The girl put her old black shoes in the box so Betty could wear the new ones.

She kept walking along King Street, very pleased with

her new shoes. They were comfortable, which was good, because it was turning out to be further to Glebe than she had thought. Eventually the shops petered out and the road became wider. She walked by the university, squeezing past a big crowd of noisy students waiting at a bus stop near the gates. One thing she liked about Sydney was the mix of races. There were so many Chinese and Indians now. Not so many Africans, but a few. It was a lot different when she was young. She hadn't seen a Negro until she had gone to America. The suburbs she had grown up in had been all white. Italians and Greeks were the closest thing to people of colour in those days of careless racism.

Beyond the university she followed a path through a large park, past lawns and big shady trees till she got to a duck pond. She sat down to rest on a bench beneath the branches of an enormous fig tree. Its buttress roots flowed out on either side of the bench, like arms. The ground beneath the tree was littered with fallen leaves and rotting figs that filled the air with a sweet fermented stench. Betty watched the antics of the ducks and water hens, and tried to ignore the noise of the traffic on Parramatta Road.

His mother wasn't at Forest Court. The apartment was just as John had left it on Sunday, nothing out of place. He went through all the rooms then locked up again, standing outside the door, looking around the courtyard. It was mid-morning but there was no one about. He checked the laundry, the drying area, the letter boxes and the common room. Nothing. He knocked on the doors of all the ground-floor units, disturbing those residents who were home. They came slowly to their doors in response to his banging and button pushing. Apprehensive women, late risers with hands clutching robes at their throats. Wary men, standing back from the still-locked screen doors. Mostly they smiled and relaxed when they saw it was him, but no, sorry, none of them had seen Betty. Not since last Friday.

John pulled out his phone and dialled Walker on the way back to the ute.

"Where are you?" she said.

John unlocked the ute and slid into the seat. "Forest Court. No sign of her here." He started the engine and pulled out into the street.

"You need to come in. To the station."

"I'm just on my way to the hospital again."

"We need to talk to you."

"No. I need to find my mother. You should be looking for her."

"We are. We need to talk to you about something else."

"What? What's going on? What's more important than finding my mother?"

"Do you know an Annette Morgan?"

"What's happened?"

"Do you know her?"

"Yes. She works for the gallery in Canberra. She was working with Mum, her photos. Tell me what's happened." John drove past the hospital on Missenden Road and turned into Salisbury.

"What was your relationship to her?"

"What do you mean?"

"Why was she at your house? Where were you this morning?"

"You know where I was. Looking for Mum. Tell me what's happened to Annette." John turned into Broughton Street and stopped the ute. The street was full of blue and red flashing light, bouncing off the police vehicles that were

221

parked up and down both sides of the road.

"She's dead. Shot. In your front hall. Come to the station. We need to talk to you."

John hung up and made a U-turn. He had to find his mother first. Then he was going to find whoever had shot Annette.

It was quite late when Betty got back to Forest Court, the afternoon sun throwing shadows across the road. She looked for blood stains on the footpath outside the gates but couldn't see any. From what John had said, she expected there would be some sign of Ken's blood. And of the other one's, the one who died. But the footpath was clean. Perhaps someone had washed it off, hosed it into the gutter, down the drain. Their blood would end up in the harbour eventually.

She let herself inside and threw the bag with the old shoes onto the bed. She was stiff and sore, and really very tired. She probably should have hailed a taxi but it was such a nice afternoon. She got a glass of water and sat down in the living room. The place seemed different somehow. She couldn't tell what exactly, but it wasn't quite the same. Through the window she watched the sun shining on the big gum tree above the car park. The white trunk was lit up in yellow, and turning pale orange as the day faded.

She didn't realise she'd been asleep until the sound of a bell woke her. It took a while for her to realise what was going on. The bell working its way into her dream, making the car and the country road evaporate so that the bell was all that was left. The countryside had been Australian even though the dream seemed to be set in France.

She tried to pull herself upright from her slumped position in the old armchair. Her mouth was dry, her lips crusty and cracked. She ran her tongue around them, trying to moisten them. How long had she been asleep, she wondered. There was that bell again. Why didn't someone answer it?

She sat up slowly, wondering why she was so stiff. Then she remembered that she'd walked home from the hospital. How far was that? She had no idea. Too far for her legs, it seemed.

The bell rang again. She pulled herself to her feet slowly and painfully, and would have sat down again but for the bell that kept ringing. *Keep your damn hat on, I'm coming*, she thought as she lurched across the room, leaning first on the back of the armchair then on the sideboard, before tottering unsupported the last two metres to the front door. God, what a wreck. She pulled the door open.

There was a big man outside. His face was badly bruised and his nose was bandaged. He was holding a red and white tube in his hands.

"Hello," he said. "I think you've got something of mine."

It was well after 10pm when John decided to check his mother's apartment again. He had spent the afternoon avoiding the police and searching by himself.

He desperately wanted to know what had happened to Annette, but he had to assume that his mother was alive. She was the priority. Stick with that. If it was a kidnapping, there had been no contact or demands. The police would have told him. It might not be kidnapping, but someone had been to his house and killed Annette. It was likely that his mother's disappearance had something to do with that. Something to do with the guns in the suitcase. The terrorist thing with his parents. What else could it be? The evening news on the car radio had mentioned the murder in Camperdown, and at the end of the bulletin a short item about police concern for a missing woman. It mentioned the amnesia but not kidnapping.

In the afternoon, John had rung Billy, and asked him to help look for Betty. He told him to stay clear of the house and Forest Court, he didn't want him running into whoever had shot Annette. Billy had taken a couple of mates and they had ridden their bikes through all the parks in Newtown, Camperdown and Chippendale. They even went along the creek through Annandale to Rozelle Bay. John had started back at the hospital again and spiralled out, driving along every street in an ever-widening search area. None of them had seen anything.

He was going to check Forest Lodge again then start back at the hospital. This time he'd do a foot search of every street and lane. What else could he do? He wasn't going to the cops, not till he found his mother.

The apartment door was unlocked and ajar. John took out the HK and backed away. He checked the kitchen window and the sliding doors that opened onto the terrace, but the interior of the apartment was dark and he couldn't see anything inside. He went back to the door and nudged it open with his foot, following its inward sweep with the muzzle of his weapon.

The apartment was empty, but furniture had been moved since the morning, and the wardrobe door was open. There was a shopping bag containing a new shoe box on the floor beside the bed, and a handwritten note on the table in the living room.

It was short: *I want the suitcase.* There was a mobile phone number on the bottom.

John used Betty's landline to make the call. He'd never

done any negotiating. He'd read the books but it wasn't his department. He was one of the guys you called when negotiating didn't work.

The phone was answered almost immediately. "Lawrence?"

John didn't recognise the voice. It was a man: deep voice, low and gravelly; Australian accent. When he replied he tried to keep his own voice level and neutral. He couldn't afford to indulge his anger and fear until his mother was safe.

"Yes."

There was a pause. John resisted the impulse to fill it. Let the other guy do the talking.

"We have your mother. We want the suitcase."

"I understand that. Is she safe?"

"For the moment. But if I don't get the suitcase very soon I am going to start hurting her. Do I make myself clear?"

"If she is hurt, you will die," said John.

"Yeah, sure. In the long run, we're all dead."

"There are different ways to die."

"I'll take my chances. Get the suitcase to me and she's yours, safe and sound. We all get on with our lives. Don't, and hers comes to an abrupt and painful end."

"Where?"

The address was in Moorebank. It was the same smash repair workshop that John had been checking out on Wednesday.

"You've got an hour," the man said.

"I need longer. The suitcase is in Artarmon. In a lock-up."

"An hour. Don't fuck around, don't be a hero. Any hint of trouble, she dies." The line went dead.

John looked at his watch: 11.03. He went back out to the ute and got the suitcase from behind the seat, and his gloves and knife from the dashboard compartment. The Škorpions seemed to be in good enough condition, a bit of superficial rust on a couple of the magazines but they looked okay. He thought briefly about using one of them, but the ammunition was too old. There was no telling what condition it would be in after all this time, and he was going to need a weapon he could rely on.

He pulled out the HK, and checked it and the spare clip, wishing he had asked Smokey for a suppressor as well. Or even better, an MP5. And some flash-bangs. He was pretty sure Smokey would have been able to deliver.

He put his knife in one sock and the spare clip in the other. The pistol went back in the waistband of his jeans. He needed to get to Moorebank – there was no time to rig a suppressor, or a pipe bomb. He put the suitcase back behind the seat of the ute. It was 11.12 when he hit the road.

EIGHTEEN

Tough Man

The M5 was clear and John made good time to Moorebank. He parked the ute in a quiet residential street at eleven thirty. The back of the workshop was about two hundred metres away, across the parkland and the creek. He checked his weapon, put his gloves on and locked the ute with the suitcase still behind the seat. He kept off the path, instead picking a line across the park that would bring him up directly behind the workshop. The creek was shallow but the water was cold as he waded across. He kept in the shadows of the trees as he climbed up towards the workshop. The rear door he had seen on his previous visit was locked. John skirted the rear of the neighbouring removalist warehouse as he made his way to the little laneway that connected the parkland to the street. He went forwards until he could see the street in front of the smash repair workshop. Three cars were parked there. The yellow glare of the street lights robbed the scene of colour but one of the cars was the same silver Commodore that had come after him on Wednesday night. And there was at least one person in the car.

John crawled up behind the sedan, taking a position just

behind the driver's door. He had the door open and his knife blade pressing up beneath the jaw of the lookout before the man could react. "I can open your throat or I can let you live. Your choice," he said. The man's eyes were wide with fear and shock. He tried to turn his head but felt the point of the knife dig further into his neck.

On the passenger seat there was a gun, along with a mobile phone, a dirt-bike magazine and an empty drink can. The gun was another Glock 19. *These guys must get a discount for buying in bulk*, John thought as he took a handful of the man's hair and pulled him out onto the road, making him lie face down beside the car. A quick search found no other weapons. John reached inside and grabbed the keys from the ignition, and the gun and phone from the passenger seat.

The last number called from the phone was the same as the number John had found on the note. He switched the phone to silent and pocketed it along with the Glock. He pulled the man up off the road and around to the back of the car. When John popped the boot lid, the man made a move, swinging a wild kick at John's knee. John side-stepped the kick, letting it brush his calf. He pivoted on his left foot, whipping out a punch that began in his knees and ended under the lookout's ribs. The man's eyes bulged and he doubled over. John tipped him into the boot while he was still gasping for breath.

There was a cardboard box already in the boot. Inside it was a black pillowcase, rags, two rolls of gaffer tape and some large cable ties. Just what you would need if you were planning to kidnap someone.

John got to work trussing the man up with the gaffer tape so his arms and legs were pulled up behind his back and a thick strip of gaffer tape ran across his mouth. The man didn't look comfortable when John was finished, but he looked even worse when John got the knife out again, and twisted the big blade in front of his eyes so that it reflected the glare from the street lights. John ran the point of the knife across the man's sweating forehead, above his left eye. The blood welled up and flowed in a red veil into the eye, puddling in the corner, before overflowing down his cheek. The man tried to shake his head but John held him fast by his hair.

"You will answer my questions or I will keep cutting. The cuts will get longer and deeper. You have to understand that I am serious about this. Your friends have my mother, so I am prepared to take all the skin off your face. And you will talk. It's just a matter of how much skin you lose first."

The man nodded desperately. John tore the tape off his mouth.

"She's inside the workshop," the man said. "She's okay. She's good, not hurt."

"How many are there?"

"Three. Me and two inside. Large and Jimmy."

"Large?"

"Yeah?"

"That's his name?"

"It's what we call him. His nickname. His real name is Phil."

"Who's in charge? Who's the boss?"

"Large is."

"Weapons?"

"They've got guns."

"What sort? How many?" John laid the blade along the man's nose.

His eyes widened. "Just pistols, nine mils."

John looked across the road to the front of the workshop. The roller shutters were both closed but the small door to the

229

side was open wide. Bright light spilled out of the doorway onto the footpath. It almost looked inviting. He held up the bunch of keys he had taken out of the car. "Which are the keys for the workshop?"

"The two silver ones. The brass one is my house key."

John wrapped a new length of tape around his head, making sure the man could still breathe before he closed the boot on him.

John went in from the creek side of the workshop. He cracked the rear door slowly and waited, listening. He couldn't hear anything but there was a smell: resin; the sweet sickly smell of resins and paints. After five minutes with no sounds he moved quickly and quietly through the door with his weapon up and the safety off. The room he was in was dark, except for a slash of light spilling across the floor from the open door to the main workshop space. It was a kitchen and lunchroom. There was a stove and a sink at the far end, and the centre of the room was occupied by a large table surrounded by plastic chairs. The walls were covered with posters, a mixture of workplace safety notices and nude women. A fire extinguisher and fire blanket were mounted on the wall near the stove.

John made his way around the room, to where he could see through the door into the workshop. It was full of cars in various stages of repair, jammed in with very narrow spaces between them. Immediately outside the lunch room was the crumpled and twisted side of a dark grey Tarago. It looked as if it had been side-swiped. John stayed still and kept listening. Still nothing. He checked his watch: 11.52, the deadline was nearly up.

He moved in a crouch to the side of the Tarago and peered

through the windows. The vehicles were so close together that it was difficult to see much unless he broke cover. He moved right, to the rear of the Tarago, where he could get a sight line along the back wall of the workshop. At the far end was a bench with shelves and tools. A man was sitting on a stool beside the bench. A thin, young man, with lanky blond hair and acne. The one who shot the bus driver, the one he had seen on Delic's Facebook page. Jimmy. He was looking at his phone, the blue glare from the screen lighting his narrow features from below. John backed quietly away and moved to the other end of the vehicle. From there he could see between the vehicles to the far side of the workshop. There was a machine there, a big steel frame with posts and chains. Some kind of rig for pulling bends out of car bodies. Beyond it on the far wall was the office and a store room. The office lights were on. Along the side wall to his left was a spray booth. He began to move past it, staying low, beneath the level of the car and spray-painting booth windows. He risked a quick glance into the booth, but it was empty. He kept moving.

The other man was near the roller doors at the front of the workshop. A big man with sandy hair and a bandaged nose, sitting on a plastic stackable chair next to a freshly undercoated Commodore. Presumably this was the one they called Large. The two men were too far apart. He couldn't get an angle on them that would allow him to take them out quickly. One of them would take cover, and he'd have to hunt him down. It was too big a risk until he knew where his mother was. He couldn't see anyone else, but there could be others. The lookout might have been lying. He moved back along the side of the spray cabinet and then started moving out into the workshop, staying low, crouching in the shadows between the cars. He was edging his way between a Honda SRV and the Tarago when the lookout's phone in his hip pocket began to vibrate. It seemed very loud in the quiet workshop but there was nothing John could do about it now. He waited.

"Shit," said the big man near the front of the workshop.

"What?" called the one at the back.

"He's here. I just called Matt, he didn't answer."

"Want me to go and check on him?" the skinny one said.

"No," said Large. "Stay where you are. I reckon our man is here. I reckon he's got to Matt."

"He might have just gone for a piss."

"He'd still answer his phone. No, something is wrong. How's Grandma doing?"

"She's alright. Breathing."

"Good. Keep your eyes open. This cunt is dangerous."

John began to move again, trying to get a line of sight to Jimmy's position, to where his mother must be.

"Lawrence," the big one shouted. "I know you're here somewhere. But there's nothing you can do. Jimmy has got your mother trussed up on the pulling rig over the back there. That big bloody machine with all the hydraulic rams."

Through the windscreen of a Falcon, John could see Jimmy standing now beside the rig. He had his arm out towards a control panel hanging on one of the posts.

"You there, Lawrence?" Large shouted. "You know anything about repairing smashed cars? It's impressive what these new machines can do with all their hydraulics. Pull an S-bend out of a frame as quick as you like. Seven cylinders this one's got, pulls up to ten tonnes. Gets the job done, I can tell you. But it's not automated, it's still very much an art form. Each wreck is different – the operator has to know just how to rig the clamps and chains to apply the pressure

232

in just the right place, in just the right order, to unfold the steel. It's a fascinating thing to watch a twisted mass of steel slowly turning back into someone's pride and joy. Turns out Jimmy's a bit of a whizz at it. Natural talent. It's hard to imagine him having talent, I know, given your track record with him."

John could see Betty now, a small figure slumped in a chair on a low platform in the middle of the pulling machine. She was surrounded by steel, her arms held out horizontally by chains from her wrists to the frames. Other chains were connected to her legs, neck and torso. A black bag was over her head. She wasn't moving. She might already be dead.

"We've discovered these machines work a treat on people too," Large said. "Sort of your twenty-first-century version of the rack. Pulls people apart, no problems. Gets a bit messy sometimes, but still nothing is perfect, eh?"

John was between Large and his mother now, approaching Jimmy's position.

"When Jimmy starts playing with those buttons, it's going to hurt her. What do you reckon Jimmy, how are you planning to start?"

"Arms," the skinny one said. "That usually does the trick."

"There was that one guy, though, wasn't there?"

"Yeah," said Jimmy. "That big Tongan guy, Brody. He thought he was pretty tough. Till I ripped both his arms off."

"Yeah, nasty that." Large laughed. "I dare say you're a tough man too, Lawrence, but how tough do you think your mother is? That's the real question."

There were three cars between John and the pulling frame. He could see his mother moving slightly, her head turning as if she was trying to hear. Her shoulders twisted, sending a vibration through the chains that held her arms out.

"Now, I'm not going to count to three or any of that shit," said Large. "Either you're going to show yourself and put down your weapons, or Jimmy is going to start pulling your mother's arms off. Right now."

As Jimmy reached for the control panel, John came up from between the cars firing, targeting Jimmy and the control panel first, three rounds. The first hit Jimmy in the shoulder, the others ricocheting off a post and slamming into the wall beyond. Jimmy screamed and fell out of sight behind a Volvo station wagon, as the window of the Falcon next to John shattered. He spun and fired at Large. Two shots, then two more, forcing Large to take cover. John turned back, approaching his mother. Jimmy was reaching up for the control panel again with his good arm. John fired. The second shot hit Jimmy's forearm. He screamed again. John turned again, but couldn't see Large. He put two rounds into the windows of the car Large had been standing behind last time he'd seen him, and kept moving towards his mother.

"For fuck's sake hit the button, Jimmy," yelled Large. It sounded as if he was behind a double-cab ute so John put two more rounds into that before he rolled across the bonnet of a grey hatch and dropped to the floor. He reloaded and listened. Jimmy was whimpering and snuffling, but there was no sound from Large.

Two shots hit the wheel he was squatting next to and the Volvo settled as the tyre deflated. John moved to his right and peered beneath the car. He could see Jimmy crouching on the other side. When he started to stand up again, John put three rounds into his ankles and feet. There was a lot of screaming. Jimmy dropped his pistol and fell back to the floor. John stayed low, moving around the car. He ignored Jimmy, picking up the Glock, dropping out the clip and ejecting the breach round. He tossed the empty weapon through the window of the nearest car and pocketed the ammunition.

There was movement to his left behind a red Hyundai. John threw himself to the floor again as two shots punched holes in the roof of the Volvo. He crawled along the floor to where the grey-painted skeleton of a car body was resting on a trolley. He gave the trolley a shove, sending it crashing into the Hyundai as he jumped up onto the boot and then the roof of a Falcon. Large was on the floor between the cars, holding a stainless steel automatic and looking the wrong way.

"Drop your weapon. Lie face down," John shouted. "Do it now. Do it now."

Large turned his head.

"Don't make me kill you," John said.

The big man looked up at John and swore. His eyes flicked from John's face to something behind him, and he started to smile. John dived forwards, but it was too late. He didn't hear the shot that tore into his legs as he fell across the bonnet of the Falcon and slid off the front into the narrow gap between the cars. He felt the pain in his legs and knew he had been shot, but he still had his weapon. He started to roll over but found himself looking up at a big dark man holding a sawn-off shotgun on him. He let his weapon clatter onto the floor. The pain in his legs was bad and getting worse.

Large watched Lawrence fall onto the bonnet of the Falcon and slide off the front onto the floor, leaving a red smear across the dappled grey paint of the undercoat.

"You're late," he said.

"Don't mention it," Pike said, breaking open the sawn-off shotgun and reloading it with two new shells from the pocket of his leather vest. The muscleman, the one called Joe, was beside him, holding a big stainless steel revolver on John. "Who is he anyway?"

"He's the one who has the machine guns." Large looked down at Lawrence. A bright red pool was forming beneath his legs, but his eyes were clear and flicking between the three men standing over him. "Shoot him again if he moves." He bent over Lawrence, picked up the HK and took Matt's Glock. He also found two spare clips, a very nasty-looking knife and a set of car keys in Lawrence's pockets. He kicked him in the ribs and turned back to Pike. "Would you mind dragging him over to the pulling frame, we need to talk to him."

Pike raised the shotgun so that it was pointing at Large's chest. "Why don't you put all those guns on the bonnet here first. Just in case."

Large grunted and put Lawrence's guns and his own Sig on the car. "We should get some help for Jimmy too," he said.

Pike put the shotgun on the roof of the nearest car and went over the guns, dropping the clips out and checking the loads. The Glock still had a full clip. He held onto it. "This guy, who is he?"

"Lawrence," said Large. "John Lawrence. That's all I know."

Joe handed Pike his revolver and grabbed John by the ankles. He dragged him between the cars over to the pulling frame and lifted him into a white plastic chair. They secured him to it with cable ties around his wrists and ankles.

Jimmy had been shot in the arm and shoulder, and both ankles were shattered. But he was alive, still crying and moaning on the floor. His feet were lying at very strange angles. Betty Lawrence was sitting still in the pulling frame, her head slumped forwards.

"If this guy's the one with the guns, who's that with all the chains?"

"His mother," said Large. "He was using her. A front for the importation."

"You took her hostage?"

"Only Lawrence knew where the guns were. I had no choice."

"Your plan's gone great so far, hasn't it?"

"Fuck off."

"So where are they?" asked Pike. "The machine guns?"

"Dunno," said Large. "That's what we have to ask Lawrence here." Jimmy was making a lot of noise, the bubbling sobs and cries, building in a new crescendo. He tried to talk but the effort made him scream again. Large couldn't think straight over, the noise. "Jesus. We need to get Jimmy to a doctor. My car's just out the front. It won't take long to run him up to Liverpool."

Pike stood with Matt's Glock hanging at his side, looking down at Jimmy. "No need for a doctor," he said, swinging the pistol out in a short arc and shooting Jimmy twice in the head.

"What the fuck have you done?" Large shouted and lunged at Pike, only stopping short when he felt the cold steel of Joe's revolver on the side of his neck.

"Do we have to shoot you too?" Pike asked. "Duggan had it coming. He was the one swinging the bat, not you. Ricky told us. Duggan was always dead, but I'm happy to kill you too, if you want to make a fuss."

Large moved away from Pike and Joe, and leaned against the bonnet of the Volvo.

"Okay," Pike grunted and turned back to Lawrence. "Machine guns? Where are they?"

"Let my mother go," Lawrence said.

"I don't think you understand, mate. I'm not interested in your mother and we're not negotiating here. I'm just going to shoot you in the legs again and keep at it until you tell me where they are." Pike lowered the pistol. "So what will it be? Right or left first?"

Lawrence looked up at Pike, glanced across to Large and Joe, then back to Pike. "They're in my ute. White Hilux, parked out the back, across the creek. He's got the keys." John nodded at Large.

Pike held out his hand and Large dropped the keys into it.

"Find the car, Joe. See if the machine guns are there." Pike pointed his pistol at Large's head. "We'll wait here, won't we, Phil."

Large stared at Pike. He wanted very badly to kill him.

John's right leg and buttock were throbbing from the shotgun wound, and he could feel his blood pooling and congealing around his arse in the seat of the plastic chair. The ties on his arms and ankles were just standard cable ties. He was pretty sure that he could snap them. He'd done it before in training scenarios, an explosive movement of his arms would do it. He hadn't done it in a chair like this, but he was pretty sure the ties would break before his wrists did.

Pike and Large didn't speak to each other while they waited for Joe to return. Pike was leaning against the Volvo's bonnet, casually holding the Glock in his hand. Large had opened the front door of the Volvo, and gingerly lowered himself onto the seat. John's mother hadn't moved. She must be in pain, with her arms pulled out like that. Jimmy Duggan was slowly leaking blood onto the paint-stained floor.

Joe was back in ten minutes with Jorge's suitcase. "The ute was across the creek. Where he said. This was behind the seat."

"Open it up," said Pike.

Joe put the suitcase on the bonnet of the Volvo. John watched them open it and pull out the guns, laying all five of them out beside the suitcase.

"Small," said Pike picking one of the machine guns up. "More of a machine pistol." He removed the magazine, then slotted it back into place.

"But easy to hide," said Large, as he climbed out of the car.

Pike was turning the gun over in his hands, squinting at the words stamped into the pressed steel frame. "Looks like they're East European." He unfolded the stock and held the little gun up to his shoulder. "Feels alright." He cocked the gun, released the safety, and put it back up to his shoulder. He fired a short tentative burst, then a sustained one that emptied the magazine. The bullets shattered the windows of a Mazda hatch and left it slumped sideways on flattened tyres. "Nice," Pike said, dropping out the empty clip and slotting in a new full one. "I'm really liking the feel of this thing." He pointed it at Large. "Real quality. Those old commie bastards new a thing or two about guns."

Joe grinned and turned back to the suitcase. His eyes widened when he pulled back the next layer of blanket. "Pike. You better look at this."

Pike stepped forwards. Large started to follow him but Pike lifted the machine gun. "Stay," he said before he peered into the suitcase. A big smile creased his face.

"Bonus," said Joe, grinning back at him.

Pike spun the suitcase around and lifted it so Large could see the bundles of US dollars that covered the bottom.

Joe lifted a cloth drawstring bag out of the suitcase, opened it and pulled out a handful of Krugerrands. "Jackpot man," he said. "Total jackpot."

John watched Large. His blackened eyes were following everything the other two did as they tried to calculate how much the money and gold was worth. Joe had put his revolver on the bonnet and picked up another bag of gold. As Large began to move around the car, John saw his own knife slip out of Large's right sleeve and into his hand.

"How much is there?" Large said, stepping up behind Joe, his voice calm, but his arm coming up fast, ramming the full length of the blade into the side of Joe's neck. Blood fountained from the wound. Large let go of the knife and reached for the revolver as Joe's legs went from under him. His arm flailed, trying to get hold of the knife. Pike was moving. Stepping away from the car. Trying to get enough space to swing up the machine gun. He wasn't fast enough. Large shot him twice. Chest and throat.

"That's for Jimmy," Large muttered, putting two more rounds into Pike as he slid to the floor.

John was on the floor now too, still tied to the chair. He had thrown himself sideways when Large went for the gun. Now he was looking into Joe's eyes. The dying man's movements slowed till he lay motionless with the knife jutting out of his neck. Pike was slumped by the front wheel of the Volvo, head tipped forwards on the bright red stain of his chest.

Large picked up the machine guns and began packing them back into the suitcase. "This is all your fault, Lawrence. You and your fucking mother."

John had nothing to say.

Large stepped forwards to retrieve the gun in Pike's hand, grunting as he bent down with one arm wrapped around his ribs, protecting them. Pike wasn't dead. The barrel of the

Škorpion lifted, and he squeezed the trigger. The clip emptied in a swarm of random fire as Large dived back behind the Volvo. John was surprised at how fast the big man could move.

The empty gun clunked back onto the floor, Pike unable to hold it. "Did I get him?" he whispered through the blood bubbling from the wound in his throat.

"No," said John. "You missed." He could hear Large swearing to himself as he crawled back to the suitcase, but Pike couldn't. His body sagged sideways, an awkward tangle of arms and legs, blood no longer pumping out of his throat, just slowly leaking under gravity. More and more red joining all the other colours staining the floor.

John listened as Large moved away from him, dragging the suitcase to the front of the workshop. The cold from the floor was seeping into his body, sapping his energy. He tried to move, using the foot and shoulder that were in contact with the floor, he arched and crabbed slowly towards Joe's body. Towards the knife that was still in his neck.

A door slammed and a new smell joined the smell of blood and gunfire. It was sharp and sweet, the smell of paint solvent. John kept working towards Joe's body but there was so much blood on the floor that it was hard to get any traction. The edge of his boot kept slipping, leaving him nothing to push against.

A soft whump, followed by the crackle of blistering paint, confirmed his fears: Large was going to burn the place. The acrid smell of burning paint reached his nostrils as the first car burst into flames. John lunged and arched, pushing himself slowly closer to the knife. His boot found a joint in the concrete floor and he was able to push himself within range. He groped his fingers out and snagged the neck of the dead man's T-shirt, dragging the body closer, jamming

241

Joe's face against the plastic arm of the chair. John stretched out his fingers again, this time trying to hook them around the bloody handle of the knife. He got hold of it and tried to pull, but the handle slipped out of his grasp. He snagged part of Joe's T-shirt, using it to wipe the knife handle, and trying again. The knife was stuck. Large must have struck bone. John rocked Joe's head, trying to release the blade, but it wouldn't come. Above him he could see black smoke lit by blue and yellow flames beginning to fill the roof space. With a fresh grip on the knife, John began pulling and pushing again.

When the knife came free, his momentum carried John across the back of the chair, and onto his other side. He lay panting for a moment, then reversed the blade and slid it back along his wrist. The cable ties on his arms fell away as the knife slice through the plastic. Seconds later he was free of the chair.

He tried to stand up but his leg wouldn't take his weight so he stayed down and began crawling to his mother, trailing his wounded leg behind him.

He was nearly there when an explosion shook the workshop, throwing a jet of flame across the roofs of the cars. John rolled beneath the nearest car as burning liquid landed around him. The flames dripped down the sides of the cars and puddled on the floor. John tried to ignore the noise and heat of the fire. He could feel it on his scarred arm and neck, could feel it burning again. He moved faster, pushing forwards but knew he was moving too slowly. He called out to his mother but he couldn't hear anything over the noise. There was a lot of smoke rolling off the burning cars, tumbling upwards, gathering in the high points, pushed around by masses of superheated air pouring off the flames.

His mother was slumped forwards against the chains,

her arms still held out horizontally. John pulled himself up to stand against one of the posts and removed the bag from her head. She was dead, a gunshot wound just beneath her left eye.

John began undoing the chain shackles, his fingers struggling to unscrew the pins, coughing as the smoke tore at his lungs. Behind him the workshop walls were alight, flames racing into the roof and along the steel trusses. Breaking glass added to the noise. The office next to the paint store was ablaze now, and it wouldn't be long before more of the car fuel tanks went up.

He got the last of the chains off, and began hauling the chair out of the machine, falling onto the floor, the chair and his mother on top of him. He stayed down where the smoke was thinner and started moving again, dragging himself with his arms and reaching back to pull his mother after him. He inched his way between the cars, to the lunch room and the rear door, moving away from the paint store. The wall frames and roof trusses were beginning to scream and groan, threatening to buckle as the heat weakened them.

The wall of the lunch room was alight but the fire hadn't reached inside yet. John shoved tables and chairs out of his way as he dragged his mother through. He pushed the door open with his head and shoulder, and they tumbled onto the dirt and dry grass outside. John sucked in cold clear air for a moment, then kept moving, kept dragging his mother in the chair till he got to the creek. Then he lay down in the water and closed his eyes. He could hear sirens and the voices of people coming from the houses on the far side of the creek. Coming to see what was going on.

NINETEEN

Smokey

John was lying face down, the wounds in the back of his leg and buttock covered with dressings.

"She's dead?" he croaked. His throat was still raw from the smoke and fumes.

"Yes. Ricochet. Caught her in the head. It would have been instantaneous," said Walker. "I'm sorry."

John just wanted her to go away. They had put him in a room on his own and now it was full of cops: Walker and Moreton and a couple of uniforms. He wanted them all to go away, everyone but Billy. He'd been sitting beside the bed when John first woke up, and had resisted all attempts by the cops to get him to leave. Walker had been the last to try. "He stays," John had said. "For as long as he wants, he stays."

Walker shrugged. "Okay. Whatever. They found three bodies in the workshop. Not recognisable – it was a hell of a fire. You were lucky to get out."

John didn't say anything. He didn't feel lucky.

"We found a guy locked in the boot of a Commodore on the street. A Matthew Peal." said Walker. "Poor bastard

244

nearly cooked. You have anything to do with that?"

"Yeah, that was me." He just wanted to sleep. He felt for the morphine button and gave it a squeeze.

"We'll have to do a formal statement when you're not doped to the gills, but do you know who the bodies are? Peal's very talkative, can't shut him up but he can only name two. He says there was a Phil Waters there, nickname, Large. Old school loan shark, we know of him but we've never had our hands on him."

"He killed the other two, not Jimmy, set the fire and took off."

"So he's not one of the bodies?" She went to the door and said something to Moreton who was talking to a uniformed cop. He pulled out his radio and started talking. Walker came back over to the bed. "What about Jimmy Duggan?"

"He's dead."

"They're mostly charcoal now. It'll come down to DNA. Duggan was a car thief and part-time meth slinger. Looks like he briefly graduated to bigger things."

"He was with this Large. They took Mum. Then the other two showed up. Never seen them before. One was called Pike, he was the boss. They called the other one Joe."

"Pike and Joe? Surnames?"

"No. Pike was the one that killed Duggan. Shot him. Then Waters killed him and the other one, Joe. Stabbed him."

"Joe was the one stabbed?"

John nodded.

"They found a machine gun beside one of the bodies. You know anything about that?"

"Pike had a machine pistol."

"There seem to have been a lot of guns."

"Yeah. There were." John closed his eyes, but he could

still see the flames. "Tell me about Annette."

"Shot. Through your front door. Dead, I'm afraid. We have a witness who saw someone fitting Waters' description leaving your house about midday. Looks like he was after you. And Morgan got in the way. What did he want from you?"

"He thought we had something of his."

"What?"

"A suitcase is what he said. This all started after our storage unit was broken into. My father's furniture, from Paris. I think it had something to do with that. But I don't know how."

A nurse came around with a trolley to take his blood pressure and temperature. Walker and the other police left. John slept.

They kept him in three days then sent him home with a pair of crutches, a lot of antibiotics and some serious pain killers. "You're very lucky it missed your femoral artery," one of the doctors said to him. *I must be wrong*, John thought, *everyone else thinks I'm lucky*.

He made a formal statement at the police station. There would be a coroner's inquiry. All kinds of inquiries and court cases when they found Waters. Not that he really cared. His story would stand up. The cops didn't like that he had gone after his mother without telling them, but they didn't know about the HK or the suitcase. As far as they could prove, he hadn't done any of the shooting.

John didn't go to Annette's funeral. He sent flowers, but he couldn't face seeing her children. They would hate him and they would be right to.

Betty's funeral was at La Perouse, the same place where

246

her own parents had been cremated. A new tradition for a family that didn't have many. John hired a celebrant rather than speak himself. A nice enough guy, who read from the bio notes John gave him. It didn't take long. They played Miles Davis's *Concierto De Aranjuez* over a slide show of images from her portfolio. No childhood photos, no family photos.

There weren't many people there. A few from the village, a couple of old newspaper people. Ken Mallard in a wheelchair with his granddaughter. He looked a lot better. "Out of hospital now," he said. "So sorry about your mum. Terrible business. She was something else, your mum."

Yeah something, thought John, shaking Ken's hand, but he didn't know what exactly, and he'd never know now. Billy was there of course, wearing a shirt with a collar. That was a first. He shook John's hand. That was new too.

"I'll miss your mum. She was awesome."

John smiled, "Thanks, mate." John had given Billy one of Betty's cameras. The Nikon. He probably wouldn't be able to get hold of any film to use it, but the boy was happy when John gave it to him. And sad too.

"Don't you want to keep it?"

"I've got the Leica. One each, eh. She would have wanted you to have it. She loved that you had started taking photos." He gave him a new digital camera as well, the camera that Betty was planning to give him for his thirteenth birthday.

The only one of his old school friends to show up was Dave Watson. "Sorry about your mum, mate," he said. "She was so much cooler than anyone else's mum."

The only people from the regiment were Sam Morris and Tommy Jackson. That was another surprise; John didn't think that either of them had met his mother, but he was grateful for the way that they ran interference with the handful of media that turned up. He saw Tommy wording up one of the photographers who was trying to get close to the small group of mourners, getting in the guy's face, a big blond threat of impending violence.

The police came too. Moreton and Timmins, sitting at the back of the chapel. They didn't bother to say hello, just nodded to him. That probably wasn't a good sign. After the service they stood in the rose garden talking to each other and watching the small crowd disperse.

A few people wanted to have a drink afterwards. "Where are we going?" Sam asked. John hadn't planned on anything, but Ken was keen, even if his granddaughter wasn't. Sam told her that Ken would be safe in his care, that he'd get him back to Glebe at a reasonable hour. Ken grinned when she shrugged and nodded her acquiescence. He suggested the Bulls Roar as a venue. "Just being selfish really," he said. "It's close to home." They dropped Billy at Annandale on the way back to Glebe. John suggested that there was still time to go to school, but Billy wasn't keen. At the Bulls Roar, they dragged a couple of tables together in the side lounge and made room for Ken's wheelchair and John's crutches. Sam and Tommy seemed to be getting on well with Ken. John appreciated them turning up, but it did occur to him that they were only there to see if Smokey showed. He didn't, of course. Dave told a couple of stories from their school days, and about meeting Betty in Paris. It was just getting dark when they called it a day and said their goodbyes. Sam and Tommy set out for Forest Court, pushing Ken in his wheelchair. Dave dropped John at Camperdown before he drove back to the North Shore.

* * *

It was August before John was able to do any serious work on the house again. In the meantime, he had got someone in to finish lining out the upstairs bedrooms and do the tiling in the bathrooms. Billy still came over each Saturday and did some work on the skirting boards and architraves. The kid really enjoyed getting the joints just right. Soon there would only be the painting, then the floors to be sanded and sealed.

The two of them were sitting on the front veranda in the afternoon, nursing cups of tea. Billy was going on about the football. In particular, whether the Tigers had any chance of getting into the finals. John had never really been a fan of league, he had played rugby at school and in the army for a while, but had never been a fan of any professional sport. Billy was excited though. It had been a few years since his team had come anywhere close to playing in the finals.

"I really think this is our year," he said.

"Yeah? You reckon they can take Manly?" John couldn't help winding Billy up.

"Manly? Of course. They'll beat Manly, then they just have to get past the Broncos or maybe Souths, and they've beaten both of them this season."

"If you say so." John stood up and bent over, stretching the muscles in the backs of his legs. When he straightened up he could see a figure in a wheelchair coming down the middle of the road. Smokey. He'd changed, but it was unmistakably Smokey. He had long greying hair now, and was much thicker in the body. Huge shoulders and powerful arms guided the wheelchair in a wide arc across the road to the driveway of the apartment building next door. He pumped the wheels a couple of times to get up onto the footpath then glided down to John's house.

"Your footpaths around here are a bloody disgrace," he said. "Had to risk my life mixing it with the traffic."

"I'd be more worried about the other road users than you," said John, grabbing Smokey's hand. "Where the hell have you come from?"

"Newtown. Caught the train."

"Jesus, why didn't you get a taxi?"

"Where's the fun in that? Who's your mate?"

"Sorry. This is Billy. He's been helping me work on the house. Billy, this is Smokey, an old friend from the army."

Billy shook Smokey's huge hand but didn't say anything.

"If I know what this lazy bastard is like, I bet you've ended up doing all the work." Smokey gave Billy a big grin then spun the wheelchair so he was facing John. "You going to offer me a beer?"

John opened the door and he and Billy followed Smokey as he bumped up the step into the hall.

"It's a bit bloody Spartan, mate," Smokey said, spinning around, taking in the living room while John got beers from the fridge.

"Don't worry, I've got grand plans. Soon as my leg is back to normal."

"Heard about your mum. Sorry."

"Thanks. I lost that USP, cops got it. That a problem for you?"

Smokey shook his big head. "No. They're untraceable, at least as far as I'm concerned." He took a drink from the beer bottle. "The reason I decided to drop in on you like this, apart from desperately missing you, obviously—"

"Obviously."

"You remember that big prick, Joni Kasuasua?"

"Fijian. The CRW guy?"

"Yeah, him. He managed not to get court-martialled

after the 2000 coup – no idea how – but he had to leave the country for a while."

"He was a fucking smartarse, I seem to remember."

"Still is. Anyway, he's back in Nadi now. I'm doing a bit of business with him, nothing too illegal. But he has offered up a bit of news that I thought might be of interest to you."

Yasawa Islands, Fiji

A dot appeared above the horizon, just west of the far headland. Only a slight increase in the helicopter's elevation gave a clue that its course was bringing it directly to the resort, to the collection of bures and pavilions strung out along the white sand of the beach that lined Palantui Bay. Jeff Palmer stood naked at the window of the bure, watching the helicopter through the wooden slats as it flew across the startlingly blue ocean. It would be coming from one of the high-end resorts further north in the chain of islands that stretched out into the Pacific. They tended to have clientele that could afford the outrageous cost of being choppered to and from paradise.

Behind him on the bed, a woman snored softly, her hand trailing on the floor, and a thin thread of saliva connecting her mouth to the pillow. He tried to remember her name and failed. She was about his age, but bloody good fun in bed. He scratched his balls idly, watching the little waves that had made it across the reef fold softly onto the beach. He wondered if she would be sticking around for a while. A few days of uncomplicated sex would be fun – and he needed some kind of hobby if he was going to live here.

Jeff pulled on a pair of swimming trunks as the high-pitched buzz of the helicopter increased in volume like an angry wasp. After it had passed overhead, he stepped down onto the beach to make sure that it kept going. The noise faded rapidly, cut off by the hills as the helicopter continued south-east towards Nadi. He didn't like helicopters. Or wasps for that matter – Fiji seemed to be full of bloody wasps. Huge ones, always busy hunting in the undergrowth and nesting under the eaves of the buildings. There was a nest in the roof of the veranda, up in the recessed light fitting just above the door. Every time he came through the door he had to watch out for the wasps coming and going. He'd asked one of the men from the village to do something about it but nothing had happened yet. Fiji time.

He took the path between the bures to the pool. It was still early and the only people about were the old men who clean up the beach each morning and the ladies who put fresh flowers on every conceivable surface. Jeff wondered if the punters appreciated the amount of effort that went into maintaining paradise for them, or if they thought it was all just according to God's plan.

There were a couple of kids at the pool already. Pommie boys by the accents, aged about nine or ten. Jeff presumed that their parents had kicked them out of their room early in the hope of getting a bit more sleep, or more likely, an uninterrupted quick fuck before breakfast. Good luck to them.

The boys were busy trying to outdo each other with the most complicated and spectacular jump from the deck into the sparkling pool, laughing and squealing as they twisted and cartwheeled themselves into the air before falling hard

253

onto the water. "Did you see that one?" shouted the elder boy, emerging from the water after a leap that involved a star jump and a full pike.

"Yeah, but watch this," said his brother, running across the yellow concrete, and launching himself into a forwards somersault, landing hard on his back with a loud slap. Jeff smiled to himself at the thought of how much that would have hurt. He slipped into the tepid water and began his laps of the undersized pool. He started slowly, gradually picking up his pace, until there were only five strokes between his slow but effective tumble turns at each end.

When he emerged from the water after fifty laps the boys were gone but Voli was there with a towel and a mug of coffee. "Morning, boss."

"Morning, mate," said Jeff, taking the towel and the mug. He set the mug on one of the plastic tables while he towelled himself down. The resort was too small to make a lot of money but it was remote and quiet, which suited Jeff. He had bought into the place just after the last round of financial embarrassments slowed the flow of cashed-up Westerners to Fiji. He had got a fifty-three per cent share of the resort for a very good price, and until recently he had been a silent partner, happy to leave Roland and Margery to run the place, just having the occasional holiday here. Tax deductible, of course. Roland and Margery had bought the place from the original owners but the financial crisis had hit them hard. They were just about to go under when Jeff met Roland at a cricket match in Auckland. Jeff had been looking for an investment opportunity in Fiji and was happy to stay out of the day-to-day running of the resort.

Roland and Margery used Jeff's money to improve the infrastructure and rebrand the resort. Now Coral Sands was an ecoparadise, targeting the backpacker market and ecoconscious empty-nesters. They had done a good job too; everyone involved was pleasantly surprised that the investment and change of name had paid off. The resort had a ninety per cent occupancy rate, and was taking bookings well into the next year.

Jeff had stayed out of the running of the place. He knew bugger all about hospitality, but he lived on site, in one of the older bures, tucked in under the headland. It really was paradise here, although he had soon learned that even an ecoparadise stinks of shit when the sewer system breaks down.

New punters arrived from the main island each day. The resort had its own eight-metre boat powered by twin 225-horsepower outboards, which made the trip to Denarau in a little over an hour. The boat took a load away each morning and returned in the afternoon with a new lot. They were greeted by some of the staff singing a Fijian welcoming song, and were prompted by the boatmen to shout "Bula!" in response. Jeff made sure he was always around to see the new arrivals step onto the beach each afternoon. He liked to know who was coming to his place.

He had breakfast sitting at the bar. They knew what he liked now and a Fijian version of a Spanish omelette was soon placed in front of him together with a glass of orange juice and his own bottle of tabasco sauce.

When he got back to his room, the woman was gone. Probably for the best, but it had been a fun night. He tried to remember her name: Annie? Dannie? It was something like that. Nice arse she had, he certainly remembered that, and very creative in the sack too.

After breakfast the punters started making for the sunlounges scattered along the beach to work on their tans, or to the pool to watch over their children. Some took snorkels and swam out along the coral reef just off the beach. Jeff went to his little office behind the dining room. He did have some actual work to do, going through the accounts and yesterday's takings. They didn't take much cash here, nearly everything was charged to the rooms, but a little bit of cash came through, particularly from the charter boats that were often moored in the bay for a few days at a time. Jeff was in the process of siphoning some of the cash off into his own safe. He didn't really need the money, it was just habit. The feel and smell of cash was reassuring, and you never knew when you would have to pay some bastard off.

With the books sorted, Jeff had run out of work for the day. Outside his window he could see Roland talking to a couple of blokes from the village, armed with shovels. There was some problem with the drains at one of the older bures. Roland was pointing at a hole in the ground and talking earnestly to the two men. He was interrupted by a message on the two-way radio that he always carried, and strode off towards the pool area. Always busy.

Jeff locked the office and went back to his bure. The bed had been made and fresh flowers put on it. He scrunched up the hibiscus flowers and dropped them in the bin before he flopped onto the bed and picked up the book he was reading. He had set himself the task of working his way through all the novels that had been left on the shelves by previous guests. He was on his third Dan Brown.

In the afternoon he sat on the veranda of the dining room with a rum and cola. A pair of terns were hunting along the shallow channel of water between the coral and the sand, wheeling and turning, their heads swivelling this way and that, looking for fish, stalling and diving, then pulling out at the last minute when their prey moved out of reach, climbing to start the search again. Hard work for a bloody fish. He wondered what their strike rate was like.

On the beach below him the bikini girls walked back and forth from the water to their sunlounges. It was a good view and Jeff was glad that the young women were intent on ignoring all the health warnings about skin cancer.

"Pretty girls."

Jeff looked up. It was Dannie or Annie, walking along the veranda towards him in an orange sarong, a bright blue cocktail in her hand. "Mind if I join you, Jeff?"

"Please do." Jeff smiled up at her, and nodded towards the beach "The girls seem to get prettier every year. Either that or I'm getting older."

"Yes, and the young blokes are getting fitter and tastier too."

"I'll take your word for it," Jeff said, watching her pull out a chair and sit down opposite him. About forty he thought, good figure, very tanned. "I didn't ask where you were from," he said.

"No. We didn't do much talking last night, did we? I'm from Melbourne, Frankston."

Jeff nodded. "Sydney," he said. "Born and bred."

They watched a young woman in a fluoro-pink bikini writing something in the sand. Behind her a young man with lots of tattoos waited with a phone to photograph the message. The girls breasts threatened to overflow her bra as she leaned forwards to dot the i's and cross the t's.

"That was fun last night," said Dannie or Annie.

"Yeah. It was ... memorable." He looked away from the girl on the beach. "Sorry I wasn't there when you woke up. I was down at the pool having an early swim."

"That's okay, I thought it would be better to get back to my own room anyway."

"How long are you staying for?"

257

"Not long enough. It's so beautiful here, I'd like to stay on, but tonight is my last night. Work calls."

The girl in the fluoro-pink bikini stood back to let the boy photograph the message. He said something to her and she pushed him in the chest, then turned and ran along the beach with the boy in hot pursuit.

"So much energy," said Dannie or Annie, sipping her bright blue drink.

"What the hell is that you're drinking?"

"Envy. It's the cocktail of the day. Mostly rum and curaçao according to the barman. Enjoy responsibly," she said, looking at him over her sunglasses and sucking the last of the cocktail up through the straw.

The tattoo boy caught the fluoro-bikini girl and tackled her onto the sand. There was a lot of squealing and laughter, followed by quite a bit of kissing.

"That's the trouble with these young people," said Jeff, "no sense of decorum."

"Oh, they should have their fun while they're young," she said. "While they've still got their looks."

Jeff drained his rum and cola, "Yeah, you're right. But they haven't figured out yet that it's dirty minds, not good looks, that you need in bed."

Dannie or Annie giggled. "Filthy minds you and I must have then."

Jeff grinned. "What do you say I grab a bottle of wine and we take a wander up the beach?"

"Why, Jeff," she laughed, "I thought you'd never ask."

Her name was Dannie. They had another memorable night together, and the next morning she stayed in his room while he went for his swim.

When he came back she was asleep. He stripped off and lay down beside her, matching his body to hers, feeling her warmth, running his hands along her back. She woke slowly, arching her back, pressing her buttocks towards him.

They ate breakfast on the veranda, overlooking the beach. It was her last day, and they promised to stay in touch. Jeff knew they wouldn't but it was nice to pretend. She finished her coffee, gave him a smile and a kiss on the cheek and left to pack.

He stood on the beach waving to her as she stepped onto the skiff. Behind him, Voli and three of the waitresses from the dining room sang *Isa Lei*, the farewell song.

"Nice lady, that Dannie," said Voli when the song finished.

"Nice enough," said Jeff.

He found the rest of the day dragged by. After lunch he took up his usual position to check out the new arrivals. They were the typical collection: about half young people from Europe or Asia. There was an American family, and the rest were Aussies or Kiwis. No one he recognised.

It was Roland and Margery's day off so Jeff had to play host at happy hour and dinner that night. It wasn't something he looked forward to, but at least he always had an excuse to move on if the conversation dried up. He nodded and g'day-ed his way around the bar with a can of Fiji Bitter in his hand. The English couple, the parents of the boys he'd watched in the pool the previous day, were there. The boys were still in the pool. "They only get out to eat," their mother laughed, shaking her head and resting her hand on the father's shoulder. Jeff could hear the boys squealing and shouting in the pool as the sun went down.

The sky put on its expected lurid display, turning shades of yellow, orange and pink. All the cameras and phones in the resort came out to capture the moment. Jeff helped out, taking photos of couples and groups in front of the sunset. When the sun finally slid behind the ocean, conversations dried up for a moment, everyone just watching the fine high clouds turn blue and gold, before starting to talk again, quietly at first but soon breaking into laughter. Jeff didn't blame them for being entranced, he still found the sunsets here extraordinary. Having spent his whole life on the east coast of Australia, the idea of the sun setting over the sea was still a novelty.

At dinner he did a bit more greeting and hand shaking, helping new arrivals find their tables. While the punters ate, he sat at the bar with another beer, watching rugby on the television and talking to Rami, who didn't think that the Wallabies would ever beat the All Blacks again. He was probably right.

The American family were sitting close to the bar. They didn't get a lot of Yanks staying – Coral Sands was too far out of the way or maybe just not up-market enough. Not that Jeff was complaining, he could do without them, although the staff would probably enjoy the tips Yanks would bring. These Americans weren't the usual young family. The father looked to be in his sixties, shaved head, fit looking. Very tanned except for his upper lip – it was pale, as though he had just shaved off a moustache. He had brought a big silver laptop computer to the table. Jeff thought having free wifi was a bloody waste of money and as far as he was concerned, having this guy in his dining room proved the argument. All through dinner the guy barely moved his eyes from the screen, his face lit blue-white, chewing and swallowing, while he followed the progress of his investments. If someone spoke to him he would talk out the side of his mouth, around whatever he was chewing on, without taking his eyes off the screen. His wife fiddled nervously with her dyed blonde hair all through the meal. The wrong side of forty, Jeff reckoned, but trying to deny it. A time-fighter, with bolt-on breasts and pumped-up lips. She was obviously bored out of her brain while her bloke moved his markers around, ensuring that the money kept flowing. They had a daughter, a skinny little thing who never took her head out of her tablet computer all evening. Didn't speak at all that Jeff saw. He hoped they weren't staying long, he didn't want to have to look at that guy talking with his mouth full every night.

After most of the guests had finished eating and had drifted away to the bar where Manoa had cranked up the music, Jeff ate his dinner alone. The bar would soon be serving free watered-down vodka shots. Jeff hated this Saturday night tradition of turning the beachside bar into a disco, but the punters loved it. When he had finished his food, he took the plate back to the kitchen and said goodnight to the staff before walking back along the beach to his bure. He had a bottle of whisky and more Dan Brown waiting for him. On the beach, the hiss and thump of the dark waves rolling across the coral and folding onto the moon-white sand filtered out most of the music. The mast-top lights from the charter boats anchored in the bay shone across the water, yellower than the light from the moon and the stars.

When he got to the end of the beach he washed the sand off his feet in the little foot bath at the bottom of the stairs and stepped onto the veranda. He had opened the door and was reaching for the light switch when something hit him in the middle of the back. He stumbled into the room. Another blow knocked him onto the bed. Jeff rolled onto his back and pulled his legs up, away from the figure silhouetted in the door. The man was dressed in a black wet-suit and was holding a familiar-looking knife.

John kept the knife out in front, making sure Waters could see the gleam of the blade.

Large Phil Waters looked up at him from the bed, taking in the knife and the black wetsuit. "Lawrence. This is this the real you, isn't it? An assassin. Not the amateur builder you were pretending to be in Camperdown." John didn't reply. "I knew it. You always looked fucking dangerous." He grunted and heaved himself up so he was sitting on the bed, leaning back against the pillows. "I presume you know what you're doing with that knife."

When John didn't respond he went on, "So what's the plan? Cut my throat? Escape by submarine?"

"Any number of ways I can kill you with this. Cutting your throat would be one of the quick ways."

"Oh, I believe you, mate."

Waters hadn't changed his appearance much. He was tanned of course, with a scraggly grey beard, and he had lost a bit of weight. Not having black eyes and a face swollen from a beating made him look much healthier too. John was surprised that he hadn't found a gun when he had searched the bure earlier. There were only two rooms: this bedroom and a bathroom at the back, with an open-air shower full of tropical plants. Everything he knew about Waters suggested he would have a gun somewhere, but it wasn't in either of the rooms. He must be keeping it somewhere else in the resort.

"So, what next?" said Waters.

"First we talk. I want to know why Annette and my

262

mother had to die."

"Who the hell is Annette?"

"She was the woman you shot at my house. She is half the reason you are going to die tonight."

"Oh, her. Yeah, I thought it was you opening the door." Waters shrugged. "Collateral, that's what you guys call it, isn't it?"

John crossed to the bed before Waters could react, driving the knife into his thigh. The big man screamed as John twisted the knife and withdrew it then stepped back to the foot of the bed.

Blood welled through Water's fingers as he clamped them over the wound.

"What about my mother?" John hissed. "What did she do to you?"

"Fuck off." Waters spat the words.

John stepped towards him again.

"No," Large said. "It was an accident. Anyway she was old. We all have to die."

"You said that to me once before."

"Did I? Well, it's true isn't it? You know that as well as me." He moved his leg and gasped from the pain. "I didn't mean for her to be killed. I liked her. She had guts. I've looked her up since then. On the internet."

"Yeah?" John didn't believe him.

"Yeah, she was a bloody good photographer. I even bought that book about her. It's on the shelf beside the door."

"Pity she's dead then."

"You know it wasn't me, don't you? It was Pike that shot her. With the machine gun, spraying it all over the shop."

"He's dead and you were the one who put her in that position. You were going to kill us both once you got the suitcase."

Waters grimaced. "I didn't have a choice. Anyway, what the hell were the two of you doing importing machine guns? You get into that game you have to expect consequences. You two were waltzing around with a suitcase of guns, pretending everything was sweetness and light."

"We weren't importing them."

"Bullshit. Anyway how did you get onto my scheme? You brought the suitcase in on my pipeline. Tried to piggyback it through customs. Did you think I wouldn't notice?"

"It was an accident, we didn't even know about the suitcase."

"Oh, of course not."

John looked at the man on the bed. He should just kill him now, end it. It would only be a moment's work. Kill him now, and be back in Sydney by tomorrow night. Get on with his life. But Waters had returned to the bure earlier than he had expected, it was still two hours before Joni's boat would be back at the rendezvous. He'd have to wait with the body till it was time to swim out to the boat. Waiting while the man's fluids decanted themselves out of his body, through the mattress and onto the floor. The man deserved to die, there was no doubt about that. His mother's and Annette's deaths were probably just the tip of the iceberg. This was a man who lived by hurting others, who sold guns to the gangs. But now, standing in front of Waters, John's rage was cooling.

Instead of killing him straight away, he told him about Rashid, about Palestinian terrorists in Paris in 1975, about his father. And about his mother and the forgotten suitcase.

"What happened to it, by the way?" he asked after he had told the story.

"The suitcase?" said Large. "Burned it. Sold the guns, burned the case. It was your dad's?"

"No. It belonged to the Algerian. Somehow it got stored

264

with my father's things. Mum just kept paying the storage bills."

"Shit."

"Yeah."

"Whole fucking thing was a cock-up then," said Large.

"Yeah, a cock-up. And you killed two innocent people because of it." He would stick to the plan. Waters had to die tonight. Kill him and wait for the boat.

He approached the bed. Waters said, "Wait, just wait, will you? I can pay, you know. I've got some money. You don't need to kill me."

Waters was wrong, John did need to kill him. To finish it.

A sound from the bathroom had John spinning and dropping into a crouch, at the same time as a man came through the front door. The man was big: broad shoulders, with a shaved head and a full grey beard. The gun in his right hand was big too, probably a .45, and the suppressor screwed onto the muzzle was even bigger. Thick, white chest hair sprouted at his neckline, above one of those loose singlets with huge armholes that people only wear on holidays. The image on the front was of a lurid sunset.

Another man came from the bathroom. This one was younger, darker. He had a broken nose and fresh scar tissue around his eyes and mouth. He was holding a big cane knife. Like a machete, but with a long, double-handed wooden grip and a wide triangular blade with a nasty-looking hook on the end.

"Evening, Large," said the one with the beard.

"Jesus, Mick. What are you doing here?"

"You didn't think we were going to let you just wander off into the sunset, did you? Not after killing Pike and taking our guns? You know that's not the way things work." The man swung the big gun slightly so it pointed at John's centre of mass. "You, in the rubber wear, I don't know what's going on here but you better drop the knife."

John dropped his knife and kicked it across the floor.

"Remember me?" said the young one to Large.

"Yeah. I remember. You still owe me twenty grand."

"I owe you a fucking kicking," the man shouted.

The one Waters had called Mick looked across but the gun didn't waver from John. "Will you shut up? Get over near the window and keep an eye out in case we get any visitors." He turned back to Large and John. "I blame you, Large, for making me have to work with fuckwits like this. Now, I don't know what bedtime games you two were about to get up to with the rubber gear and all, but you'll have to wait. Ricky and I have a bit of unfinished business with Large."

"What's it got to do with him?" said Waters.

"For me, it's personal," Ricky said.

"Yeah," said Mick. "He owes you a beating, and there's the fact that you killed his brother-in-law. There's a lot of sympathy in the clubhouse for Ricky. Especially from Pike's mob, and only because they haven't had to work with him. But he's been brought into the fold, made a prospect, being groomed for full membership."

"Yeah, well I wouldn't lend him any money if I were you," said Large. "He doesn't pay his debts. This whole mess only started because of that prick not paying up."

Ricky came across the room, bringing the knife down in a double-handed axe-swing between Large's legs, slicing into the mattress. "I'm going to cut you into little pieces, old man, feed you to the fucking pigs."

"Take it easy," said Mick. "First Large is going to give us the money. If he does that, well maybe he survives, maybe we

266

just chop up rubber-man, here. You know me, Large. It's just business. I always liked you and we got on pretty well, but I have been told loud and clear that you are my mess to clean up. We can't let you get away with fucking the Chiefs, killing our people, and ripping us off. The world doesn't work that way, mate. It would send the wrong message."

"I don't have any money. I sank it all into this place."

"That would be a pity if it were true, because then I would have no reason to stop Ricky from chopping into you. But I don't think it is true, Large, it's not the way you operate. You always have contingency plans, and I'm sure you've got a bundle of money stashed away here somewhere. And whatever that is, now it's ours."

John watched the other men carefully. They obviously knew each other, and Mick obviously knew what he was doing with the gun. John was a bit surprised that he was still alive at this stage; he didn't have anything to bargain with, and even without the big suppressor on the gun, there was little chance that a shot would be heard over the music and the waves. He wasn't too worried about the cane knife. It was sharp but it was long and unwieldy, requiring a big swing. No, the .45 was the problem.

"What money there is, is outside in the ceiling of the veranda," said Large. "Go on. Take it and piss off, the lot of you."

"Where? Show us." Mick twitched the gun in the direction of the door. "You too rubber man."

John followed Waters out the door and onto the veranda. "It's up there," Waters said, pointing at a recessed light in the ceiling. "Couple of zip-lock bags. US dollars. You can reach it if you take the light bulb out."

Ricky put the cane knife on one of the armchairs and dragged the chair across to the middle of the veranda beneath the light.

"Hang on a sec, Ricky," said Mick. "Anyone on the beach can see us out here."

"There's no one there, and if there was, so what? We're just changing a light bulb."

"Alright." Mick moved to a position next to the door where he could see along the beach and cover the veranda with his gun. "You two over against the end wall where I can shoot you if I have to."

Waters and John moved to the end of the veranda.

"In the corner," said Mick.

John and Waters shuffled back further. John could sense the tension in Waters as Ricky climbed onto the chair. Standing with a foot on each of the wide timber arms, he reached up to unscrew the light bulb.

"It's a bayonet fitting," said Waters. "You have to push it a bit then twist."

"Okay, got it." Ricky removed the bulb and tossed it underarm to Waters, who was caught off guard and fumbled the hot bulb. John caught it just before it hit the veranda floor and put it down on the other chair. "Good reflexes," said Ricky. He reached up again, pushing his arm past the light fitting. "Which side is it? Hang on here it is ... Got it. Oww, what... Fuck. Oh fuck—" He screamed and pulled his hand out of the hole. It was followed by a dozen large yellow wasps that began attacking his head.

He fell off the chair and tumbled down the steps onto the beach. Mick turned, watching Ricky screaming and waving at the wasps. This was what Waters was waiting for. He lunged for the second armchair, sliding his hand into a slit in the side of the seat cushion. The gun John had been expecting to find inside the room was in the cushion. Ricky was still shouting and batting at the wasps with his hands as he stumbled towards the water.

Mick swore and turned back to the veranda, firing the .45. The gun kicked back in his hand, but neither John nor Waters were where they had been, and the rounds buried themselves harmlessly in the wall of the bure. John was on the floor reaching for the cane knife, as Waters fired through the cushion cover. Mick slumped down onto the decking, a big red wound in the centre of his chest. Waters pulled the gun out and swung it towards John, but stumbled on his wounded leg, firing wildly. John threw the cane knife in a scything horizontal arc, and went for Mick's gun. Waters ducked and lurched off the veranda, stumbling on the stairs, firing and missing as he went.

John twisted the .45 out of Mick's hand and rolled behind the armchair. All he could hear now was the music from the bar and the hiss and thump of the waves. There were two more shots from the beach. He stayed still, listening. Then he heard Waters crashing through the undergrowth, making his way up the hill behind the beach. There was a path there that led over the headland to the village.

John wiped the gun clean and put it back in Mick's lifeless hand. He retrieved his knife and left the bure. On the way down the beach he checked to see if anyone had responded to the shots. There was no one there, and the music was still thumping away. Ricky was face down at the edge of the water with a hole in the back of his head. His blood had turned the moonlit water black. John checked his GPS watch and waded out through the stained water. He would swim out to one of the skiffs moored in the lagoon and wait there till it was time to set out for the rendezvous point. He was going to have plenty of time to think tonight.

Acknowledgements

Thanks to all those who helped with encouragement and advice along the way, especially my father for reading a book of fiction for the first time in many years, and my mother who doesn't read anymore but was sure it was very good anyway. Thanks also to my wife and daughters, and (in no particular order), Ian Davidson, James Renwick, Matthew Stephens, Fiona and Rénald Navilly, Ashleigh King, Paul Bennett, Chris Searson, Emma Renwick. Many thanks to Kylie Mason for helping a first time author.

CPSIA information can be obtained
at www.ICGtesting.com
Printed in the USA
LVHW090256310321
683046LV00006B/129